UNLIVED HISTORY

Vivian van Zwol

Book cover by Vivian van Zwol.
First edition 2024.

For the woman who inspired me to write a book.
This is for you, Oma van Zwol.
I will forever carry you in my heart.

Preface

My writing journey began shortly after the passing of my dear Oma (grandmother). The day started off like any other, until a whiff of nostalgia hit my senses – that undeniable scent I had grown up to know and love whenever I visited my grandparents. It was a sensation of joy and sadness, and more than that, it did something to me. It *inspired* me!

Soon after, words started playing in my head like lyrics to a melody. This was further amplified by the oh-so-familiar sound of the wood pigeon blessing me with its cooing through my open window. As a little girl staying for sleepovers at my grandparents' house, in the morning you were often greeted by that same sound, which is not so common where I live now. Here the caws and cries of crows and seagulls are the dominant ones. Yet the wood pigeon left the nearby woods and honoured me with its calling.

I am certainly not one for believing in faith; however, these events and my parents' upbringing, where creativity was embraced, unleashed a desire in me to create a piece of fictional writing. That desire to write pulled so strongly at my heartstrings that the prologue of this book was born soon after.

During my writing journey, I have reminisced about the fond times I spent with my grandparents as a child, especially with my grandmother. I cherish the small treasure chest filled with her handwritten letters and postcards. The letters were written as if you were looking through a looking glass; it would transport you to her world in great detail. Whenever I close my eyes, I can still see her sitting at the dining table writing away at length, her hair always in the same style, two side plaits neatly pinned up over her head. That's my Oma.

Now, over a decade later, having *finally* reached completion, following a writing journey that has been a source of joy and inspiration throughout, I honourably share this book with you. May you be transported through the looking glass of the *Unlived History.*

Prologue

As I heard car tyres driving over the gravel road fading away into the distance, almost complete silence took over. The slight rustling of the leaves from the old oak trees controlled the atmosphere. It was the most calming, therapeutic sound I had heard in a long time.

When I walked further down a narrow path lined with overgrown bushes and a range of the prettiest wildflowers on either side, I approached a tunnel shaped out of low, overhanging trees. Wandering in was like entering a magical world from one of the fairy tale stories my mother used to tell me as a child. Beams of sunlight shone through the gaps in the branches, which cast stunning shadow shapes around me while I was drawn to the bright ending.

There it was. So beautiful, I couldn't believe my eyes.

As I stood there, the two heavy suitcases slid out of my sweating hands onto the ground. I did not spare a glance towards them. All the quirky, slightly gothic features were like nothing else I had seen before. Windows – so many that at that moment, I didn't care to count. Little towers stuck out from the roof spaces, and a vast porch supported by four beautifully carved columns drew me in.

Chapter 1

Two weeks earlier

"Wake up, honey! Wake up, honey!" called a deep, sexy voice. The sound made me groan and feel like screaming inside as I pulled the pillow over my head.

"When are you going to change your alarm tone, Liz?" Su asked, taking hold of my bedsheet and dragging it off me. This had become the usual morning routine lately. "You're just torturing yourself listening to his voice. He's a jerk! Remember?" Her exasperated tone was something I was getting used to.

I sighed deeply, knowing she was right. I sat up in bed, watching her scurry around the room.

"Later, I'm going to take you out to that new place down the road, so wear something nice!" she ordered while placing yesterday's post on the nightstand.

"You know that I do *not* want to celebrate my birthday, Su," I mumbled, slightly annoyed.

"I know," she sighed, shoulders drawing down; but I knew she was ignoring my wishes. "That's why it's just the girls tonight, and we are going to have a bit of fun!" Throwing my closet open, she tossed a few dresses out of it onto my bed. "Are you not going to open your post?" she pressed, pointing towards the pile of envelopes, which were probably all birthday cards – and the reason I had ignored them when they arrived. Noticing my silence, she slowed down and turned to look at me.

"Look, Liz, I know you have been through a lot lately, and that you miss her a lot, especially today." She walked over to sit next to me on the bed, holding my hand in both of hers. "I'm not trying to make you forget her, but I know she would want you to celebrate your birthday, or to at least enjoy yourself." As she spoke, I couldn't help the tears from rolling down my face.

My mum and I had this tradition since my eighteenth birthday, where on that day, we would do something we had never done before. We were always up for a new experience. I remember when we first thought of the idea. It was on a bus journey from Galway to Dublin. She was taking me shopping there so we could spend some proper time together after my busy college year.

During the journey, she told me I had grown into a beautiful, independent woman with a wonderful career ahead of me. Although I don't remember her exact words, it was something along those lines. What I will never forget is the way she reached for my hand, holding it firm, when we decided no matter how busy my life got, or where I ended up living, birthdays we would spend together and make it into a day we would always remember.

We had followed through with this for the past eleven years. Oh, and the fun we had! Horse riding on a beach in Dingle, which left both of us sitting on gel coolant pillows for our sore bums in the evening. The oil painting workshop with a dark, handsome, nude model, who got more attention from all of us beginner painters than the brush and canvas ever got. Cupcake baking lessons, salsa dancing . . . to last year, when my birthday was on a Friday.

We decided to make it a three-day camping trip "in the wild," as we called it. Of course, for most people, "the wild" would be somewhere in sunny Tanzania on a safari with lions, leopards, and elephants. Ours was in Connemara with wild sheep and rain. But it was a trip I will never forget.

We had both taken the Friday off work. We left at six in the morning – I don't know what we were thinking. We spent an entire week making lists over the phone and discussing what to bring. The list was so long, it could have been a three-week holiday we were planning for.

My mum bought this cheap tent. “We only need it for two nights,” she informed me as she argued her position for buying the most unreliable tent, which was more like an indoor play tent for young children. That would have explained why it started leaking as soon as the rain poured down, and we ended up sleeping in the car for the first night. We laughed so much that night while being sandwiched between the load of luggage we had brought.

The following morning, we woke up stiff and aching, which is when we decided to go to the nearby hostel to have a shower and make some breakfast. Inevitably, we concluded we would stay there for the last night. Of course, then the weather had turned around and was unusually nice that day. We spent it mostly outside, having the most wonderful of walks, conversations of fond memories and plans for the future.

That night while we lay in bed, Mum said, and I recall so well: “Liz, plans for your thirtieth birthday will be a surprise.”

We always had a close relationship. I wasn’t sure if it was because my father wasn’t around, or because my mum was so young when she had me, but we could relate easily to one another. It would have been fair to say that she was as much my friend as my mother.

Su held me until the tears let up. I stared up at the photograph hanging on the wall. It was me and

Mum sitting on the beach with our arms around each other's shoulders, enjoying a beautiful summer's day. I sighed, suppressing a fresh bout of tears. "You're right, she would have wanted me to celebrate, she would." Su gave a little encouraging smile and left me to it.

For a moment, I wondered what Mum's birthday surprise would have been.

Reaching down to the foot of the bed, I pulled the pile of dresses and with a little burst of enthusiasm, decided to give today my best attempt.

I took a shower, applied some makeup, straightened my hair, and even sprayed some perfume. All that, and it was still only the morning.

Su tried to disguise the surprised look as I walked into the kitchen. Since my mother died, there was not one Saturday where I left my bedroom before noon, despite her consistent efforts.

She ushered me into a seat at our dining table which had my favourite doughnut, paired with bright, fresh strawberries on a plate waiting for me. We ate breakfast together with the radio playing in the background.

#

"Liz, would you like if I came with you today?" Su inquired in a gentle voice as she picked away at her doughnut after she finished a healthy bowl of porridge.

"I would." I smiled appreciatively, looking up at her, my eyes starting to get watery again.

Every Saturday afternoon, I visited my mother's grave to bring fresh flowers and speak to her about whatever had happened that week, from the huge electricity bill that arrived in the post, to her old neighbour who came by the shop again to buy flowers for his mistress. Or maybe this time they were for his wife. We had always wondered if she knew about her husband's affair. Mum thought she must know. "Oh, Liz, things are almost never just as they seem," she would affirm.

The lovely weather made us decide to walk the short journey to our shop. It'd been almost six years now since we opened our floral boutique, Ms Bouquet. The business had really taken off since we expanded to the online market, and we even discussed the prospect of opening another chain around the county.

Su does most of the business side of things, and I am more the hands-on person in the partnership, making arrangements for all occasions and hosting floral design classes.

After graduating from the floristry school in Dublin, we spent around a year planning, getting to know the business, before we had set up shop in Barna in County Galway, where we also rented an apartment. I liked being back in the small, picturesque seaside village where I had spent much of my childhood. It's been about two months now since I moved back into the old apartment with Su, after calling off my engagement to Gordon.

I barely noticed the walk there until the chime jingled as Su opened the door to our shop. Adrianna was cutting flower stems at the worktable and raised her eyebrows, clearly surprised to see me in this early. "You look lovely, Elizabeth!" she said, pushing aside the sheared stems on the counter.

"Why thank you, Adrianna," I replied as if it was the kindest thing I had ever heard.

"It's her birthday!" Su blurted out in an upbeat voice.

"Happy birthday!" she exclaimed, the surprised look never quite leaving her face. *I must look like hell the other times if she's this surprised.* I thanked her, focusing on the flowers, pretending it was no big deal.

Adrianna worked in the shop on weekends, and occasionally during weekdays if we had a big order for a wedding or on special days like Valentine's Day and Mother's Day, when the shop would be busier than usual.

Browsing around, I started to pick the flowers for my mother's bouquet. The scent of the flowers always enchanted me, and all the colours were a feast to the eyes. "The shop looks great!"

Adrianna smiled, pleased as she met my gaze.

"No compliment for me?" Su joked.

"Best birthday breakfast ever." I winked at her. As we exchanged a little light banter, my bouquet turned out beautifully. *Just as she would have liked it,* I told myself. I always made sure to include white roses, as she adored them, and this time, I complemented them with white germinis, chrysanthemums, and gypsophila, and for some colour, purple lisianthus and blue statice. The creations you could make are endless; that's what always inspires me and why the job never gets boring.

Su and I left the shop just as a customer walked in, and we set out together toward the cemetery.

#

When we arrived there, I noticed, to my amazement, it appeared much more visited than the other times I had been, which was generally later in the afternoon. It made the place feel less lonely. The bright weather also helped.

Walking slowly past the rows of headstones, I always noticed which graves were unvisited and left unattended. Seeing those made me sad.

There was one grave in particular which caught my eye. It read: David Mo–. A True Friend 1814–1877. The *M* and *O* were the only letters from his surname I could make out from the old, disintegrating gravestone. I wondered if anyone knew this man or even attended his funeral, other than his friend. What had happened in his life? Sighing, I drew one white rose from my mother's bouquet and laid it on his grave.

At my mother's funeral, there were no direct family members. Her mother – my grandmother – had died when she was only sixteen years old, and she never knew her father since he left them when she was only a baby. She also had no siblings.

Mum never told me much about my grandmother, and whenever I asked about her, she would quickly change the conversation or make herself busy. I never pushed her much on it, as it seemed to upset her. On the other hand, she had a big circle of friends who all attended the funeral. *She was well loved*, I told myself, walking to her grave.

It occurred to me that I was just like David now. No family. The thought made me shiver.

Finally approaching Mum's grave, I noticed a man kneeling in front of it, appearing to be crying, as he rubbed his eyes vigorously. "Who is that?" Su whispered, stopping in her tracks.

"I have no idea. No man has visited my mother's grave since the burial that I know of," I answered, bewildered.

He must have heard us because he got up and walked away quickly. We exchanged confused glances but continued until we stood side by side at the foot of my mother's grave.

"Probably a friend," I told Su when I saw the flowers left on her grave. I crouched down to inspect them. It was a beautiful bouquet of pink scented lilies. I saw a flash of paper underneath as I touched a stem and unearthed the card.

"Oh, it's not from him," I said, reading the note. The flowers were from Margret, my mother's best friend. The card read: I miss you, Heather, x Margret.

"Look!" Su called out in a louder voice than you would usually use in a cemetery. She pointed towards the ground at a paper attached to a single white rose, a small distance from my mother's grave. I walked over and picked it up. "Well? What does it say?" Su asked, giving me a fright as she stood right beside me now.

I scanned around, but he was gone. I passed my mother's bouquet to Su and opened the little, nameless envelope to read the card.

"Sorry."

Frowning, I turned the card over to check all its faces.

"Sorry?" Su repeated, confused, lengthening her neck to get a better look at the message.

"Yes, Su. 'Sorry.' That's all it says.".

"He must have dropped it when he walked off," Su reasoned.

"Sorry for what?" I questioned aloud, half expecting more words to materialise on the card.

"Are you sure you didn't recognise him, Liz?" Su asked, pacing by my mother's grave, likely looking for more clues.

"No, I definitely didn't." I once again looked around to see if he was still about, but the cemetery suddenly looked very empty. "One white rose, a card that says sorry, but no name, nothing," I said aloud, again hoping futilely that something would come to me. "He must have been someone special," I mumbled, staring at the symbolic white rose.

"You didn't know all her friends, Liz," Su replied, although it came out more like a question. She was right. It's not like we shared *everything*, even though we were very close. "You didn't tell her about Gordon until four months after you started dating. Remember?" Su pressed, trying to catch my eye.

This was true. Nonetheless, I would have liked to believe that she would have shared anything – or anyone – important in her life with me. "You're right." I nodded. "The flower and card could even have been for someone else. Mum's not the only one who likes white roses," I added, unconvinced.

I mentally shook myself and turned back to my mother's grave. Removing last week's wilted flowers from the vase, Su passed me the bouquet and I arranged them perfectly in place. As per ritual, I read the lines engraved in the small marble plaque.

Heather Elizabeth Hayden
1964–2010
Mum
How much I miss you,
Is a quantity I cannot describe.
How long I will grieve for you,
Endlessly.
You will never leave my mind.
How much I love you, and

Long to have you back in my life.
Mum,
How much you mean to me,
There will never be words that can describe.
Love,
Your daughter, Elizabeth

Two days after she died, I wrote that poem while sitting in her favourite chair. Every day I carry the original piece of paper, now wrinkled from my dried-up tears, with me in my handbag.

We stayed for a while at the cemetery, breathing in the much-appreciated summer weather and letting the moments of being in her presence count.

Once back home, sheer exhaustion came over me. Lying down on the couch, I thought briefly about the man in the cemetery, wondering who he was and what the note meant until I got tired of thinking about it and decided to let it go again. My eyes felt heavy and began to close as I cuddled up on the couch in a fleece blanket like a little child.

#

"Liz? Liz!" I heard as my shoulders were gently pushed back and forth.

"Huh?"

"You have been sleeping for four hours, Liz!" Su said.

"What?!" I replied, confused and surprised as I sat up in one quick motion. Then I remembered what day it was.

"We're leaving in an hour," she said in a no-nonsense tone, like a parent to a child. I knew I had no way out of this. I didn't really mind though, as she meant well.

Still surprised at the length of time I had slept, I checked the clock, rubbing my eyes to make sure I wasn't seeing things.

I quickly freshened up, changed my outfit, and added a little bling with some shiny, silver dangle earrings, and we were off to the restaurant.

When we arrived, Claire, Vi, and Aoife were already seated at a table by the window. The place was busy and buzzing with chatter, laughter, and clinking glasses and cutlery. "Hey! Happy birthday, Liz." Vi walked over to me with open arms. "You look lovely! I am really glad you came," she added as we walked toward Claire and Aoife, who were now also standing with beaming smiles.

They hugged and congratulated me as if we hadn't seen each other for a whole year. "I have already ordered a fine bottle of champagne in your honour!" Claire smiled. "The big three-o, how does it feel?"

Aoife frowned and nudged Claire. "You don't ask her that!" As if it was an offence to do so. "You see, for the next nine years she will be twenty-nine when anyone asks, and when she turns forty, she will be thirty-nine for those following nine years," Aoife explained with a slightly serious demeanour.

We all burst out laughing because till this day, none of us were fully certain of *her* real age.

"Anyway, how do you feel, Liz?" Claire asked more seriously after we had composed ourselves again and sat down.

"I'm all right," I said, picking at the tablecloth. "I miss her so much." This came out in a whisper and I stopped talking, trying not to get upset.

"Let's celebrate your birthday and your mother's life," Su said, sensing I needed some support.

I nodded. "Yes, that would be lovely. Thank you, guys, for doing this! If not for you, I would still be in the apartment, probably in bed already." I gave them a grateful smile. We all have been such good friends for quite some years now, and they were my only constant support in this difficult time.

#

The following morning, everyone was still asleep when I woke up. My head was throbbing like mad. The bottle of champagne wasn't the only alcohol we had drank. After the restaurant, we all headed back to the apartment, continued drinking, and consumed a huge amount of chocolate, probably more than the weekly intake nutritional guidelines would recommend. We watched several episodes of *Sex and the City* and finished the night with a good dose of gossiping about old boyfriends and lovers – not touching on my ex-fiancé. We all had fallen asleep, cozied up in front of the fire with lots of pillows and blankets. I hadn't laughed and enjoyed myself like that in a long time.

After taking two paracetamols and a strong cup of coffee, I managed to drag myself into the shower. It did wonders. Sitting on the edge of my bed, wrapped in a towel, I reached for the pile of envelopes that was still lying on my nightstand. The first one I opened was from Margret; since she and my mother became friends, which was for as long as I can remember, she'd never forgotten one of my birthdays.

"She's so kind," I said aloud, suddenly guilt-stricken for not having returned her call. I gave the card a special place on my nightstand. I picked up the next one and immediately recognised the handwriting on the envelope. It was from Gordon.

For a while, I hesitated, wondering if I even wanted to open it. Trying to get over him had been so hard, and this certainly didn't help. Nor did the countless phone calls from him which I kept trying to ignore. In the end, my curiosity – and admittedly, lingering affection for him – made the decision for me.

Tearing open the envelope, I pulled out the card with shaking fingers. I didn't even look at the front of it. Only the inside mattered. "Happy Birthday" was printed in the centre of the card, followed by his own handwriting which said: I miss you, honey, Love, Gordon x.

Right then, I wanted to call him and let him know I missed him as well. My heart still ached for him since calling off the engagement. Even though he hurt me so deeply, love doesn't just disappear. Sometimes I wondered if I was wrong in ending the relationship. Other people have similar complications and still found a way to overcome them and continue to live a happy, fulfilled life with each other. Was I just naïve wanting more?

I reached for the handle of my bedside cabinet, pulling it open, and withdrew my diary. Browsing through the pages, as always, I stopped at the same one. The day we met.

Not looking for you, just having fun, no care,
Suddenly, you were standing there.
So confident, yet poised,
The words you spoke with such intelligence,
But not for show.
That dance, like a movie scene
A gentleman's kiss was your exit choice,
I eagerly await for tomorrow to hear your voice.
20-11-09

I signed off with my rose lipstick kiss. Corny, maybe, but when you are so captivated by someone, anything goes. Meeting him was so unexpected, which had made it even more thrilling. That night, I was truly on cloud nine.

I hadn't written much new poetry in my diary for some months now. One of the last entries was when my relationship with Gordon was going downhill rapidly. I remember the way I could barely keep my words on the lines as my hands shook with despair. Taking a deep breath, I turned the pages to that day.

Do you still have feelings for her?
Does she for you?
What are her intentions?
Shared custody, or does she want more?
What are your intentions? Are you even sure?
I don't know what worries me more,
You, her, or me,
My insecure thoughts that just accumulate more and more.
Did you laugh with her as you do with me?
Do you share a deeper history?
Truthful answers are what I need.
Don't you realise how much this is hurting me!
You talk about your baby's future, but it isn't with me.
You walk around with secrecy and provide nothing to inform me.
That is a lot you ask from me.
I should be the one carrying your baby!

Reading that again made me feel sick with anger and I threw his card aside. "Let him go, he isn't worth it!" I said, irritated that I was getting upset again and even ever contemplating the thought we could have made it work. Never!

#

I shook myself and picked up the next envelope. It was brown, A5 in size, and had my old address from where I lived with Gordon crossed through with marker and my current address written underneath. Strangely, it was stamped from England. It didn't look like a Happy Birthday greeting would be inside, nor did I know anyone in England, even though I was born there.

Opening it, I pulled out a folded, expensive-looking cream letter. The page had a crest printed at the top centre, with Jones & Thompson Solicitors, Colchester, printed underneath, followed by:

Re: Ms H. Hayden

Dear Ms E. Hayden

I'm writing to inform you that I have completed the administration of Ms H. Hayden's estate. To finalise the transfer of your inheritance, please complete and sign the enclosed form and return with the required documents listed to the address below.

On receipt of these, we will provide you with the deed of the estate and relevant papers forthwith.

Yours sincerely,

David B. Jones

I read and re-read the few sentences over and over. It didn't make any sense! All my mother's affairs were put in order. I had overseen the sale of her house, which sold quickly, and she didn't have any other assets, and definitely not in England.

I scanned the page for a phone number so I could ring them when it occurred to me that it was Sunday, and the office would be closed. Annoyed, I silently wished I had opened the post earlier.

"What are you reading?" Su asked, startling me. I hadn't heard her come in. She leaned in to peer over my shoulder.

"It's a letter from a solicitor's practice in England about my inheritance from Mum. It says I have inherited her estate, I think." Baffled, I let my own words sink in.

Su pulled the paper out of my hands and read it for herself. It took her a good few minutes just to read those short sentences. She looked as tired and hungover as I felt earlier. "It looks legit," she finally said, examining the paper once more as if it was a hundred-euro note and she was looking for the watermark.

"Give them a ring tomorrow to find out what the deal is," Su said quite carelessly and out of character.

"I was already planning to do so," I snapped back, getting inexplicably annoyed. Su looked back at me.

"Sorry, Liz, my head is throbbing like mad. I'm not used to drinking like that anymore," she said, holding her head in her hands, the paper getting crumpled.

"Tell me about it," I sighed. "We overdid it a bit."

"A bit!" With a hint of a smile, she handed the letter back.

"Get some paracetamol, and I will make us my special hearty breakfast." Her smile widened at that and she turned, strolling toward the door. "And, Su!" I called after her. "Thank you. I had a great time!"

#

Monday morning at exactly 9:00 a.m., I rang the number. It went straight through to a recorded message informing me of their business operating hours, which were nine to five from Monday to Friday, and then it disconnected. They should be open. I was about to call again when Su shouted from the kitchen.

"Gordon is at the door!"

He was the last person I wanted to deal with today.

Steeling myself, I marched toward the front door like a soldier and pulled the door open with such force, he stepped back in surprise. We spent a moment just staring at each other in silence until he broke eye contact.

"Hi, Liz," he said, obviously nervous.

"This really isn't a good time!" I spat, and turned my attention back to my phone. I was dying to find out more about the letter, and he was not going to derail me from my mission. He ignored me though, powering on.

"I didn't expect you to be home. I was going to leave this by the front door," he said as he held up a pink gift bag with a gold glitter border.

"What is it?" I asked impatiently, wanting him to leave, my last diary entry still fresh in my mind.

"A present for your birthday," he replied as he slowly placed the bag on the ground, knowing very well I wasn't going to take it from him. He opened his mouth as if to say something else but then cleared his throat. "Anyway, I'll be going now. Wouldn't want to make you even more late for work." He hesitated at the door before turning around and walking back to his car.

I didn't bother to say that I wasn't late for work. Su had rung Adrianna to ask if she could cover for a few hours so we could have an easy morning.

I slammed the front door, consciously leaving the bag outside. My muscles relaxed as I slumped against it. When I turned to open the door again, bringing the bag inside, his car was already gone.

Dumping it on the floor I pressed redial, still standing in the hallway. After three rings, someone answered.

"Good morning, Jones and Thompson, how may I help you?" said an overly cheerful voice for a Monday morning.

"Hi, good morning, can I speak with David Jones?" I said, reading the sign-off from the letter.

"What's your name please?" she asked, her voice tinkling in my ears.

"Elizabeth Hayden."

"One moment please, Ms Hayden, and I'll put you through."

Her voice was followed closely by a beep and then the most soothing music I ever heard on call waiting. *They probably need it to calm unhappy clients*. I waited for a while, listening to it; and just about zoned out when a deep voice cut through the music.

"Elizabeth Hayden?"

"Yes?"

"David Jones here. How can I help?"

"Uhm, yeah, I . . . I got your letter," I started off, forgetting my words entirely now that I was actually on the call.

"Yes, I have the file pulled up in the computer here. Is there a problem with getting the documents?"

"No . . . no, I have them. It's just that I didn't know about the inheritance and frankly, I'm quite confused. I don't know why she never told me . . ." I trailed off, embarrassed. "Sorry, I know this isn't your problem. I was just wondering if you could tell me a bit more about it?" I said, thankful that there was a phone – and an ocean – between us.

"Right, of course. Well, Ms Hayden . . ." he began very officially, as if she was an acquaintance of mine and not my deceased mother.

"She owned a property in Colchester, in Essex. Do you know the place?"

"Uh-huh, I do. I was born there," I replied, surprised again that I never knew my mother owned another property, and in Colchester of all places.

"So you know the area then?"

"No, I actually don't. We moved to Ireland when I was still a baby."

"Oh, I see. Well, the property is on the edge of Colchester, in a lovely rural setting," he detailed, as if he was trying to sell it to me. "Ms Hayden paid all the necessary fees. She didn't want to leave you with any financial burden, and as stated in the letter, the entire estate has been left to you."

Tears welled up in my eyes. I reached for the tissues in my handbag hanging on the coat hook to dab them away, but new ones kept coming. It was such a big inheritance, and my mum never mentioned it. Why hadn't she? It wasn't like her. I felt overcome by it.

"Hello? Ms Hayden?" he broke the silence.

"Uh, yes, sorry. Thank you for the information. I will post everything to you as soon as possible," I blurted quickly and ended the phone call, not wanting to cry to a complete stranger.

When my tears stopped, I picked up the gift bag and made my way to the kitchen. Su held a tray full of delicious foods for our breakfast at the ready, making my stomach rumble. “Perfect timing. Well? What did he say?” she asked curiously.

I looked up at her, and her face morphed into anger when she saw mine. “What has he done this time?” she demanded to know. “Get that man out of your life already!” She put the tray on the counter with a bang.

“It isn’t him, Su! He just came to drop off this.” Vexed, I held the bag up. Su looked at it disapprovingly.

“If not him, then what happened?” she asked a bit softer, still an edge in her voice. She really didn’t like Gordon.

“Let’s sit down first,” I breathed.

Once our plates were filled with sweet, delicious pastries, I started relaying what Mr Jones had said during the phone call and noticed Su going pale. “Are you feeling all right?” She gave the slightest of nods.

“What’s wrong?” She avoided my gaze for some long seconds before sighing and glancing at me.

“Look, Liz, I’m going to tell you something. I’m not sure if I should, or if it will help, or maybe clarify some things, but . . . I-I don’t even know if this could be related to it . . .” She trailed off, looking down at her hands.

“Spill it, will you?” I said in a low but impatient voice, feeling riled up by the mere thought of there being more secrets. "Whatever it is, I can handle it." I hoped those words came out convincingly because I sure didn't feel so.

"Okay!" she said, sitting up straight and finally looking at me, as if she was ready to release a bombshell. Just in the way Gordon had done. Suddenly, I felt sick.

"Your – Your mother was going to bring you to England for your birthday this year," she said in a rush. "Sorry I didn't tell you before. I thought it might upset you, but now I think she might have planned to bring you there to . . . to . . . show you the place, maybe?" She faltered, guilt lacing her words.

"How did you know?" I whispered, not really sure if I asked loud enough for her to hear.

"Some weeks before your mother died, she told me her plans for your birthday and asked if I would come as well. She said you might *need* me there. I thought it was a strange invitation at the time, but didn't think about it much further. But now . . ." She took a deep breath. "It just seems a bit coincidental. That's all."

I processed this information. "Maybe . . . she was going to show me around Colchester where she grew up, and the property," I said wistfully. That would have been a wonderful present.

On second thought . . . "Why would I *need* you there?" Su's puzzled expression likely mirrored mine. "Maybe . . . she was just inviting you to come along to celebrate my birthday. My mum and my best friend." I explained it away. The thought filled me with love and sadness. Su looked unconvinced, but I didn't care.

"Thank you for telling me, Su."

We didn't speak about it any further as we devoured our breakfast, feeling absolutely famished, but my mind was still distracted with thoughts of England and my mother.

"Well, are you going to open it?" Su asked after a while.

"What?" I replied reflexively, knowing very well what she meant.

"Gordon's present!" She lowered her voice a little, then declared, "You know that I think you shouldn't." I nodded, looking down at my plate. "Why do you keep doing this to yourself, Liz? Cut him out of your life! Hasn't he caused you enough misery?"

"I'm trying to do that!" I replied, getting annoyed at her constant drilling. How could she possibly know how hard it is?

"Well, try harder! Your mother would have told you the same," Su said, raising her voice.

"Leave her out of it! Stop telling me what I should or shouldn't do!" I snapped, pushing my chair back from under me and grabbing the gift bag from the ground so roughly one of the straps flung loose. I stormed to my room like an unreasonable teenager, opened the present, and got ready for work.

#

When Su and I arrived at our shop, we only spoke to each other if we had to. It was a short day since we started later than usual, but it felt as though it lasted forever. Adrianna had stayed for a while, but she was noticeably uneasy by our lack of communication, and she kept to herself more than usual.

We had our disagreements and arguments from time to time – we live and work together, after all – but this one was so unnecessary. I left the shop first and Su locked up after me. We walked home in the same manner, several feet apart.

Back at the apartment, I cooked dinner, making more noise with utensils and pots than I normally would. When nearly done making the meal and thus taking out my anger on the kitchen cupboards now, Su walked in.

"What did he give you?" she asked, her voice neutral.

"Pink fluffy slippers," I mumbled, embarrassed that he gave me such a stupid present. Su tried to contain her laughter but couldn't, and after a while, I couldn't either.

"I'm so sorry, Su." I reached out before hugging her tightly. "I am a bit all over the place."

"Yes, you are." I pulled back and gave her a stern look, while her face softened. "Me too. I'm sorry too. You know I just don't want to see you hurting," Su said, almost whispering. I nodded, and with that we had made up.

Dinner tasted horrible, probably from the lack of love I put into it, so we ordered pizza. We ate in front of the TV, watching Comedy Central's *Roadshow* to lift our spirits.

"We should give Adrianna a call to apologise," Su said.

"Yeah, we should," I agreed heartedly, feeling guilty for putting her through such an uncomfortable day.

#

The following morning, I got all the paperwork ready for Mr Jones to put in the post box on my way to work. Su had made a delicious breakfast again. Her famous omelette with goat cheese and fresh rocket salad. I scuffed it down quickly as we spoke about the day ahead. My ringtone broke through our conversation. I glanced at the name and rolled my eyes, leaving it alone.

"Are you not going to take that?" she asked as my phone kept ringing.

"No! It's Gordon. He has left four voicemails already."

"Right, it's time you change your number. This is getting ridiculous!" Su picked up my phone and started to listen to the voice messages and broke out in laughter. I felt inexplicably embarrassed.

"I'm sorry, Liz, but there's no way you would want him back after hearing this!" I could feel my face getting flushed. "Liz, he gave you the wrong present; that one was for Monica! He's asking for it back and hoping you haven't opened it, and if you did, he says he's 'really sorry'." She bent her fingers into air quotes. "Come on, Liz! Do you really want to stay caught up with this eejit?"

I pulled the phone out of her hand and listened to the voice messages myself. He sounded pathetic, rambling like a child in trouble. I awkwardly laughed while tears were welling up in my eyes. "You're right, Su, I feel so stupid. How could I have allowed myself to be so blinded?"

"Because you still love him, Liz."

"No!" I said with determination I didn't know I had in me. "Today after work, I am going to let him go for good!"

"Good!" Su smiled, unable to hide her surprised expression while leaning over to hug me. She picked up her phone and began texting the gang to invite them.

Pls come over this evening at 8, we r getting rid of Gordon!

I looked over at her phone and quickly took it, adding:

Symbolically that is!!! x Liz

In case they wondered if they were being invited to be an accomplice in a murder. They texted back in record speed.

Violet – *Won't miss it for the world! x*

Claire – *About time! See u this eve x*

Aoife – *I'll bring the firewood and matches. You go girl! X*

#

During the day, apprehension and doubt tried to creep in, but I wouldn't let it. I forced myself to think back over everything that had happened, how much he hurt me, and even listened to the voice messages again, reminding me of the sad little man he is.

After work, I packed everything that was tied to Gordon in any way into a large garbage bag, including the pink fluffy slippers. It felt surprisingly good.

Everyone arrived at the house at almost eight on the dot, which was rather unusual. They seemed almost more excited than I was. "You ready to dump him with Liam?!" Aoife asked. Liam was her last boyfriend; their relationship had ended quite badly.

"I sure am," I said, beaming at her.

"That's what I like to hear!" shouted Su from the kitchen with delight.

"You have all his things?" Violet asked. I pointed at the bag against the wall, her eyes following my finger. "Brilliant!" She nodded approvingly and made her way to the front door, yelling over her shoulder, "I have everything else we need in the car. Let's go!" We all rushed out after her to the car, ready to head off.

Violet drove us to Trá So Lin, a beautiful little beach just off the main road not far from our place. It was completely deserted, and the only sound came from the small waves rolling in. We nestled ourselves between the rough rocks, where Claire and Su started to get the fire going. It was still bright out. The wind wasn't blowing too hard, so they got it started with relative ease. Of course, with the assistance of a serious amount of firelighters.

"You brought cigarettes?" Aoife asked hopefully.

"What do you think?!" Violet said, never being one to miss a single detail.

"Just asking!" she said with a smirk. None of us were full-time smokers, but on certain occasions, we wouldn't do without.

As we sat around the fire smoking our first cigarette, Su reached out a pen and my diary. I shot her a surprised look. "Write down everything you want to get off your chest, girl!" she said, motioning for me to take it from her. I honestly could have cried then; I truly have the greatest friends.

Sitting cross-legged, using my lap as a table, I began writing, starting to feel the heat of the fire which burned high with sparks flying in the dusk, providing a lively artistic scene.

After almost a packet of cigarettes smoked between us, I finished. Instinctively, I stood up and silence fell as I began to read aloud.

Gordon,
I might miss your touch, your gentle stroke over my back.
I might still have a love for you, but don't delude yourself,
I will never take you back!
How dare you have treated me this way,
And then be sorry after the fact.
Did you ever think of me when you fucked her?
Or was she so enticing your brain got a defect?
And now you say you're sorry.
Where were you when I buried my mother?
I think we both know!
So, what.
The day you found out she was pregnant,
My mother is dead, and you go?
How dare you! You ASSHOLE!!
I need to let you go.
You're an addiction, bad for my soul.
I hope you hurt as much as I have!
I hope you will forever live with a feeling of regret!
YOU. GIANT. ASS.

Tears rolled down my face as I tore the page out of my diary and threw it in the fire, which I followed with more pages.

"Do the honours, Liz?" Su said, passing me the horrible pink slippers once I was finished with the diary. They were consumed by the fire in seconds and released an awful stench, which felt fitting. I then tossed in his shirt, which I used to sniff most nights just to feel close to him.

Next, the photographs of our great times together, or so I had thought – burned! Presents he had given me – burned! My engagement ring – "NO!" Aoife shouted, a second too late. "You could have sold that," she said with a huff. I noticed Claire poke her in her side with her elbow.

Valentine's cards and entry tickets to places we had visited – burned! Everything went up in flames, my materialistic history with him erased in minutes. Tears still streamed down my face as I released my anger, which turned to sadness, and finally acceptance.

I sank down to my knees, overwhelmed and relieved at once. Claire and Su held me.

"He was the one. I was going to spend the rest of my life with him," I said, choking back more tears. Forever letting go of the idea.

"I know, Liz, I am so sorry," Su said, hugging me tighter.

"This calls for a drink," Aoife said as we all looked towards Violet, who was already rummaging through her massive picnic bag. In no time we were sipping some cocktails, fitting for a celebration for new beginnings.

The atmosphere lightened as we allowed ourselves to get lost in the sound of the ocean and the flickering fire shining brighter by the minute as the sun disappeared behind the horizon.

Aoife stood up to make a toast. “To Gordon and Liam, may you become best mates!” We all fell into laughter. “Wait! Wait, I’m not done yet.” She turned to me, her expression soft. “More importantly: to a fresh start and an exciting future.”

“To you, Liz!” the rest called out.

“Thank you, guys,” I said, smiling, letting out a deep breath.

#

The next morning, I felt a little numb and emotionally worn out. The relief I hoped to feel was chalked up to a more disappointing acceptance of what is.

Arriving at work, we were wrecked. We had considered ringing Adrianna to ask her to cover for a few hours again, but after our behaviour yesterday, we decided not to. We had a busy day ahead of us. A big order for a wedding to prepare for delivery tomorrow, some smaller orders, and I was teaching a class later in the evening. I normally loved doing classes, but today I was so exhausted, I was dreading it.

Then of course there were the people who just came in from the street. The first person to walk into the shop today, of all people, was my mother’s old neighbour, always wearing a long overcoat and walking with a cane that was purely for show.

"Hi, Elizabeth! How are you today?" he said, his face brightening at the sight of me.

"Not too bad," I answered as standard. "So, Mr Connolly," I said, never wanting to be acquainted with him on a first-name basis. "What can I do for you today? Flowers for your wife or mistress?" I said with a roll of the tongue. Shockingly, he hardly flinched.

Suddenly, there were several bangs from the storeroom which got both our attention. Su trampled out as if she had just fended off a burglar. "Mr Connolly!" she blurted, all but plunging herself behind the counter and elbowing me aside. "Lovely for you to visit our shop again," she said hastily, straightening her clothes and hair while making obvious gestures with her eyes for me to leave.

"My apologies, Mr Connolly, she has been going through a lot lately. What can I get you today?" I overheard Su say as I took my leave to the storeroom.

"No bother . . ."

He bought his bouquet and then left rather quickly, as I heard the bell from the front door chime probably no more than a minute later. I picked up the clipboard Su must have discarded and busied myself with taking note of the ribbon stock.

Su stormed into the room shortly after, clearly unimpressed. "What's wrong with you! You might not approve of his lifestyle, but he is a damn good – and frequent – customer." I felt my defiance fade and instead felt flushed with embarrassment as it dawned on me how callous I had been.

"Oh God, I'm so sorry, Su. I didn't realise I was going to say it and then it was just . . . out," I said, feeling guilty. Turning away, I sped out of the shop to see if Mr Connolly was still around so I could apologise, but he was nowhere to be seen. I walked back into the shop regretful.

Su stood at the opposite end with her hands on her hips. I shook my head. "Well, we probably won't see him back anymore," Su said, going back to work.

"I'm really sorry," I said, unsure how to make this up.

"I know you are." Her tone still had a hard edge to it. My mother would have been extremely disappointed in me, I thought, picking up a vase and getting back to work as well.

Later in the evening, as we sat on the couch with a glass of merlot, tired from the day, Su was the first to laugh about it. "Imagine him, worrying that you might tell his wife!" she said, giggling into her hand.

"Well, serves him right!" I said, grinning back at her. "Of course, I have no intention of actually doing that," I quickly added.

"I am glad to hear it. But honestly, he kind of deserves it."

#

Gordon hadn't rung for a whole week now. Maybe he finally got the message. It was good not to be constantly reminded of him, but I was still hit with bouts of loneliness. Did he not care anymore? Was that all he could do to try to get me back? Not that I wanted or would have taken him back. But somewhere, I guess, I hoped he would have tried harder. But now seeing that he hadn't, it in return gave me confidence in knowing I deserve better than him.

"There is post from England!" Su shouted from the hallway with excitement.

"Already? That's fast!" I rushed to the door.

"I signed for it!" she said, waving the large envelope in her hand. We had spoken about my inheritance quite a lot since the now famous letter, wondering what kind of property it is. We had even gone as far as talking about future holidays and using the house as a base to explore the city of Colchester and further afield. It's supposed to be really beautiful there, "a thriving modern city, with unique heritage and history, inspiring nearby countryside, award-winning museums, a castle, and even a zoo," or so we had read doing some research. Not that I had any interest in going to the zoo. I hadn't even visited the Dublin Zoo before, but nevertheless, one was there.

I never had an interest in finding out more about my birthplace until now. I always felt one hundred percent Irish. This had been and still was my only home for as long as I could remember. Yet now I welcomed the distraction, and I couldn't deny it was exciting.

The envelope felt stiff and rattled a bit as Su handed it to me. I quickly tore it open, and a set of weathered silver keys fell out onto the ground. Su picked them up as I pulled out the stack of pages still caught in the envelope. "Well?" she asked impatiently as I quickly glanced through them.

"Nothing," I said, seeing only tightly packed writing. "Just a lot of legal mumbo-jumbo, no pictures at all!" I rechecked the duplex-printed pages a little slower. There was no way they only sent me a bunch of words and no *real* details on the property itself. I saw a flash of a box-like shapes on one of the pages and pulled it out from the rest. "Here! I think it's a blueprint."

For some moments we just stared at it, stunned. I counted eight bedrooms, five bathrooms, three drawing rooms, what seemed to be a large kitchen and a smaller one, and some extra rooms with no clear description.

"It's huge! That can't all be mine. Can it? It's probably split up into several apartments," I observed in disbelief.

"They wouldn't have sent you this drawing if you only owned a section of it, now would they?" Su said, half stealing the page from my hands to get a better look.

“Wow! Oh my God! I own a property! And it’s enormous!” I shouted, nearly dancing with glee.

“Check again if there is a picture,” Su said, matching my excitement.

I rifled through them once more but there was nothing. “Nope. Not even one.” This reminded me again of the mind-blowing fact that my mother never told me she had a property in England, and this large! Why did my mum never share this information with me? As amazing as it is, I wished she’d told me. This definitely wasn’t the small, one-bedroom apartment she’d spoken about, where we lived briefly after I was born.

“Your mum would have told you, and probably shown you on the trip to England she was planning for your birthday, if given the chance,” Su said, noticing the change in my mood, reading me oh so well. I nodded, shaking myself of questioning thoughts.

“You know, she hadn’t been to England since we moved here. The property can’t be in the best condition.” I shrugged, suddenly imagining a large, derelict house with broken windows, roof with fewer tiles than it should have, and drains falling down from overgrowth. “I will have to arrange somewhere else to stay when I go see the place.”

“Yea, that may be best, till you know the state it’s in,” Su agreed a little dispirited, both our excitement dampened by the prospect of a half ruin.

That night, I didn't sleep much. My mind was filled with thoughts. Every explanation I conjured felt a bit off. It was all overwhelming.

"Have you booked yet?" Su shouted from the kitchen. She had asked this several times now. The uncertainty of not knowing what to expect, I found unsettling, and had made me a little hesitant. It wasn't supposed to be this way, going without my guiding mum. The only good thing about it all was that I had no room in my head to spare a thought for Gordon.

"Are you sure two weeks isn't too long? We have so many orders, and you'll need to take over my classes," I repeated. I didn't want to leave them with overwhelming responsibilities.

"It's fine! Adrianna and I will manage without you," she reassured.

"Will you bring flowers to my mother's grave while I'm away?"

Su peeked her head around the door, her expression briefly changed into a softer one. "Of course I will, Liz. Now go book your ticket!"

"Yeah, yeah, I'm doing it! I can fly direct to Southend Airport. Says here it's only forty miles away from Colchester!" I shouted in her general direction, each click taking me closer to my destination.

"Great. Now book!" she said sternly, appearing again at the door, this time waving a spoon.

Chapter 2

As I reached down to pick up my suitcases, a shadow of a person was visible on the ground. I rushed to look up and froze. A man stood beside me, holding one of them. He was tall, of slender build, slightly rough-looking, and wearing dirty, torn, light-coloured denim jeans with a navy T-shirt covered in paint stains.

"Hi! You must be Elizabeth. I'm Andrew!" he said in a deep voice and stuck out his free hand to shake mine. I stared at his hand for a beat too long until the man, somewhat unfazed, pushed it back into his pocket. "We expected you to arrive yesterday!" He half gestured to the house. "But I'm glad you're here now."

With my body still stiff with shock, only my mouth managed to move, stammering over my words as I mentioned that I wasn't supposed to arrive yesterday. While my only thoughts were, who is this man? And how does he know my name?

He cleared his throat, breaking me out of my internal line of questioning. "I'm here to show you around, didn't they tell you?" he asked, a frown breaking across his features.

"*They*? Who are they? And – and what are –" I blurted when the man, *Andrew*, suddenly interrupted me.

"Everything is always left to me," he muttered, annoyed. "You can't trust some of those big-shot city folks to get things done as asked. Just pass on a simple message! They are always so caught up in their own lives!" he ranted, his face turning red as he progressed. "No offence," he said belatedly as he looked down, staring straight into my eyes.

Aside from the fact that I did take offence, although more so from his arrogance in pretending to know me, his blunt statements about some city folks did have some merit. Having lived in a busy city for a while myself, I could understand what he meant.

"My apologies, Lizzy," he suddenly said in a much calmer tone of voice, his face relaxing as he looked at me with an expression resembling sympathy. "You must be *really* confused right now. You don't mind if I call you Lizzy, do you?"

I felt a rush of anger flame my cheeks. Only my mother and my closest friends ever called me by my nickname, Liz, and certainly not Lizzy. This stranger stood here talking to me like we were the greatest buddies catching up after a day of hard work.

But instead of voicing my true feelings, which I would have likely done in any other situation, I replied unsurely with, "That's fine," as I mentally kicked myself for not saying that I certainly did mind. Andrew's expression brightened.

"Come, let's sit over there and we can talk." He pointed at an old, cast-iron bench under a beautiful, large willow tree. I dragged my suitcase behind me while he carried the other as if it was as light as a feather.

Once we sat, there was a short period of silence. He must have noticed the shocked and confused state I was in, my body shaking as if I was outside on a cold winter's day without a coat on. "Sorry, let's start over," he said tentatively while reaching out his hand again to introduce himself. "I'm Andrew."

"Elizabeth," I replied, emphasising my full name as our hands shook.

"Nice to see you, Elizabeth!" he said, using my given name, which was more considerate and appropriate, in my mind. "Did you have a good journey?"

"Yes, not too bad," I replied, not giving any more details. Like how the man who sat next to me in the airplane had the worst case of smelly breath and an incredible interest in starting a conversation. Or the terrible cup of coffee and almost stale sandwich I bought in the airport for a whopping €13.50, a total rip-off! Those were the details I would reserve for my *friends*.

"The weather is lovely," I said, gazing toward the bright sky, trying to break the awkwardness that had become apparent again.

"Isn't it!" he confirmed. "The weather has been great so far this summer. What about in Ireland?" he asked, relaxing into a much gentler demeanour.

"So far, we can't complain, but we generally don't expect good summers in Ireland." I placed my hands on my knees to stop the involuntary bouncing.

"Well, I hope for the duration you are here, it stays like this," he said sincerely, with a hint of a smile. I gave a little appreciative smile in return.

"So, you are here to show me around?"

"Yup. Thought it might be nice someone is here to welcome you."

"Would be nice if I was told," I mumbled under my breath, before quickly adding, "The garden looks beautiful," not wanting him to go off on another rant. I stared at the finely pruned hedges and the many flower beds. "I thought no one had lived here for many years. I expected an overgrown garden and a . . . somewhat derelict property?"

Andrew looked at me in what I could only describe as disbelief, his ocean-blue eyes not leaving mine. He opened his mouth several times as if he wanted to say something but didn't know how.

When he finally overcame his surprise enough to speak, he stammered hesitantly, "What – What do you mean, years?"

"Well, I presumed that the house was left to my mother when my grandmother died and that my mother, for some reason I can't imagine why, didn't want to do anything with it since she had never mentioned anything about it to me. And since my mother died . . ." I took a pause, taking a deep breath and trying to compose myself, "I now have inherited this place."

Andrew's eyes widened even further. I rambled on uneasily to fill the silence which had once again descended between us. "Or, well, that was the conclusion I had come to. Has she been renting it out then?" I asked, unsure.

"She?" he asked, finally rediscovering his voice.

"Yes, my mother."

Andrew shook his head.

"No, your grandmother has lived here until she passed away last month," he spoke cautiously, his frown slowly returning.

"Sorry, you said what?"

Andrew slowly repeated the same words again and I let out a squeal of laughter to the ridiculousness of what he was saying. "Is this some kind of joke!?" I said in a louder voice as I stood up, glaring down at him.

"Excuse me?!" He matched my expression. "You *are* Elizabeth Hayden, right?"

"Yes," I answered impatiently.

"And your grandmother was Hilda Hayden, correct?"

"Yes!" I said again, my annoyance bordering on anger. At this point, Andrew was standing as well, towering over me. "Why did you say she died last month?" I demanded.

"Because she did," he answered matter-of-factly.

"Impossible! IMPOSSIBLE!" I shouted while I hastily backed away from him.

"Lizzy!" he called out, following me.

"It's Elizabeth for you!" I snapped, enraged.

"Sorry! Your grandmother always called you Lizzy when she spoke about you," he said, somewhat apologetic.

"You never even knew her. *I* have never known her. She has been dead for decades!" I yelled even louder while darting off towards the porch of the house. I turned and collapsed onto the steps, my hands covering my eyes as hot tears rolled down my face. This *has* to be a dream, I told myself, even though I knew it wasn't. "Why? *Why*?" I asked aloud. "Why the lies?"

As I heard Andrew approaching, I wiped my face and tried to get a hold of myself. He kneeled in front of me, dropping my suitcases at either side of him. "Elizabeth?" he began. "I don't know what you have been told, but your grandmother has lived here for as long as I can remember. She passed away only last month."

"Impossible," I replied again but softer, not hearing him. He didn't say anything and sat next to me on the foot of the porch.

Growing up, my mother always taught me to be vigilant and careful of strangers. She would always say, "There are a lot of good people in the world, Liz, but strangers are called that for a reason." And now there was this stranger talking to me, telling me things that I could not trust. But the distressing part was, I got an inkling I couldn't trust my mother's stories either. I wanted to just run away and cry until no tears could come anymore, but I felt so exhausted and confused that I wouldn't have been able to even run past the tunnel of trees. Not to mention, I was in a foreign land.

"Where are you staying?" he asked, as if he was reading my fleeting thoughts, looking quite uncomfortable.

"In a B&B not far from here," I mumbled, rummaging through my handbag to find the details and handing it to him. "It's the nearest B&B to here," I told him with certainty, having spent a long time searching to find the closest place to the property to stay. Even though the house seemed to be in immaculate condition, I had no interest in staying there, or even looking inside at that moment.

"Ooh, great! You're staying at my place," he said with awkward excitement.

"Excuse me?" I snapped.

"My wife and I own The Slumber. Let me give you a ride. Unless . . . if you want to . . ." He glanced up at the house. My face must have said enough, as he stood up and carried my suitcases down the path to his car.

Unbelievable. First, this person tells me something incomprehensible, and now I will be practically living with him.

I watched from a little distance as he loaded my suitcases into the car. When I approached closer, he was holding the door open. I gave him a small smile to show my appreciation, but judging from his drawn expression, he didn't notice.

It was a swift drive, during which the uncomfortable silence had returned. I didn't know what to say. Every thought that popped into my mind, which were many, seemed ridiculous and inconceivable to me. If there was a level rating for confusion and state of mental destruction like what countries have for the threat of terrorism, mine would be substantial.

The B&B looked closely like the image online which I had studied when I booked, just not photoshopped, and the door colour had changed from green to sky blue. It was a charming double frontage house.

"Sorry for the mess. We should have finished renovating inside last week, but I am pleased to tell you the bedrooms are ready, and not to worry, we won't charge you the full rate," Andrew said as he put my suitcases down in the hall. I didn't reply and stepped over two large pots of brilliant-white paint and some smaller ones of other colours on an unfinished wooden floor.

"Is that you, Drew?" a woman's voice called from another room. We followed her voice and walked into the kitchen diner where she was preparing a meal.

"Why didn't you tell me Elizabeth was staying with us?" Andrew asked, moving toward the woman and kissing her on the cheek. The woman looked confused.

"Elizabeth, this is my wife, Gloria," he said in my direction when she didn't respond to his question.

"Hi." I held up my hand in greeting.

Gloria walked over to shake it, now that the penny had dropped. "Elizabeth, I am so glad you're staying with us." She demonstrated such elegance in her movements, even with the apron and a spatula in her other hand. She was stunning. Not a sexy beautiful but an effortless, all-natural beauty with eyes only a blind man wouldn't notice.

It dawned on me how unflattering I must look. No makeup, my eyes probably red from crying, and my hair – I didn't want to think about. The last time

I'd looked in the mirror was in the airport bathrooms.

"Can I get the key for the room? I am really tired," I asked, longing to be alone.

"Of course."

"You will have dinner with us later, won't you?" Gloria asked in a melodic voice. The invite from her was hard to refuse. Andrew was looking at me too, awaiting my response. I nodded, and he smiled and left to get my key.

"Six okay?" Gloria queried as I was leaving the room to follow Andrew.

"Yes, thank you," I called back. Moments later, Andrew held out a shiny, gold key.

"Here you go. First floor, second door on your right. I hope it's to your liking." He spoke in a business-like manner, giving me a quick nod. I gratefully took the key from him and went to get my luggage.

"Let me help you with those," he said, having followed me and reaching to take them off my hands.

"No. No, thank you. I'm fine," I said briskly as I pulled back and climbed upstairs to my room. As I fiddled with the key, the door couldn't open fast enough. I dropped onto the bed with a heavy sigh. Momentarily I thought of calling Susan, but didn't know what to say, I felt so confused, and opted for a quick text instead. *Hi Su, arrived safely. B&B is nice. Feeling very tired. Chat later x*

For an indeterminate amount of time, I just laid there, unaware of anything but my thoughts, which circled around what Andrew had said. When I did check the time, it was already ten past five and I was feeling in no mood to have dinner with Andrew and Gloria. But since I would be, I did want to look more presentable.

Forcing myself to sit up, letting out an involuntarily groan, I took note of the room for the first time. The space had lots of character with exposed beams, wooden floor, and shutters by the windows. While also having a modern twist, with the use of chrome fixtures and fittings and the glass-brick feature wall leading to the en suite bathroom. It was all tied together tastefully with a subtle blue theme.

I had a quick shower, quick because the water pressure was so strong it felt like getting a scalp massage, as my hair was washed in no time at all. I went for my easy-go-to messy bun style, being in no mood to fuss with the hairdryer. Adding a pair of small hoop earrings and a little touch of mascara and lip gloss, I felt ready. Or, as ready as I was going to be.

#

As I walked down the stairs and approached the kitchen door, it was open the slightest bit and Andrew's distinct voice drifted through the crack.

"She said Hilda died *years* ago," he whispered in disbelief.

"Why would she think that?" came Gloria's voice, almost matching Andrew's confusion.

"I don't know! But her mother died only recently, I think. She thought her mother left the house to her."

"Weren't they in contact? Hilda spoke about her, no?"

"I don't get it either. She rarely mentioned her daughter. She was always a bit evasive about her."

"Maybe they had a falling out?" Gloria posed, her whisper becoming fainter.

As I leaned closer to the door to hear them better, the floorboard creaked underneath me. Their voices went even quieter and seconds later, Andrew swung the door open.

"Hi, Elizabeth!"

My face felt red as I stumbled through the doorway. "Hi." I bashfully tried to compose myself.

"You look lovely. Sit down." Gloria pointed at a chair. "Dinner is almost ready." They both snapped into hosting role. Andrew looked almost unrecognisable. Well-dressed, in casual fitted jeans with a suit jacket over a crisp ironed shirt which added that element of sophistication.

"Thank you," I replied, taking my seat and crossing my arms in a poor attempt to hide how underdressed I felt in their presence with my floral oversized dress, doing nothing for my shape, paired with sandals. It was more of a beach day outfit, not casual chic like Gloria pulled off with a wide-legged, belted black jumpsuit and heels. Little good my effort did.

The table setting was extraordinary, something you would expect to see in a five-star restaurant. A silk table runner, swan napkins, more cutlery than I would know what to do with, and fancy-looking tableware. But the most impressive was the centrepiece, a bouquet with an arrangement of green anthurium, hot-pink roses, violet calla lilies, and gerberas. It was then that I noticed the table was set for four.

"Andrew, will you call Annie in?" Gloria asked, looking over at him expectantly. I turned to look at Andrew too, confused. "Annie is our daughter," Gloria filled in before I had a chance to ask.

"Oh, right." I nodded and turned my attention back to the table, reaching for something to say.

"The table looks beautiful. Especially the flowers," I said, gesturing at the bouquet.

"Glor always goes overboard when it comes to dinners," Andrew said knowingly.

"I like entertaining! There is nothing wrong with that. Now please get Annie, dinner is ready!" she said, making a fanning motion.

She must be the image of a perfect housewife. Beautiful, elegant, organised, loves to cook; one of those women that can do it all, I pondered a little begrudgingly.

Moments later, Andrew walked in with Annie. Her name was very appropriate. With her fair skin, curly red hair and freckles, she reminded me of the Broadway musical Annie, which my mother and I watched numerous times on DVD. The only thing missing was the red dress.

Andrew introduced us with pride only a father can have for their child. She spoke and moved with surprising grace and sophistication for her age, probably around eight, when we shook hands. This was clearly Gloria's influence.

"You can ask," Andrew said, gesturing at his daughter, patting her shoulders gently. "She knows."

I looked from him to Annie, not having a notion of what he meant.

"She's adopted," Gloria said fluidly, stepping in next to Andrew. As I looked at them, the obvious became clear; they shared no resemblance at all. Unless a miracle DNA mutation had happened, there was no way they could have been the biological parents. "I see," I said, unsure how to respond. Mentally kicking myself for the no pun intended. "You're a very beautiful girl, Annie." She smiled at the compliment and took her seat at the table.

The three-course dinner was sensational. If Gloria cooked like that every evening, all men and some women would want to marry her. We never spoke about my grandmother or anything else that happened or had been said during the day. I felt uncomfortable asking questions with Annie there. Thankfully, Annie kept the conversation flowing as she spoke a lot about her friends and a sleepover she went to the previous day. We all listened with great interest, or at least I hopefully showed it. My mind was wandering all over the place. Nevertheless, she was bubbly and polite. This was the family setup I thought I would have in the near future, not so long ago.

Almost eight o'clock, stuffed and tired of socialising, I got up to make my leave. "Thank you for this wonderful meal, it was delicious. And lovely to meet you, Annie," I said, crouching down a little.

"You're a nice lady," she affirmed.

I smiled, despite myself. "Well, thank you. You have a good night now."

"Goodnight, Elizabeth." And to my surprise, she got up and hugged me. I patted her on the back and looked up to see Gloria and Andrew smiling at their daughter.

Being around them for a few hours had been quite an experience, but as soon as I left the room, my brain went into a whirlwind of questions I wasn't even sure I wanted to know the answers to. I craved a smoke. This was one of those occasion that justified harming my lungs, or so I told myself.

I softly knocked on the door I had just left through. Andrew opened it a beat later. "Sorry to disturb, I was just wondering if there is a nearby shop that is still open?"

"There is a local shop, a few roads down." He looked at his watch. "But that closes just about now. The petrol station is still open though. Can I get you something or drive you there?" he kindly offered.

"No, thank you. Just point me in the right direction." I really wasn't looking for company.

"It's about a thirty-minute walk. Are you sure?" Andrew said, eyebrows raised.

"Yes, I'm certain."

#

The evening air brought a little sense of calm as I made my way. The light was slowly fading, and a warm breeze was still present. Andrew was right, it was quite a walk, one you would do in the morning when you're full of energy, not late in the evening after a huge meal and when exhaustion had already hit. Nonetheless, after asking the few people who were out and about for more detailed directions, I arrived.

"You're not from around here, are you?" the lady behind the cashier said in a rich British accent.

"Ireland," I said, fumbling with my wallet to get out some cash.

"Of course you are," she said, taking the notes from my hand and placing the pack of Marlboro back into it. "Well, have a lovely stay. That is, if you are here on holiday?" she said with curious eyes, leaning across the counter slightly.

"Yes, I am." I mustered a polite smile. I sure wasn't going to tell a total stranger why I was really here. And it was sort of a holiday. Not that it was particularly restful since arriving.

On my walk to the petrol station, I had seen the perfect spot to sit down and have a smoke in peace. The bench was situated under a large tree on a small stretch of green beside a quiet road. Having made my way back there without taking a wrong turn, I'd just sat down and lit my cigarette when a car drove slowly by and then reversed back to my location. It took me a few wary moments before I realized it was Andrew. He stuck his hand out of the window and waved.

Startled by his sight, I coughed out the cigarette smoke I tried to hold in and quickly hid it behind my back.

"Are you all right?" Andrew asked, now with his head out the window and car engine turned off.

"Just fine, thanks." *Please, please don't get out of the car*, I wished silently.

He got out.

"No need to hide that from me," he said with a slight smirk. Caught red-handed, and unsure why I was hiding it in the first place, I slowly brought my arm back from behind me.

"Would you like some company?" he asked, standing next to the car hesitantly.

“Sure, why not,” I said courteously while shouting a firm no in my head. Andrew sat down on the bench, reached into his back pocket, got a lighter, and pressed it down to relight my cigarette, which had gone out.

“You like one?” I offered.

“If you don’t tell Glor!” he chuckled, taking one from my outstretched hand and lighting it with practiced ease.

“My lips are sealed.”

For some time, we sat in silence. I listened to the wind rustling the leaves in the trees and the odd car driving by, trying to soothe my brain.

“I am sorry for upsetting you earlier today,” he eventually said. “Your grandmother would not have forgiven me if I didn’t make sure you’re all right.”

I turned to face him and gazed straight into his blue eyes, scrutinising him for a moment. The sincerity in the emotion he showed made me come around that he was telling the truth.

“You really knew her, didn’t you?” I asked cautiously.

“Yes.” The word almost caught in his breath.

“And . . . she – she died only recently?”

“Yes,” he replied with tears springing to his eyes. “She meant a lot to me.”

I started to tear up as well, not from grief, but from having been lied to all these years and not knowing why. He put his arm around me. I wasn’t sure if he did so to comfort me, himself, or both.

Whichever it was, it felt oddly good, and I was secretly a little grateful that he had come to look for me, even though we only just met.

After we had our tearful moment, I warily asked him if he could tell me a bit more about her. His face brightened by this and almost every sentence he spoke began with Hilda, followed by some nostalgic story or fond memory. She had been a sort of grandmother to him since he was a small boy. I couldn't help feeling a little pang of envy as he spoke, but despite that, it was surreal to get to know her just a little through his memories. She loved music and for her age, she was still quite hip and up to date with the music world, Andrew had shared with a chuckle.

"Gardening was a passion of hers, but with her deteriorating health the past few years, I helped her out. She was quite bossy, you know," he laughed softly. "Oh, and she was a real perfectionist too. Pushing you *to be your best*," he imitated her voice along with a fisted swing of his arm.

"How did she die?" I asked almost in a whisper.

"She eventually died from a heart attack, but she had been battling with the aftermath of a stroke she had two years prior. She never fully recovered physically, and she found it hard to accept the help she needed." He sighed heavily. "In her mind, she was still a young woman, her body just wasn't." He spoke as if he had told that story several times before. I nodded in understanding, and we fell quiet for a while.

"Who was supposed to tell me that you were going to meet me at the –" Andrew's phone rang. He gave me an apologetic look and got up to answer it.

"Will be home soon, Glor," I heard him say before ending the short call and sitting back down beside me. It was getting late, and we had been talking for more than an hour, yet it felt like nothing.

"Can I give you a ride back?" he offered, appearing eager to leave.

In no mood to do any more walking, I accepted appreciatively and reached in my handbag to offer him some gum. He took it with a knowing yet rigid smile. We didn't talk any further about Hilda during the short ride.

Since the phone call, Andrew had gone quiet and seemed somewhere else. I could have kept talking, but to my disappointment, it would have to wait for another day.

Gloria was waiting at the door when we arrived at the B&B. She gave Andrew a soft lingering kiss on his cheek, enlaced her fingers with his and greeted us back in and offered me a drink. If she was upset or had said something that changed Andrew's mood, it didn't show on her.

Despite her hospitality, I kindly declined and went to my room and got ready for bed. Within minutes, I had fallen asleep.

#

The day started off sombre, with grey skies which turned the wind colder. Even so, I was eager to go back to the house and explore the inside. Gloria had mentioned that Andrew could give me a drive up but judging by her less than thrilled tone of voice, I didn't feel comfortable accepting. Andrew was comparatively cheerful this morning and gave me his mobile number if I should need anything.

It was a complete role reversal from late yesterday evening. Whatever it was, and it had become clear there was something, it wasn't my concern. I had too much on my mind, for one; besides, it wasn't my place to get involved in other people's lives. I did briefly wonder if she might be the jealous type.

By the time I arrived, feeling invigorated yet slightly breathless from the long walk, the place still looked as magical as before. The tunnel of trees on the approach were darker without the sunlight, but it added an element of drama to the grounds, and the change in weather made no difference to the impression of the house.

It took me a while before I found the right key to open the front door. It unlocked with a satisfying audible click, and I slowly pushed the door open.

For some reason, I wanted to shout, “Anyone home?” but of course, there wasn’t.

Standing on the threshold, it took me a long moment to take in the grandeur of the hallway – if you could call it that. There must be a posher word for it. The stunning good morning staircase trailing down from either side with beautifully carved wooden posts was a feature on its own. You would expect to see a princess walking down in her ballgown. Numerous paintings in possibly gilded frames, which you would expect to find in the Louvre Museum, not in someone’s home, filled with landscapes and some still life, decorated the walls. The beige tapestry with a small floral detail covering the stairs gave it a warm and welcoming feeling.

I stepped in and softly closed the door. It was then that I noticed a collage of photographs displayed meticulously on the wall just beside me. Some black-and-white, some coloured. To my dismay, there was a photo of me as a little girl. I must have been around three or four. Seeing it here, and the implications of it, made me a little lightheaded.

Inspecting the photographs further, for the first time, I saw my grandmother; a lot older, that is. My mother had a few photographs of her as a teenager. Even in old age, she looked so much like Mum, no doubt it was her. *Andrew was telling the truth.* Although I was no longer doubting him, this proof was undeniable. My grandmother was still alive for all those years. She was standing next to an older man and looked so happy, with a genuine smile reaching her eyes.

There was a black-and-white photograph which was from when she was much younger, early twenties maybe, all dressed up, smiling, with a dapper young man beside her. I wondered if he was my grandfather. I would ask Andrew; he might be able to tell me more about the people in the images, since he clearly knew her well.

Finally peeling my gaze from the collection, I looked around and noticed the numerous doors which were all closed. I hesitated, frozen on the spot. What would they reveal? I thought about the close bond my mum and I shared all those years. The memories. It all seemed to be based on a lie or secret. *But why?* With a pit in my stomach and all eagerness to explore gone, I felt a wave of unsteadiness and anxiousness that was unsettling. Fresh air was what I needed. Fast.

Swinging the front door open, I took in several long, deep breaths before I walked out and sat on the porch steps, where just yesterday Andrew had broken the truth. So much had changed in only 24 hours and for a moment, it felt like a dream that I couldn't wake up from. After some minutes, I got my phone out and rummaged for the piece of paper Andrew had written his number on and dialled.

"Andrew? It's Elizabeth," I said, folding the slip of paper and pushing it into the pocket of my jeans.

"Oh! Hi, Elizabeth," he said, still sounding upbeat. "How are you getting on?"

"Uhm. Honestly, I'm not feeling so well at the moment and was wondering if you might be able to collect me? If you're not too busy, of course . . ." I said, trailing off a bit, suddenly feeling a little weird for asking.

"Sure. I'll be there shortly!" he said with not a moment of hesitation. "Can I get you anything? Medication?" I could hear his key jingling in the background.

"No. No thank you."

"Okay."

#

I heard a car door shut in the not far distance and moments later, Andrew emerged from the tunnel. He looked no different from when I first met him, same clothes, and a bit of a wild look. A far cry from the groomed man at the dinner table. I felt a sudden regret for having taken him away from his renovation work.

"You look pale. Have you seen a ghost?" he joked, his face falling slightly when he noticed my unamused expression.

"Come, I'll make you a cuppa." He reached out his hand. Instead of taking it, I placed the keys in his palm, needing a moment. He disappeared inside.

After a few breaths, I got up slowly and made my way to the threshold. Not even allowing myself a glance to the photographs, I noticed the second door to the left was open. "Andrew?" I called out, unsteadily nearing the door.

"In here!" his voice came from the room. I peeked inside before entering. The kitchen was huge. "Sit." Andrew pulled back one of the rattan chairs by the solid wood table.

I sat, getting my bearing slowly while stroking my hand over the many dents in the table before looking up and taking in the room in detail. It was decorated in soft shades of blue, not dissimilar to my room at the B&B, with gold accents dotted around. This was complemented by whitewashed kitchen cupboards and a Belfast sink placed in a kitchen island that was as big as my kitchen at home. The countless plants which lined each windowsill gave it a homely feel, although some were in desperate need of water.

Andrew knew his way around, opening all the right cupboards and drawers and in no time, handed me a cup of tea. "Well, what do you think of the place?" he asked while sitting across from me holding a steaming mug for himself.

"This is the second room I have seen, the hallway being one of them . . ." I said, my eyes fixed on the exquisite China pieces displayed on one of the shelves. "It looks very nice," I quickly added.

"Mm-hm . . . so do you remember this place?"

I frowned at him, perplexed. "How would I? I've never been here before.

"Follow me." He promptly got up and walked out of the kitchen. Leaving my tea behind, I left the room after him, stopping abruptly as he stood by the collage of photographs, busy taking a frame off the wall.

"You see this?" he asked, holding it up to me. Having immediately recognised it I walked to him, closing our gap.

"Yes, it's me," I sighed.

"No. Well, yes, but I mean the swing you're sitting on." My eyes zoomed in on the makeshift swing hung by two hemp ropes tied onto the branch of a tree.

"Yes . . . what about it?" I asked, my words coming out laced with hesitation.

"It was taken here, in the garden." I looked from him to the photo and back again, shaking my head slowly.

"W-What? That's not possible." I laughed at the ridiculousness.

"Let me show you," he said, ignoring my shock, once again opening the front door and jogging a little down the steps of the porch. Hesitantly, I followed him and we walked through a part of the garden I hadn't explored yet. Consumed in thought, I almost bumped into Andrew when he stopped abruptly. Turning toward me, he held out the photograph and pointed towards the tree ahead.

The swing still hung on it, although looking a bit worse for wear. To say I was flabbergasted would be an understatement. *I so need therapy*. He took my hand and somewhat dragged me towards the swing, gesturing for me to sit down, first giving it a strong pull to show it was safe. If my legs weren't shaking, I might have protested, but feeling so overwhelmed, I sat down, my hips barely fitting between the ropes. Seeing a photograph of myself in my not then deceased, but now deceased grandmother's house, was surreal. Now, furthermore, I had been here, here in this place, implausible if not for the photographic proof.

Andrew walked behind me and began to push the swing. The cold breeze on my face cooled down my overloaded mind and I found myself getting swayed into a daze.

"We had some great times here," he said in a faraway voice after some time.

Knocked out of my trance, I stopped the swing with my feet and looked back at him.

"What do you mean *we*?"

"The four of us. You, me, Glor, and Brian. As children, we played here in the garden. I can't remember you very well, but I remember playing here with Glor and Brian, having the greatest adventures," he said nostalgically. "My parents do remember you though, and have several photographs of us four playing here. We must have been around four or five at that time." He went off on a tangent, telling me how he and Brian are still best of friends till this day.

I mustn't have blinked at all as he spoke because I could feel my eyes starting to burn. How my legs managed to carry my bodyweight to get off the swing and sit under the tree escapes me. Andrew followed and kneeled in front of me, apparently waiting for me to speak.

"Why can't I remember any of this? I have never been back to England since I left when I was only a baby. It doesn't make any sense." My voice wavered, and I just about stopped myself from crying.

He soothingly stroked his hands over my arms. The sensation I could feel right through my bones. It was comforting.

"I can show you the photographs someday?" he asked a little apprehensively.

I gave the littlest of nods and shivered.

"Can I make you a new cuppa?"

Taking a deep breath, I sat up a little straighter, attempting some composure. "No, no, thank you, I'm fine. We should go. You should go back to work. I am so sorry for taking this much of your time. I, I really hope Gloria doesn't mind?" I asked, feeling a pang of guilt.

"Any time, Lizzy – er – Elizabeth," he said, looking apologetic.

"Liz is fine; that's what my friends call me," I said softly.

"Okay, Liz," he repeated, giving me a small smile. "And about Glor . . . you shouldn't worry. She will understand. She isn't the jealous type."

"Of course not. Sorry, that – that wasn't what I meant," I lied. "It's . . ." Andrew smiled light-heartedly as I felt heat rising to my face. If I had only just stopped there, but my mouth ran off. "It's just – she seemed upset this morning and yesterday, you . . . you . . . I know it isn't any of my business," I backtracked, suddenly unsure how he would react. He took a deep breath and had a pained look across his face. "I shouldn't have said anything. Sorry –"

"We got some disappointing news . . . and we're processing" he whispered, his voice cracking, with sadness written all over his face.

"I am so sorry!" Without a second thought, I pulled him in for a hug. To say I felt foolish would be an understatement. What was I thinking? God, had I become so self-absorbed in my own drama that I thought every relationship had infidelity and jealousy issues?

He said nothing for a few moments, after which, he pulled back. "Now if she saw that, she might be a bit jealous," he smiled uncomfortably. It was only then that I realised the position I embraced him in. Me sitting slightly elevated against the tree with my legs stretched out long, with him kneeling in between them as I had pulled him into my chest, holding him tight. I felt heat rising to my face once more.

"Oh God. I'm so sorry," I said, squeezing his arm only briefly, hopefully making it less awkward. "Do . . . do you want to talk about it?"

"No. Thanks." He cleared his throat and his sadness vanished from his expression almost entirely and was replaced with what I now knew to be his carefree disguise. "So . . . who hurt you so badly?" he asked, changing the subject.

"Excuse me? Is it that obvious?"

"Uh . . . well, yeah," he said in a manner that made me feel a little defensive. "Well?" he asked more softly when I didn't elaborate. Still staying quiet, he tilted my chin and looked at me with reassuring eyes, and to my own surprise, I poured my heart out to him. While I spoke and explained the situation with Gordon, I could tell he was listening attentively. His eyes never left me as he sat cross-legged on the grass in front of me, quietly taking it all in without interrupting. Just giving a heartfelt sorry after all was said. "You're a good listener."

"I know," he said with a cheeky wink.

Talking about it did me good. As I heard myself out loud, I could see what a jerk my ex-fiancé was. It felt good to be reminded of that. After some time of just being silent in each other's presence, Andrew looked at his watch with some trepidation. "I'm sorry, but I do have to go soon. Do you want a ride back or are you going to see the rest of the house?" he asked, his voice slightly teasing, already presuming my answer. After locking up, we walked back to the car side by side and once again, I was struck by how quickly life can change.

We stayed clear of heavy topics during the short ride. Instead, the mood was light as we spoke about music. He had quite a unique selection of CDs in the car, many of which were his own playlist. One for every mood, he explained. "Put on the 'upbeat'," he said, referring to the name he had written on the CD with a black marker. I soon found it and put it on. I couldn't help but laugh as he sang along to some country-style song unknown to me.

Back at the B&B, Andrew hugged Gloria, which lasted longer than just a quick, "Hi, love." Whatever it was. *None of my business*. They were coming to terms.

"See you at dinner again?" Gloria called as I was halfway up the stairs. I turned around, gauging them. Didn't they need some alone time? As if reading my thought, Andrew gave a subtle nod.

"That would be nice."

"At seven?"

"Sounds good."

"I've invited Brian as well . . ." I overheard her tell Andrew. *Guess it's going to be a reunion.*

#

From the clinking of the glasses and laughter I heard when I approached the door, dinner was in full swing. They were so punctual.

Steeling myself, I opened the door. Immediately, all eyes were on me. This time I was more appropriately dressed for these dinners, but their piercing stares made me wonder if I had left a clip in my hair. Or maybe there was a tear in my dress? Or worse, did I have more cleavage showing than intended? I discreetly touched my hair and fiddled with my black dress. Thankfully, the corset and the spaghetti straps were still in place, all was fine.

"Hi, Liz, we were waiting for you. You look nice," Andrew said cheerily, breaking the stares.

"Well, you know us Irish, we're never on time," I said, slightly nervous.

"This is Brian." Gloria gestured to him.

"Hi. You have aged very well from the little girl I remember," he said, smiling wide when our gaze met. He had perfect teeth and a strong handshake. Andrew cleared his throat rather obviously, telling him not to go there.

"Well, you're not too bad yourself, not that I remember you," I shocked myself by saying, the words rolling off my tongue.

"Touché."

I sat on the chair beside him and could feel him looking at me. Daring to face him, noticing his hazel eyes for the first time, he still had a broad smile imprinted.

He reached for the wine bottle and poured me a glass, without even asking if I wanted one. Noticing the near empty glasses on the table, they'd definitely been here for a while. He handed it to me, not letting go straight away as our fingers touched and our eyes met again; his twinkled. He was putting on the charm. The attention was flattering. I felt flutters of excitement in a place which had been absent for some time.

Gloria got up to get the food, and I took another moment to check him out. He was handsome. I felt an instant attraction. His dark brown hair almost touched his shoulders, and a few wavy locks fell over his forehead. I wondered what it would feel like to run my fingers through it.

He noticed me staring and I felt heat rising, not only in my neck . . . *Get a hold of yourself! You met him practically seconds ago.* But – and there was a big *but*. He just ignited something in me. I had almost forgotten what it felt like to feel desire. I recalled what Susan said just before I left, about having a rebound. "Where better than in another country, where nobody knows you? There are definitely no strings attached then!" she proclaimed in her oh-so-subtle way. Right now, I was open to the idea of something.

"How was your day?" Gloria asked, placing a dish with roasted vegetables and fish on the table, snapping me back.

"It was good," I lied. "And this food looks good too!" I said, taking the focus off myself, suddenly feeling hungry. I had no interest in talking about my day or any more drama this evening. Briefly, I wondered how much Andrew had filled her in on, but since she didn't ask any further, it didn't matter. I just wanted to forget about it all and have a good time.

Annie had gone for a sleepover at a friend's house again, so it was just adults having a grown-up dinner. Their strong friendship became quickly apparent from the openness with which they talked, laughed, and teased each other. Much to my delight, the trio stayed away from any serious topics. Momentarily, I wondered if they were warned off from doing so by Andrew. *Probably*. Either way, I greatly appreciated it.

Brian kept up the charm and I secretly revelled in it. We were all a bit tipsy by the time we finished the crème brûlée that tasted to die for.

"How about it, Elizabeth?" Brian reached for my hand under the table, subtly stroking my dress skirt before enlacing his fingers over mine. His most intimate move yet.

"How about what?" I said croakily, his touch awakening me again.

"How about we leave these lovebirds and go elsewhere?" he suggested. Gloria looked sheepish as she lifted her head she'd rested on Andrew's shoulder while sitting on his lap.

"Let me get my coat," I said without a moment of hesitation, and thanked them for the lovely dinner as we staggered out of the room, leaving them to it.

Upstairs, I quickly touched up my makeup, sprayed some more perfume, and wiggled my breasts into a more "out there" position and changed my shoes for something more comfortable. *I can't believe I am doing this!* My excitement at a high and adrenaline pumping through my body like wildfire, I felt like a teenager again. As I walked out of my room onto the landing, I heard Andrew's and Brian's voices down in the hallway.

"Mate, don't treat her like the others! She is going through enough already," Andrew whispered almost urgently.

"Here you go again. What makes you think I'm going to hurt her?" Brian said, sounding put out.

"Your track record says enough." Andrew's voice raised above a whisper.

"Seriously, that again. Maybe I'm exactly what she needs. Did you consider that?"

I didn't care to listen any further and made my way downstairs, stepping a little louder onto the wooden steps. They both looked up in shock, unsure if I overheard them.

"Don't worry, Andrew, I'll be fine." I tapped him on the shoulder once I was down. Overhearing what I did would have made me run for the hills any other time, but not today.

"I'm not as bad as he makes me out to be, you know," Brian whispered in my ear.

"I'm sure you are." I winked. *OMG, where did that come from.* "So . . . where are we going?"

"Just you wait and see."

#

When we made it to his car, I was surprised he drove a Mini Cooper. Not even one of the newer versions, the true old classic. I had him pegged as a race car kind of guy, like a Honda Civic complete with a range of spoilers, huge exhausts, and flashy alloy wheels that he would show off with pride only a man could have for a car, and probably entertain countless women in. Well, that sure wasn't going to happen in this one. Even the backseat driver position would be impossible without risk of a concussion and spinal injury.

He opened the passenger door and placed the bag with leftovers Gloria had rustled up for him inside and rummaged around. Of course, he wouldn't be driving anywhere with all the alcohol in his system.

"You seem like the outdoorsy type," he said, reemerging with a bag and locking the door behind him.

I said nothing, letting him take the lead. As we walked, we didn't say much to each other but exchanged the occasional glances and smiles made visible only by the streetlight and the odd car passing. The back of our hands touched several times as we walked side by side, lingering a little longer each time until he took hold of my wrist, pulling me back.

"We are here," he said, his voice sounding deeper than I had heard it before. We stood in front of a high metal gate, mounted between even taller stone walls, dimly lit on either side.

"I'll help you over?" he said, letting go of my wrist and interlacing his hands, leaning down, gesturing for me to climb on.

"I am looking for a fun night, not to get arrested for trespassing," I laughed a little uncomfortably.

"You *won't*," he promised, giving me a ridiculously charming smile. "Come," he said, gesturing to his hands again.

"I better not regret this." I stepped on his hands and made my way over the gate in a nonathletic move, feeling very grateful my dress didn't get stuck on the way down.

"Catch!" Brian tossed the bag to me, the contents light, and he quickly followed suit with relative ease. It was almost pitch-dark ahead. The only thing I could make out was some big trees, a pond, and a bench lit by the moonlight.

"Over here." He reached his hand and without hesitation I held it, letting him lead me to the bench. It all reminded me a bit of the scene in the romantic comedy *Notting Hill* where Hugh Grant and Julia Roberts climbed into a communal garden. This bench didn't have the soul-touching engraving, and their situation was incomparable, but the same feeling of excitement was there.

We sat close together, his leg touching mine. My eyes adjusted to the dark and my surroundings became more visible as I was trembling with nerves and anticipation. Waiting for him to make his move, or at least say something, felt like an eternity. Trying to distract myself, I focused on the soft shimmer reflected by the moonlight in the water.

Lost in a trance and trying to breathe calmly, I almost missed it when Brian stroked my hair away from my shoulder. Our eyes met. Gently, he held his hand behind my head, leaned forward, and placed soft kisses on my neck, trailing down to my collarbone. The sensation ignited my entire body. He came back up, his mouth inches from mine. I could see the want in his eyes, but he halted, silently asking, are you sure? I ran my fingers through his hair; it felt better than I imagined. He still waited for me, as if that wasn't enough of an answer.

Holding his face, I leaned in and kissed him softly. "Yes," I breathed, biting his lower lip before tracing it with my tongue. He parted his lips and we kissed, slowly first, getting to know each other, then deeper and more passionate. Coming up for air, he grabbed the bag, pulling out a blanket, and lay it on the ground. As I stood up, he was back with me in seconds, kissing the sensitive area on my neck, and one hand reaching for my dress zipper, slowly pulling it all the way down. Sliding the straps off my shoulder, the dress slid off me and he paused, taking me in. “You’re stunning.” His voice was heavy with lust.

He guided me onto the soft blanket. From there, I got lost in his touch and let him explore every inch of me with complete submission before returning the favour. “You’re driving me crazy,” he’d groaned as I teased him at length with my body, pinning his hands down. “I want you.” His plea urgent.

I lost my resolve to make him wait any longer. “I want you too.” My words laced with need. He reached for a condom, and I rode him until we climaxed together. Afterwards, we lay intertwined, breaths heavy and our heartbeats racing. It wasn’t until we came back from the state of pre-lustful hunger that the cold the evening brought started to penetrate our bodies and we got dressed. Fully clothed, albeit slightly dishevelled, Brian sat back onto the bench. I followed and lay with my head on his lap, looking up at the moon and stars, and occasionally at his face, brightened by the moonlight. I could see him smiling.

We struggled to start a conversation, as several attempts from either of us resulted in laughter. I felt confident that he felt as blown away as I did. A while later, I finally broke the silence.

"So . . . how many girls have you brought here?" I asked light-heartedly. He looked down at me, as if he was contemplating the answer. "I don't mind. I know why I left with you tonight. No regrets."

He stayed silent for a few more beats.

"You don't have to tell me."

"You're actually the first. I come here often by myself to clear my head and enjoy the silence." He paused for a few seconds, taking a deep breath. "I am not the person Andrew made out to be."

"Am I *really* your first here?"

"Yes. Is that so hard to believe?"

"Well . . . I don't know you, other than that you know how to satisfy a woman."

He let out a chuckle and traced his finger over my lower lip before whispering, "So do you."

"Presuming I believe you, I should probably admit this was my first time outdoors. I am *not* the outdoorsy type you took me for. The closest I have come to doing *it* al fresco, was in a yurt."

"That's not outside."

"My point exactly. But you might have just converted me."

"My pleasure."

"And mine." I grinned.

"Can I ask you something."

"Sure."

"You did overhear us talking, right?"

" . . . Yes."

"So . . ."

"So what?"

"Nothing," he eventually said.

My stomach made a lengthy rumble.

"You're hungry?"

"Yes. Sex like that does that to me." I sat up and kissed him, feeling him smile against my lips.

"I was that good?"

"You know you were." I bit his lower lip again.

"You're amazing, Elizabeth," he breathed, and we kissed so deeply it took our breath away.

"Wait here," he whispered when my stomach made another sound. "I'll be right back."

"You're going to leave me here alone in the dark?" I asked, slightly alarmed as he let go of me.

"Don't worry, you have nothing to fear," he said, turning around. "Just snakes!"

"Ha-ha, very funny." Obviously, he was joking, but I still pulled my legs up onto the bench, just in case. Which I knew was ridiculous since they could just slither up anyway. The thought sent a cold shiver down my spine.

I looked behind me and it felt darker than before. For some time, I listened to the occasional car passing by in the distance and the leaves rustling in the breeze, my senses heightened. It started to feel eerie. Brian took his time, and my mind began to play tricks on me, convinced I heard something moving several times. "Brian? Brian. Are you there?" I called out, trying my hardest to peer through the darkness in the distance, in vain. "This isn't funny . . ." I said, while trying to convince myself it was just a squirrel.

A shrill tune broke the silence and I jumped off the bench with a scream, my heart racing. That's when I noticed my jacket pocket was vibrating; it was just my phone. Breathing a sigh of relief, I reached to retrieve it and continued to look out into the darkness for Brian as I answered it.

"Hey."

"Hey? That's all you say?! Why haven't you replied to my texts or called? I'm sorry to ring you at such a godforsaken hour, but I couldn't sleep. I have been worried sick about you! Are you okay?"

"Text? Yeah – I – yeah . . . I think so," I said, struggling to focus.

"You think so? You think so – what? What is going on? Where are you? Are you not in the B&B?" Su asked, her voice rising.

"No . . . I–I'm sorry, can I call you back later?"

"No! Not until you tell me what's going on!" she all but screamed down the line. I moved the phone away from my ear to protect it.

"Okay, okay!" I let out a breath I didn't know I was holding. "You remember what you told me before I left?"

"What? Uh – yeah, to have a good time? What does that have to do –"

"Yes, that *and* having someone on the rebound," I said, raising my voice to drown out her stream of questioning.

"You're with someone *already*?" Su said, all anger draining from her tone.

"Well, yes and no. I was with someone just earlier. I'm outside in some garden and he left saying he'll be right back . . . but he isn't back yet and it's really dark and I'm kinda starting to freak out. What if –"

"Just *starting* to freak out?" a deep voice whispered.

"AAAAAH!" I screamed so loud the birds flew out of the trees. Reflexively, I turned around and hit the person behind me as hard as I could and ran in the opposite direction.

"Ow! Wait – it's only me! Brian!"

I stopped in my tracks, feeling disoriented. and turned around, making my way back. Sure enough it was him, holding a bag. I was shaking. He immediately pulled me in for a hug. I gave him another small punch on his shoulder for scaring the life out of me. He retaliated with a kiss that made my knees buckle, my heart rate calm and then rise again. Coming up for air, we became aware of a faraway voice.

"Liz? Liz! Are you okay? Where are you? If you hurt her, I will kill you! KILL YOU! Do you hear me? You –" Looking around, I followed the sound that was getting louder and more panicked by the second until I found my phone on the ground. Which I must have dropped when Brian scared me shitless. At this point, Su was screaming curses and threats down the line that I can honestly say I never heard her say before.

"I'm fine! I'm fine! I am FINE!" I shouted back, trying to get her to listen to reduce her state of utter rage and panic.

"I'm going to need a few minutes," I said to Brian. He led the way back to the bench, where we sat down.

While I spoke with Su, he opened a bottle of wine and brought out the containers filled with Gloria's leftovers. Su and I spoke for much more than just a few minutes, during which she made me promise to call her later more than three times. Finally, after one last half-hearted threat from Su, we hung up. I turned to face a bemused Brian taking a swig from the open bottle.

"Sorry that took so long," I said, placing my hand on his knee.

"That's okay. So . . . I am your rebound?" he said playfully, giving me a little nudge.

I climbed on top of his lap and leaned in to whisper, "You said you might be just what I needed, and you were right."

"You're different," he whispered back.

"Tell me about it."

He handed me the bottle and I took a sip. "How is your shoulder?"

"I can handle a little bruise."

"Don't ever scare me like that again."

"Not when your friend is near, I think she might have a stronger arm than you," he said, amused.

"Hey!" I punched him again. "So, what do you do when you're not entertaining a woman?"

"Well, for your information, I haven't entertained anyone for some time." He kissed me with a cheeky smile.

Chapter 3

Quietly opening the door to the B&B in the early hours of the morning, I tiptoed to my room and rested my head on the pillow as soon as I got in. I only just managed to set the alarm for breakfast before nodding off.

I woke up in a daze, replaying the night and smiled to myself, even pinching myself. It was real. A small hour later, all freshened up, I made my way down to the breakfast room. It was quiet. There was a young couple holding hands over the table and an older man sitting alone reading a newspaper. The breakfast buffet was plentiful, and no doubt Gloria's doing. The older man greeted me with a nod, peering just above his newspaper as I walked by. I replied with the same gesture, not that I think he even noticed with his face buried in the pages again. I was so hungry I could eat a breakfast and a half. While I was deciding whether to go order a full English or a healthier option or both, Gloria drifted in.

"How are you this morning, Willie?" I overheard her ask the older man.

"Good today. I can't complain," he said in a rich voice which carried across the room.

"Anything special I could make for you this morning?"

"If you keep feeding me like this, I will have to make my strolls in the park into those power walks young people do," he grinned and Gloria laughed, flattered.

It dawned on me that I was listening in on the conversation. It was hard not to overhear in a small room with few people, however, my staring was no doubt intrusive. I turned back around to the buffet, taking in the many options in more detail.

"Good morning, Elizabeth!" Gloria said a little later in a cheerful voice, unknowingly having creeped up on me. "How are you this morning?"

"Not too bad, thank you. The food looks great!" I gestured at the stretched-out table loaded with pastries, breads, fruits, cereals, yogurts, cheeses, and more, all displayed like an advertisement for a five-star breakfast at a fancy hotel. She beamed, her eyes shining with modest pride.

I ordered a full English and started to take some healthier choices from the buffet.

"You know that man sitting over there," Gloria said in a low voice, nodding in the direction of the older man I had overheard her call Willie. "He was a good friend of your grandmother's." And with that said, she turned around and disappeared back to the kitchen.

Having finished my food selection, I stood with my tray in my hand looking back and forth between the empty tables and Willie's spot, contemplating whether I should introduce myself.

"There are plenty of empty chairs," he said, eyeing me over his newspaper, having noticed my indecision.

"Actually, sir, I was wondering if I could sit with you?"

". . . why not? I am always happy to have breakfast with a beautiful young lady," he replied, looking a little surprised, folding his paper and gesturing for me to take the seat across from him. "So, what can this old man do for you? It cannot be my good looks!" He grinned.

I smiled politely, placed down the tray and reached out my hand.

"Elizabeth. Elizabeth Hayden," I said as we shook. His bushy eyebrows shot up to his hairline as his face had shock written all over it. "Er – William, but everyone calls me Willie," he replied but didn't blink for an uncomfortably long time and just peered at me.

At a loss as to what to say next, I sat down and opened my little blueberry yogurt and took some spoonfuls. All the while, I could feel him staring at me. He ignored his own food. "Gloria mentioned that you knew my grandmother, um, Hilda?" I prompted to get the conversation going.

"Yes, yes I did. My sincerest apologies, Elizabeth." He reached for my hand and held it in his. "It's truly a pleasure to meet you." His eyes began to water. "Will you be here for a while?"

"Yes, for another –"

"We will meet again then," he said. He got up swiftly and left unsteadily on his feet out of the room.

Baffled by his quick departure, I sat gazing at the closed door for some moments, and then impulsively decided to follow him. I just managed to see him get into his car and within seconds, he was gone. Defeated, I stood in the door opening. I wanted to run after him, but what was the point? Letting out a loud, audible sigh, I was suddenly gripped with a feeling of dread and fear; fear of more revelations.

"Hey."

I whipped around, startled from the tap on my shoulder, not registering the greeting.

"Does everyone here just sneak up on people?!" I snapped, and afterwards felt immediately regretful as Andrew held his hands up in the air in peaceful surrender.

"Oh. I'm sorry. I'm just . . . I'm . . . oh, I don't know. But I didn't mean to snap at you."

"I am sorry I startled you again." He dropped his hands down. "But what is going on, Liz? Are you okay?"

"No. Truthfully, I'm not. Why don't –"

"What has he done this time? I warned him!" Andrew said abruptly, his face instantly filled with anger. For a moment, I was confused by his words until I realised that he must be talking about Brian.

"Oh, I don't know what the problem is between you both, but keep me out of it," I said, slightly annoyed. "I was talking about my grandmother, my mum, and Willie, who I just met."

Before he could reply, I strutted past him back to the breakfast room. It was empty now; the loved-up couple had left. Gloria brought out my full English as soon as I sat down and I started to dig in, appreciating the quiet to gather my thoughts.

Halfway through my plate, Andrew stood in the doorway. Our eyes met and he hesitated before making his way to my table. "How is your breakfast?"

"Delicious. Gloria is a great cook," I said calmly, meaning every word.

He smiled fondly. "Her food can do wonders." I nodded, taking a sip of my orange juice.

"I'm sorry, Elizabeth," he said sincerely, taking the seat Willie had departed from. "Willie was a close friend of your grandmother's. They knew each other for as long as I can remember. Her passing has been particularly hard on him. I'm sure you will get a chance to talk one of these days. He comes in here almost daily for breakfast or lunch."

"How close were they?"

"You mean . . . if they were doing it?" Andrew smiled playfully.

"Eww! No. Well, yes, I mean," I said, giving him a light kick under the table. I missed.

"Ha! Got you to smile. You should try to do that more often," he said triumphantly. I shook my head at him.

"I *meant*, could he be my grandfather? Did my mum lie to me about that as well?" I mumbled, looking down at my plate.

"No, Liz. Your grandfather died a long time ago. Of that, I am sure." I heard him, but I didn't know what to think anymore, these past few days had been so confusing.

"I wish I could talk to my mum." I sighed heavily. The only noise in the room for a long minute or so was from my fork scraping the plate as I played with my food, until Andrew cleared his throat.

"So . . . how was your night with Brian?" he asked. I looked up, frowning at him, but the tentative smile on his face told me that he was trying to change the mood, so I smiled back but stayed quiet on any details.

"How about I drive you back to the house today, so you can explore? Would you be up for that?" He looked at me encouragingly, obviously hoping to move some conversation along.

"Yes, I would, actually. Thank you for the offer, but I will walk though. I could do with the fresh air," I said, desiring some alone time.

"All right, give me a call if you need someone to talk to." He lightly touched the back of my hand, got up, and left the room.

#

Back in the house, feeling uplifted from the walk, I felt ready to do some exploring. The wooden panelled door next to the kitchen caught my eyes first. It squeaked lengthily as I pushed it open. Stepping in the room, rays of sunlight entering through the windows illuminated the dust hanging in the air, as well as a smell that was distinct, yet unrecognisable to me. There was a large antique desk with a green inlay and a colour-matching captain's chair by the window. The room was of grand proportion, with high ceilings and detailed cornicing, and a fireplace no one would dare to cover up whichever style was fashionable at the time.

Yet the space felt warm with all the soft furnishings and knickknacks displayed. It had the grandeur of the hallway, or more appropriately named the entrance, but with a cosier, homely feel to it.

Moving slowly, I walked to the desk and lifted the quilted throw that was neatly draped over the chair, held it up to my face and inhaled softly. I felt close to my grandmother in that moment, as if we met for the first time. Cautiously, as if afraid it would crumble beneath me, I sat on the captain's chair and looked out of the window. She must have sat here many times, admiring the breathtaking view out to her garden, a beautiful display of flowers and plants Monet would have loved to capture on a canvas.

An old typewriter stood in front of me, positioned ready for use with a paper loaded, and many more papers and books lay on the desk. It was as if she had just popped out of the room and was going to be back any minute now. I let out a heavy breath at the heartbreaking thought.

Exploring the books, the first one that caught my eye, and made my heart skip a beat, was a novel by Wendell Berry. I'm not very familiar with the novels he had written, yet I have enjoyed reciting some of his poetry from time to time. One of his poems, my favourite, "The Peace of Wild Things" I'd learnt off by heart in no time at all. The last line, 'I rest in the grace of the world, and am free,' always gave me goosebumps. I held the book close to my chest and sighed, feeling a wave of affection. The fact that we had a common interest was comforting.

There was something about this room, something that I couldn't place; it intrigued me to keep exploring. I wanted to discover more and more about her. As I stood up, the next thing that caught my eye was the mahogany piano. Upon closer inspection, the keys had yellowed with age and the wood was covered with markings and small dents. I softly glided my fingers over the keys, pressing a few down, listening to the different tones. I never learned how to play.

Following that, my gaze was captured on the chunky, ceiling-high wooden shelf cabinet. At eye level, I noticed a huge collection of CDs. Andrew hadn't been kidding when he said she loved music, and was certainly right she was quite hip and up to date with the music world. Although, there were many older music albums with names I hadn't heard before, and even a stack of vinyl records, probably from before I was even born. There was a row of CDs with familiar names with the likes of U2, Coldplay, Pink, Madonna, Alicia Keys… The collection made me smile with surprise. The shelves also held many more books placed like a jigsaw puzzle to make them all fit.

Standing back, on one of the higher shelves I noticed a little wooden box nestled between some books. By going on my tippytoes, my fingers could just about graze the side of the box, allowing me to push it to the edge of the shelf and take it down. Studying the little locked trinket, my curiosity was piqued. Running my fingers over the notches in the wood, I noticed there were tiny numbers engraved at the side: 20-07-1981. It took me a second to register.

"My birth date!" I gasped, surprised, tracing the engraving with my index finger. I excitedly and somewhat frantically started searching for the small key that could unlock it. Starting with the shelves, I moved books which would take a genius to put back in the same order and stood on a wobbly stool to get a clearer look at the top shelves, to no avail. The search of the desk drawers also came up empty and with the many nooks and crannies in the room, it was like finding a needle in a haystack, if it was even here.

I conceded to not finding it and sat down on the dark-brown Chesterfield leather couch placed in perfect position by the fireplace. I took a long, hard look at the little box in my hand. If only I had x-ray vision powers to see through the wooden facade. With a surrendering breath, I placed it in my handbag. Maybe Andrew could help me open it.

Walking out of Hilda's study, I briefly looked back at the kitchen door until I was drawn forward to a set of high, dark, wooden double doors, carved in an arch shape at the top. I pressed the cast-iron handles and slowly pushed the doors open.

What I met was a feast for the eyes. The abundance of textiles and busy wallpaper had created a drawing room of sophistication. It was like stepping back in time. The bold reds, golds, and rich blue colours took centre stage while being harmoniously balanced with a softer colour palette. It was a statement room. A room where one would invite important guests to show off their wealth, or possibly host suitable men interested in courting one's daughter long ago. The opulent curtains and valance were draped flawlessly, as if someone meticulously placed each crease at the same distance.

A deep-red velvet chaise lounge stood beside the fireplace, with other beauteously crafted armchairs and ottomans padded with lush material and bold floral prints creating an exquisite seating area. A bespoke mahogany table and several smaller side tables, each one completely unique from the other, were placed in the perfect position to entertain. The decorative ceiling was dressed with chandeliers and the dark wooden floor with oriental rugs. Ornaments were placed around as prized possessions while the walls displayed what looked to be more gilded frames holding paintings of an era that was easily eons ago. There was so much to take in but compared to the study, this grand room was cold. The sunlight hadn't reached this side of the house yet and before exploring any further, I was craving a warm drink.

The kitchen had a bit of familiarity to it now, although I had to open several cupboard doors to find what I needed. Once I had my tea made, I sat down on the porch step and enjoyed the warmth and view of the garden. All I could hear were the birds singing, rustling leaves, and an occasional car in the distance passing by. It felt so peaceful. Sometime later, the crunching sound of car tyres that grew louder brought me out of my zen. To my surprise, Willie appeared from the tunnel of trees shortly after.

"Willie!" I called out, setting down my cup and getting up to greet him. He stopped in his tracks and seemed hesitant to come further. Not giving him a chance to walk away, I closed the distance between us.

"How are you? I am having a cup of tea; would you like one?" I laced my arm through his, prompting him to walk with me, pleased to see him. He mumbled something inaudible. "Why are you here?" I asked while coaching him to the steps, ready to walk inside.

He hesitated. "I come here sometimes to sit in the garden . . . to feel close to her." He unlaced his arm from mine and turned around, gazing out at the grounds for some time, as if he was reminiscing events from the past. "We had many good times here." He turned back to me, his eyes saddened with grief.

I knew exactly how he felt. The waves of immense grief and sadness, the reminiscing of good times followed by the black hole of emptiness, repeated endlessly. I reached for his wrinkled, sun-spotted hand and placed it in mine.

“I’m so sorry for your loss, Willie. I . . . I know how you feel. I lost my mum four months ago.” My eyes started to well up as soon as I spoke the words.

With his eyebrows raised and with his mouth agape, he stared at me.

“. . . . Heather, dear Heather is . . . dead?!” He shed tears that came faster and faster. I couldn’t help but do the same. There we stood, sniffling away our tears in a close embrace.

“You have her eyes, you know,” he said after a while in a shaky voice. I unlocked from the hold and we looked at each other. “Actually, I don’t know. I don’t know anything. I didn’t even know Hilda . . . my grandmother . . . was alive all this time.” He gently tilted my chin up and had another look as if to confirm his words.

“Are you my grandfather?” I asked softly without forethought. Under the circumstances, and with his aggrieved reaction to the news of my mother’s passing, it didn’t feel too far-fetched to think he might be my grandfather. I knew Andrew had said otherwise, but I needed to hear it from him. He took his handkerchief from his breast pocket and dabbed his eyes, studying me for some moments, keeping me in suspense. With a heavy sigh, he finally spoke.

“My dear, I am truly sorry, but I am not your grandfather. I couldn’t have been.”

"Oh, that's okay," I said, unsure of how I was feeling. *Did I want him to be?* It would have been nice to have family.

I nodded to the front door to go inside and we slowly made our way into the house, to the kitchen. He unsteadily took the first seat at the table. "I was going to make us a tea, but would you like a cooler drink instead?" I asked, noticing he looked a little sweaty and pale walking in.

"What?" he said in a strained voice.

"Would you like a tea or something cold to drink?" I repeated a little louder, but he didn't respond. "Are you all right, Willie . . . Willie?"

He slowly craned his head up and beads of sweat stood out on his forehead, and then as if I was watching a movie scene in slow motion, it happened. He clutched his chest and leaned sideways on his chair. I just about managed to break his fall to the ground as he gasped for air. "Oh my God, Willie!" I let out a scream. Carefully and quickly laying him down, I loosened his tie and shirt and rang the emergency services. The person on the other side of the phone asked me questions and talked me through what to do, as she reassured me that help was on the way. It all happened in a blur.

I was shaking when the ambulance arrived; he had started going in and out of consciousness and it looked as if he was about to give up. As I stood back while the paramedics worked on him, I quietly sobbed into my hands. In an unknown time, he was rushed into the ambulance, machines hooked up to him and beeping, while he lay motionless on the way to the hospital. I was in a state of quiet panic. I hate ambulances, it brought back awful, painful memories. Memories I couldn't cope with.

My mind started racing between past and present. What if he died? He might be the only link to my family left. Although he said he couldn't be my grandfather. What did he mean exactly, with "couldn't"? Regardless, he was close to Hilda.

#

Andrew arrived at the hospital a short time later, after my hysterical phone call to him. As we sat on the cold, hard steel chairs waiting for news, he made some calls. My mind was still in a whirlwind of thoughts, I couldn't stop it; not even a psychologist could have made sense of it. I wasn't ready to be back in this environment, but then, who would be? It's not like anyone would come here for fun.

With all my attempts to gain some calm and control failing, I felt my breathing getting laboured and waves of panic and anxiety flooding my entire body.

"I must get out of here. I–I can't be here –" I said, tapping Andrew's arm, my words barely audible. Standing up, feeling light on my feet, I took a few steps in the direction of the white double doors which led to the outside.

"Wait, Liz," Andrew called out, and before I could say anything, my legs failed me and I landed in a heap on the floor. Every sound around me had muffled, there were only the cries in my head.

"Wake up, Mum, wake up! Please?! I need you! Open your eyes, please! Please, Mum. Please!"

"I am very sorry, Miss Elizabeth, there is nothing more we can –"

"NO! No, no, no, try again! Try again, she can't die, she – TRY AGAIN!"

"I am so sorry, but she's gone, there is nothing more we can do."

"No, I need you to try something, please?! PLEASE DO SOMETHING! SHE CAN'T DIE!!!"

Chapter 4

The knock on the door was a mental wake-up call. My mind had been racing and my head was pounding from the stress.

"Can I come in?" Gloria called out softly from beyond my room.

"Yes," I answered, matching her voice, afraid to make my headache any worse. She opened the door, carrying in a tray loaded with food and drink. Eating hadn't been on my mind since the hospital yesterday.

She placed the tray on the side table and handed me a glass of water. "I brought you some paracetamol."

"Oh, thank you!" I gratefully took it from her.

"Any news on Willie?" I asked as soon as I swallowed the pills.

"Andrew spoke with the doctor again about an hour ago," she started off while meticulously arranging a few mini sandwich bites on a plate. "They're optimistic, which is a good sign considering he had a massive heart attack and emergency bypass surgery." Her voice broke as she said the last words. I took an anxious breath, letting her words sink in.

"Is he going to be okay?" I looked at her for reassurance.

"I think so." Her lips curled into a weak smile. "It was very lucky you were there with him, you know." She met my gaze. The unspoken words hung thick in the air for several uncomfortable beats.

"Thank you for all this." I gestured to the food while she poured me a steaming cup of tea, the sweet scent of fennel tickling my nostrils. "I know B&B's don't do room service." I smiled a little sheepishly. She bashed my words away as if it was nothing and got ready to leave, having served all the little delicious foods beautifully on small dishes.

"I'll be staying in my room for a while. Really no need for cleaning today," I told her quickly, wanting to lighten the load of her jobs and truthfully there was no need, regardless.

"If you're sure. I'll let you know if there is any more news." And with that, she quietly left the room.

Taking careful sips of tea, I took a few mindful moments to close my eyes and imagine myself on a beach, watching the rolling waves hitting the rocks and sandy shore, the soothing sound combined with the fresh air allowing me to breathe calmly. I was here for four days now, and it had been a lot to take in and deal with. Su was a great comfort yesterday and this morning on the phone; she even offered to come over several times. "Adrianna can handle the shop for a few days, and I can do the orders from anywhere, you know that!" she'd argued adamantly. As sweet as that offer was, it just didn't feel right to accept.

Even Brian had called to ask how I was doing and offered to come over. Which was incredibly sweet of him. But right now, I craved to be alone, in this room, to let my mind and body relax. After finally dozing off to sleep, once my headache had eased and my tummy was full, the sound of banging woke me up. The renovation was going on downstairs and reminded me that it was daytime, although half of it had already passed at this point.

Slowly, I got myself out of bed, dressed, and went downstairs. Making my way straight to the open front door, my face was touched by sunrays. With closed eyes, I took in the wonderfully warm feeling. The blissful moment was soon interrupted with more bangs of a hammer. Squinting my eyes, adjusting to the brightness, I observed Andrew. The black-metal-fenced garden had a makeshift workshop on one side, where he was hard at work.

"Coffee?" he asked with a grin when he finally spotted me, having come out of deep concentration.

"Coffee!" I smiled.

He put down his tools and picked up a rather fancy-looking flask and sat down on the little wooden bench by one of the bay windows. “You have coffee on the go, while your kitchen is five seconds away?” I said bewildered.

“That’s Glor for you.” His lips curled up into a smile. “I even have two mugs!” He held them up a little smugly before pouring in the coffee and handing me one. “How are you, Liz?” He patted the space next to him on the bench. I placed my handbag on the ground and sat down, softly blowing at my mug of hot deliciousness before answering.

“Uhm . . . I’m okay, I think.” I carefully took a little sip and the fragrant, rich taste awakened my senses. “Sorry about yesterday, it all became too much, you know . . . thank you for your help.” I gazed up at him, hoping he would see my sincerity.

“I am so sorry about your mother, Liz. She must have been a wonderful woman,” he said earnestly, meeting my eyes.

“She was. She really, really was.” I sighed, reminiscing about her for some time as we silently sipped our coffees.

“Liz?” Andrew said, breaking my magic spell.

“Yes?” I replied a little cautiously, hearing the seriousness in his tone.

“I don’t know why you were told what you were told about your grandmother, or . . . or why things were kept from you, but I am a firm believer that it's better to know the truth than to speculate." He paused. I waited in anticipation for him to continue.

"And?" I prompted when he didn't fast enough.

"Well, I have a feeling that Willie knows something more about your family."

"Why do you say that?" I frowned, my curiosity piqued.

"You see, I went back to the hospital last night, when he was out of surgery. Willie wasn't fully coherent but there is something he said over and over that made me wonder. 'It's her. It's her.' I think he was talking about you, Liz. I don't know why; I suppose you can call it a gut feeling, since you're the new person here. He did mumble a few other things, but I couldn't make sense of it," he finished, shaking his head.

"I had the same inkling from the first time I met him in your breakfast room. I wonder what he meant?" Suddenly remembering the small wooden box I'd put in my handbag, I fished it out and showed it to him.

"I found this little box yesterday high up on a shelf in Hilda's study. I totally forgot about it after what happened with Willie. It has my birth date engraved in it." I stroked the writing before passing the little trinket to him.

"I haven't seen it before," he said, inspecting it.

"Would you be able to open it? I have searched around in the room for a little key but found none."

Meticulously, he studied the little lock, then grabbed one of the tools lying around. "I *will* have to break the lock?"

"I know." And with an anticipating nod from me, with a grab and a pull the lock was free, just like that. My hands were shaking with suspense as I took it back from him. The tiny hinge made a creaking sound as I carefully opened it. There was a small brown envelope with Lizzy Hayden written on the front with long, loopy strokes, in black ink.

Lifting it out from the box, I turned it around and with much care, opened the envelope. First, I saw a little lock of brownish-blond hair, which I touched with my fingertips before taking out a yellowed card with slightly smudged baby feet prints. Turning back to the box, I noticed an old-looking brass key. I held it up to show Andrew. He shrugged and shook his head. I carefully placed the envelope with the belongings back in the little keepsake box.

"Hmm . . . surprising she had this, but not much of a revelation," I said, somewhat disappointed after closing the lid. "Except maybe this key." *What is it for?* I held it up again, my hope and curiosity rising. Andrew gestured for the key, to have a closer look.

"Very big and old," he said unhelpfully before giving it back with another shrug.

"Hey, you had really tiny feet," Andrew smiled, nudging me with his elbow. I took the card out once more.

"They are cute. I had cute feet!" I said, having scrutinized them a little.

"Yes, you had cute little duck feet." He grinned, pointing at the smudges between my toes.

"Ha-ha, very funny!" I nudged him back, just that bit harder in the ribs.

"Ouch." He professed pain.

"She *did* call me Lizzy!" I said with a soft chuckle, staring at the writing on the envelope.

"Did you really doubt me about that!" Andrew said, placing his hand on his chest and letting out a mock gasp. Smiling at his theatrics, I reached for the coffee and took several large gulps.

"Seriously good!" I moaned in pleasure. "So, Gloria is a culinary genius and makes excellent coffee too. Is there anything she can't do?" I asked somewhat seriously.

Andrew beamed at the compliment of his wife and even blushed a little. "So . . . what are your plans for today?"

"Well, I would like to talk to Willie, but since that won't be possible right now . . ." Andrew hummed in agreement. "I suppose I'll go back to the house and maybe find out what this key is for," I said, holding it up again.

"Listen, why don't you take a break? Do something fun for the rest of the day? Whatever the key opens, won't go away. I am planning to visit Willie this evening, but tomorrow morning, I'll be visiting my parents. Maybe you'd like to come? She might remember something . . . and of course, my mother can show you the pictures."

I took another large gulp from the mug, momentarily in thought, which led to Brian. He's *fun*. "You know what? I might just take you up on the offer. Thank you! And . . . could you tell Gloria not to count on me for dinner?"

"Going to visit your rebound?" He smiled and put an arm around me, my thoughts transparent.

"He told you? Oh no!" I covered my face, tamping down my rising blush.

"We talked," he said with a chuckle.

"What's the story with you guys, anyway?" I asked quickly. Even though I didn't want to know earlier, curiosity had gotten the better of me.

"That's for another time, Liz." He gave my arm a squeeze, got up, and went back to work.

#

Brian was pleased I called. His concern was touching and to my delight, he was free and interested in spending some time together. I had hinted I was looking to have a nice time, a distraction from everything.

Going through a second outfit change, hoping to convey an effortless, casual look with a little va-va-voom, took effort to pull off with limited choice. I settled on a short, playful, slightly flirtatious dress, complimented with white flats and my long, wavy curls up in a loose ponytail. Minimum makeup, but enough to shine.

When it was time, I stood slightly posed, leaning against the windowsill outside, waiting for him. Andrew stopped sawing and couldn't contain the large grin on his face. I held my head high and looked away, praying I wasn't flushed. To my relief, moments later I heard the saw back at work.

Brian pulled up shortly after. It was obvious he checked me out as I walked towards him. His gaze said it all and I felt flattered. A quick wave to Andrew from both of us and we were away in his cosy car. If there was a slight awkwardness between us initially, it didn't last long. I felt a self-confidence around him that was liberating.

"How are you, Liz?" He smiled and placed his hand on my lap. With my short hemline, he touched my skin, giving it the subtlest of strokes, awakening my body while sending heat to my cheeks. Our eyes briefly met and he read me like a book. A little gentle touch and I longed for him.

Without a second thought, I placed my hand on his lap, veering just a little. He definitely liked it; that much was clear. I didn't ask where we were going, but I could have guessed; we both knew what we wanted. The desire to take off his clothes and have his naked body against mine was like an avalanche – nothing could stop it from happening.

Once we stepped through his front door, that's exactly what I did, and didn't hold back. He had this sexual aura that drove me wild. It was passionate and urgent. He had me stark naked in his living room, my bits and pieces spread across the floor, before making our way to his bed. The way his body reacted to mine was like fire to oil.

As he pushed himself against me, I could feel his heart racing. Oh, how he satisfied me! It was a dopamine overload. His many groans, lip-biting, and eagerness to pleasure me in different ways was almost too much to take. I never thought this happened in real life; not in mine, anyways, but twice now, it did.

Lying breathlessly on his bed, the bedsheets distorted, for the first time I started to notice the room. It had a red brick feature wall and a white voile curtain hanging from a black industrial pole for some privacy, separating the room from the rest of the apartment. His table lamp was knocked over from our excitement, and I made a reach for it to set it up straight. He grinned wildly as he pulled me back into him, still breathing heavily.

Some time passed when a thought popped in my head, how little I knew about him. After all, this wasn't a one-night stand situation anymore. "What is it that you do? Outside being very good at this, of course?" A fact already established.

"Very good, you say!" he echoed, milking the compliment and adding a little chuckle. "I . . . I run my own business in web design and advertising." He reached to take my hand and pulled me closer to sitting. "Come, I'll show you." He shuffled out of the bed, our hands still locked together, pulled me up and began leading me to his office.

I couldn't help but stare at his bare bottom as he moved. As he quickly turned around in front of the white door, he caught me looking at a different view. "Eyes up here," he smiled, and opened the door wide and led me inside.

It took me some time to take it in. "Wow, are these all your designs?"

He nodded. I studied the many advertising posters on the wall in more detail. They ranged from sunny getaways and cruises, a man's shaver, clothing, fitness studio, and many more, all displayed in large A2-size prints. When my gaze turned back to Brian, his was firmly focused on my naked body. "Eyes up here, you." I gave it back to him.

"You . . ." he murmured, eyeing me up and down, not listening. "Are beautiful, Liz." Giving me a seductive smile, he turned around and pushed his office chair in front of me to sit on. I eagerly obliged. He spun me around and around, playfully, until the posters in the room all merged into a continuous array of colours. When he stopped the chair right in front of him, his excitement was obvious – and so was my next move.

We were laughing after we finished again. Our tiredness had become apparent in our performance and we both agreed we were *really* done now.

He started to tell me more about his business. He spoke with such passion, especially about some particular clientele, dropping what he said were big names, yet many were unfamiliar to me. It was clearly a big deal for his business, which put his name on the map he said with pride of his achievements.

I told him a bit about Ms Bouquet and how Su and I had made our business dream come true. He nodded his head, seemingly impressed by what I was telling him. "You can never do enough advertising," he said just at the right time, as if he had been waiting to put himself forward.

"Like you're doing now?"

"Sharp." He winked. I smiled cockily. As we dived deeper in conversation, I started to share more personal things, from my childhood growing up in Ireland, my mother, and even brushing on past relationships. Talking with him felt easy and natural. I divulged more than I normally would, especially with someone I had only just met. Granted, we'd had sex numerous times. *That was different.* I did leave out most of the details about the past few days. I preferred to bury that for just this little while.

Brian looked sexy in his afterglow. His hair was handsomely messy, with locks of his dark-brown hair covering part of his hazel eyes that were sweet and dreamy; they smiled, even when he wasn't. But when he did smile, his eyes were lined with perfect creases that you couldn't even call wrinkles. He's one of those guys that only get more handsome as the years pass.

#

It was well into late evening now and I didn't feel like going back to the B&B. Normally, I wouldn't have asked, but I was doing many things I wouldn't have done before these past few days, so *to hell with it*. If his reaction was any bit hesitant, or an outright no, I would feel bruised, no doubt about it, but that wasn't going to stop me.

We were in the kitchen. I sat on the high breakfast bar chair, legs crossed, tall posture softly swinging. He stood across from me at the counter, his sexy, toned body on display as he only had a pair of trousers on while he navigated the kitchen proficiently as he made us something to eat. I stared at him for a while, hooked. I almost forgot what I wanted to ask.

"Brian?"

"Yes, Lizzy?" he said, looking up from washing the tomatoes, with his smiling eyes. Lizzy sounded different coming from him and I kind of liked it.

"Can I stay the night?" I hoped it came out confidently and my voice did not waver, feeling nervous for his reaction.

Without a pause, other than surprise, he said, "Sure, that would be nice." I smiled and watched him pottering around once more and took in his apartment.

It was open plan and had a real industrial look about it, with exposed brick walls, steel beams, and even some pipes running down the walls like a feature. He had decorated the place with some retro-style pieces, from his curved four-door low sideboard cabinet to his unusual floor lamp that looked like a round fan mounted on tripod legs shaped like stiletto heels, taking pride of place in the living area.

Only his office and bathroom were separate rooms. Every other area was either open or divided by a partial wall innovatively doubled up for storage and decoration, or with curtains. The whole space had a relaxing feel to it. I walked over to his couch and made myself more comfortable, covering myself with the throw. Finished taking in all the little details of Brian's place, I turned my attention back to him,

"I can see you watching me, you know," he said with delight.

"Well, it's a nice view."

Now and then he looked up from what he was doing, and we smiled at each other when our eyes met. The smell of the sizzling bacon started to fill the room.

"Lizzy?"

I smiled at the sound of my name.

"Yeah?"

"I like you," he said with a wink. The words fluttered around in my head and my stomach.

"I like you too, Brian," I said, smiling and blushing. I covered my face slightly with the throw.

"You're cute when you're shy," he said, giving me a smile that made my insides swim. Embarrassed, I covered myself fully.

"Smells good!" I said from under the throw, deflecting.

"Thank you. Why don't you come over here and try some?"

I was ravenous, so despite my embarrassment, I uncovered myself and wrapped it around my body. He stared at me as I did so. "Here, have a taste." He blew on the wooden spoon before feeding it to me. The sauce had a serious kick of spiciness to it.

"Not too bad," I said while trying to not be overcome by the heat.

"Not too much sauce for your sandwich then." He smiled.

"Can I take a shower before we eat? And maybe . . . do you have a shirt I could wear?"

He switched off the hob, took my hand, and led me to his wardrobe, handing me one of his white shirts after eyeing the length, and a towel. His bathroom had a luxurious hotel feel, with a walk-in shower easily fit for two people, and a large showerhead.

Not long after I wetted my hair and started to wash myself, Brian joined me. He took the loofah from me and slowly washed my body, paying special attention around my sensitive areas and laying a gentle kiss here and there. My body quivered as he did so, my tiredness a thing of the past.

He admired my body and I enjoyed every bit of it, letting out a moan here and there. It was such a release being with him. Something about being intimate with him set me free of all my doubts.

When he finished satisfying me, I eagerly returned the favour. His enjoyment was mine. It was the most sensual experience. I never had a shower with someone that felt like *that* before. He had a way that was exhilarating and liberating.

We stepped out looking slightly pink. Once I dried off and put on his shirt, he stood behind me and slowly buttoned it up, his hands gently caressing my breasts. He knew exactly how to entice me. It was close to 11:00 p.m. by the time we ate, cosied up on the couch, and not long after, so exhausted, we barely made the short distance to his bed and fell asleep.

#

We were greeted in the morning with the sounds of birdsong and light traffic coming from the open window. The curtain slowly swayed in the draft. My body was kept warm by his embrace. "I will have to get up soon," he whispered in my ear. I sighed, enjoying the sound of his morning voice.

"I do too. Andrew is bringing me to visit his parents." I matched his whisper. "He said they have some pictures of us when we were little." Brian hummed and kissed the back of my neck. I turned around in his arms to face him. "How is it that you remember me?"

"Truthfully, I only have a few memories of you. I remember playing on the swing together in your grandmother's garden. Andrew and I would take turns pushing you girls. We would also run around the plants and trees and have races through the tunnel. You were a fast runner and beat me a few times."

"The tunnel of trees?"

"Yes." Brian's lips lifted into a small smile. "You remember?"

"No," I replied, unable to hide the disappointment in my voice. "But it felt like magic walking through it when I arrived at the house. It's so beautiful. My . . . my mother used to tell me stories about fairies when I was little, and when she described where they lived, that place reminded me of it," I said, closing my eyes briefly, imagining them flying around there. "Come to think of it, it could be *the* place."

Brian kissed me softly on my lips and got up and we fell into comfortable silence as my thoughts drifted away.

"I'm going to the Lake District for a couple of days, walking, hiking, that kind of thing," he said, putting on his trousers. "Would you like to come?"

"Uhm," I smiled, sitting up, dazed while thinking of how impulsive I'd been these past few days. "When are you going? And where will we be staying?" I asked eventually.

"Tomorrow."

"Tomorrow!?"

"I know it's short notice. Have a think about it. I have a place booked and there is plenty of room." He winked. "Would you like me to drive you back to the B&B?"

"Yes please, thank –" He kissed me again, passionately and for longer this time.

"Just, think about it. Okay?" he whispered, sounding hopeful. I nodded, breathless and unable to form a single word.

#

Andrew was busy working in the garden when we pulled up at the gate. "Hey, I wasn't sure if you were still coming!" he said as soon as I stepped out of the car after yet another passionate kiss. I gave him a quick smile. "Of course I am!"

Making my way to the door, I lingered a little as the men caught up; to my disappointment, I couldn't make out what was being said. They looked up almost simultaneously however, grinning. With an undoubtedly flushed smile, I rushed upstairs for a change of clothes.

Not long after, we were in Andrew's car on the way to his parents' house. "How is Willie doing?"

"He is recovering well from the surgery, but he will need someone to take care of him for around six weeks once he gets home. He can't strain himself in any way until the area with the stitches is fully healed."

"Does he have any family he can stay with?"

"No. Not that he has ever mentioned. We decided he can stay with us."

"That's kind of you," I said, reminded once again of their generosity.

"So . . . how was your time with Brian?" he asked with a knowing smile.

"Good," I said, not wanting to divulge more.

"Just good?"

"Okay, it was great," I said, smiling wide and letting out a laugh. He shook his head, chuckling.

"So you like him then?" Andrew asked after a moment. Feeling sheepish, I looked outside of my window to disguise my face from view.

"Are we almost there?"

"Do you recognise the road?"

"I think so . . ." I said, taking in the cobblestoned road which was paved between red bricked houses. "It's really close to my grandmother's house, isn't it?"

"You see over there?" He pointed to a little lane off the side of the main road, wedged between overgrown shrubbery. "If you walk through there, you end up at the gravel road to her house. My parents live just around the corner at the end of this road."

"Oh, you lived really close," I said, feeling a brief stab of envy for not having had the same experience. "How is it, actually, that your parents got to know my grandmother?"

"Well . . . she used to mind me, Brian, and Glor, but I am not sure how they initially met, to be honest." Andrew parked right in front of the house. The garden was immaculately kept.

"Shall we?" he asked, opening his door.

I let out a breath I didn't realise I was holding. "Yeah, sure." I got out of the car, meeting him at the foot of the short path leading to their aqua-blue front door with a round, stained-glass window detailed with a floral design.

"The garden looks lovely," I said, admiring the abundance of violas, geraniums, and even the rhododendron on its last leg still made an impression. It was a joy of colours.

"My dad's work," he said with pride in his voice.

"Hmm, like father, like son." He smiled, a faint blush flickering across his cheeks.

Andrew pressed the doorbell, which made a high-pitched ding sound with the expected dong absent. I felt a little nervous meeting his parents, or – I suppose I wasn't so much nervous about meeting them as I was apprehensive about what they might tell me.

Andrew's dad opened the door. There was no mistake; he had the same-shaped blue eyes and jawline. "Andrew," he said to his son, placing his hand on his shoulder.

"This is Elizabeth, Dad," he said, gesturing toward me.

"Nice to meet you, sir." Timidly, I stuck out my hand for a shake.

"Call me Harold," he said adamantly and shook my outstretched hand with a strong grip.

"Who is it, darling?" a high-pitched voice called from inside the house.

"Andrew and Elizabeth!" Harold called out while he beckoned us to follow him down the hall. The walls were lined with framed photographs. I didn't get a good look at them as I followed the two men into the bright kitchen.

"Elizabeth! It has been so long! Let me look at you." A short woman with grey hair tied in a bun dashed toward me and took my hand, studying me for a few seconds. "The last time I saw you, you must have been around four." She looked me up and down, and her freckled face broke into a fond smile. "You, Gloria, and the boys got on so well. They wanted to be your boyfriends, you know!" she whispered towards my ear, unfortunately loud enough for everyone to hear.

"Huh. Nice to meet you, Mrs –"

"Call me Selina. I hope you're taking good care of her?" she directed at Andrew.

"Very much so," I assured her. "They both are. I have never eaten so well."

"Oh, Gloria is a cooking marvel. Luckily for Andrew, as he never was any good." She poked a jab at him, joking, but still matter of fact as she placed cups and saucers on a tray. Andrew laughed it off. "Let's sit."

Selina led the way, and we sat down at the oval wooden table with an old-fashioned, off-white lace table runner. Andrew sat opposite of me and gave me a friendly smile as if to ask, are you okay?

"I still can't believe I have been here, and I never knew," I said in a shaky voice.

"You were very young when you left, dear," Selina said. She put the tea down and poured us a strong cuppa, noticeable from the dark colour.

"I just don't understand why my mother never told me – and lied about it," I said, fiddling with the table runner.

"I can't answer that for you, but what I can tell you is that you lived with Hilda, your grandmother, from when you were born, and then left one summer. It left her heartbroken. She would just say you were with another family now."

"What? I lived here? Not visited?"

"Yes, you lived with Hilda." She said it so matter-of-factly it blew me away.

"And . . . and my mum wasn't here with us?"

"No, she wasn't, and it was not something Hilda would ever talk about. It wasn't my place to pry, dear. It clearly was a weight on her heart that she carried around, whatever it was."

"Another family?" I said, confused.

"She must have meant you went to live with your mother," Andrew replied, getting up to move the chair out for his mother to sit on.

"Why the secrecy?"

Everyone was quiet for a few seconds. Clearly, no one knew.

"Would you get the photo album? It's on the shelf by the fireplace," she asked Harold, who now sat across from her, quietly holding his drink. He nodded and got up, hardly making a sound.

"How is it that you knew my grandmother?"

"Brian's mother introduced us to your grandmother because she was going to mind him when she went back to work, and at the time I was looking for someone to mind Andrew." Listening, I took a sip of my tea, adding sugar and milk to dilute the strong flavour.

"You see, I was going back to work too. You met Brian, right?" I felt myself flush at the question. Andrew's big grin didn't help.

"Yes, we met."

"Yes, they met, Mum," Andrew confirmed smugly, which was met by a kick under the table. Andrew's mother seemed to notice this and smiled.

"You know, if you had stayed, dear, you might have ended up with him, as Andrew ended up with Gloria. Or maybe the other way around." Andrew shot a displeased, "Mother!" at her.

"She is just joking," Harold said, lowering himself back into his seat next to me, the album in his hand. "Selina has a big imagination and a strange sense of humour. Don't take any notice." Selina frowned at him and he winked back at her.

"Aha, now I know where Andrew gets it from," I said, sending a teasing grin back his way. Harold and Selina laughed.

"Well, do you have someone special in your life, dear?"

"No, I don't," I said, taking a quick sip of tea, tasting much better now.

"You don't!?" Andrew said as we locked into a stare, leaving his parents confused.

"Right. . . one day, you might meet someone special."

"Thank you, Selina." I shifted uncomfortably in my seat.

Harold passed the photo album to her. "Ah. This is from when Andrew was small, but you're in some of the photographs as well." She browsed through it until she found some. There I was, in my grandmother's garden, like Andrew had said.

Picking flowers and playing with a ball. And even one by the swing.

"This is you?" I turned the album around to Andrew. Before he could say anything, Selina confirmed. There was a small Andrew pushing me on the swing. There was no denying the truth anymore. It was easy to make out Brian and Gloria in the photographs as well. We all looked so adorable and happy.

"I don't have one just of you, but you can have one of these if you like," she offered, already removing the photo from the plastic pocket.

"I would love that. Thank you," I said, meeting her eyes.

"I am sorry I can't tell you more." I could tell she was genuine, as Andrew had been. I swallowed back my emotions.

"Thank you for your time in showing me this and for inviting me to your home."

"You're very welcome, dear. Maybe Willie can shed some light on things for you. He was a very close friend of your grandmother."

"So I have heard. I hope he can, once he feels better."

"How is he now?" she asked her son.

While Andrew explained Willie's condition to his parents, I had another look at the photographs, staring at my younger self, wishing I could remember. We didn't stay much longer after we finished our tea, and on the drive back to the B&B,

I held onto the now cherished photograph of little me and Andrew in Hilda's garden, holding a bunch of flowers in my hand. *I loved flowers from a young age.* The thought warmed my heart.

#

I had already spent an hour on the phone with Su when the call for dinner interrupted us. Much of our conversation was more of an interrogation. The only difference being that instead of a reluctant interrogation subject, I was easy and eager to answer the questions, especially about Brian.

The past five days felt like a dream, yet so real too. "Don't forget to send a picture of Brian! And go with him!" she made me promise before she let me go for another *fancy meal.* I had done some boasting about Gloria's elaborate dinners.

"Some good news!" Andrew said as soon as I entered the dining room. "Willie will be allowed home most likely in three to four days –"

"– and he will be staying with us for a while, so we can take care of him until he is fully recovered," Gloria interjected, shooting Andrew a smile as she placed a piping-hot dish on the table.

"That *is* great news! And very kind of you." I smiled at Andrew, who had already shared that last bit of information. "Has anyone else visited him?"

Gloria shook her head. "No, not that we know, do we, Drew?" She looked at him.

"No, he hasn't mentioned anyone."

As much as I wanted to talk with Willie, he was not allowed to have any stress, which, clearly, my presence and desire for information about the past caused just that. Maybe a few days away was precisely what I needed to get off the roller coaster that was the past few days.

"Three days, you said?"

"Yes, maybe four."

"Um . . . I will be going away for a few days," I mumbled, a little nervous. "I'm going to the Lake District with Brian." I felt as if I was telling my mum I had my first boyfriend and was afraid of her reaction.

Andrew and Gloria looked at each other, surprised. "Oh, you will love it there!" Andrew said a moment after they collected themselves.

"It's stunning!" Gloria added with a nod.

"You have been?!" They smiled at each other.

While Gloria was putting the final garnishing on the plate, I quickly texted Brian to let him know the news.

(Brian) *Great, I will pick you up at 6 am;)*

"Six a.m.!" I said out loud unintentionally.

That evening, back in my room ready to pack my suitcase, I felt uneasy. Willie was on my mind. I had so many questions, and as thoughts occupied my restless brain, putting pen to paper came to me as my only possible saviour to quiet the noise.

Dear Willie,

I am so pleased to hear you're recovering well, and you might be able to go home in a few days. I have not visited you, not wanting to cause you any more undue stress. I hope Andrew has passed on my get-well wishes.

I will be going away for a couple of days and was hoping on my return, we might be able to talk? I have questions I would like to ask you and I have a feeling you have more to share with me. I can understand it might be painful, as you miss my grandmother dearly. However, I do hope you could find it within yourself to share some of the memories you have of her with me so I may get to know her. I was unaware that my grandmother was still alive until recently . . . and I have no recollection of ever living with her.

Andrew and Gloria told me you will be staying with them when you're leaving the hospital. Maybe we can meet there upon my return?

Love and get-well wishes,
Elizabeth

It was before midnight by the time I finished writing the letter, packing, and my head was more settled. I quietly went downstairs to leave the letter with a note on the table in the kitchen for Andrew. To my surprise, the light was still on.

"Hey, night owl," I whispered.

Andrew looked surprised. He was in checkered navy blue and red pyjamas, working on his laptop.

He stared me up and down and a smirky laugh escaped him. I was in my bunny-covered dressing gown, which I self-consciously fastened tighter, as if that would disguise the childish print.

"Aw, you look lovely," he said, widening his grin.

"Well, so do you." I gave it back to him. Unfortunately, this did not have the same effect, as his pyjamas weren't that bad.

"You have something for me?" he asked, eyes fixed on the paper in my hand.

"Uh, yes, yes. I was wondering if you could give this to Willie?"

"Of course! A love letter," he teased, reaching his hand out to take it from me.

"Ha-ha, very funny."

"Would you like some tea?" he asked, pointing to the seat across from him. I considered for a second that I ought to go to bed if I was going to wake up before six, but I wasn't sleepy.

"Sure, why not. Working late?" I asked, sitting down in my designated seat.

"Not so much working as just unwinding from the busy day." He got up to boil the kettle.

"Thank you again for bringing me to your parents. It was lovely to meet them."

"They enjoyed meeting you as well." He got two mugs out from the cupboard and dropped a teabag in each. "So, you really like Brian, huh?" He turned to me, awaiting my response.

"I do," I said quietly.

"You're blushing!" His grin was as wide as it could be.

"Thanks for that!" I replied, dizzy with the blood rushing to my head.

Chapter 5

Six hours and one pit stop into the drive, with a soft tapping on my leg, Brian woke me up. A little disorientated, staring in the mirror on the sun visor. I could tell from the car door impression on my face that I had slept for some time. My hair looked a mess with my long, flowy, spiral-shaped curls anything but defined, and when I did the hand breath test, *oh boy,* it smelled terrible. *At least I didn't drool.*

Brian reached down the side of his door and handed me a small box with little mints, which I gratefully accepted and popped several in my mouth.

"This is a little town called Keswick," he said, gesturing out the window in front of us. "We are about twenty minutes from Seatoller, but I thought we'd get something to eat here and do a little shopping, since this is the nearest place with amenities."

The charming, bendy streets were lined with pretty character houses and cottages. A quintessential English town, as I imagined an English town to be. "Sounds good," I said, tightening my hair in a ponytail and patting down the stray hairs. "The nearest place, you said?"

"Yup. And if you'd like to make some calls, you should probably do it now. You might not have reception later." I looked at him to see if he was messing with me. He wasn't.

Moments later he parked, and we walked to what looked like the main shopping street. The street was paved with areas of red and grey bricks and had a little church in the middle that was now a tourist information centre. There were many pretty shops dotted around and places to eat, but Brian took my hand and ushered me to an outdoors shop. "What size are you?" he asked, opening the door, signalling for me to go inside. I gave him a look.

"*Shoe* size, Lizzy," he said, giving me a playful nudge.

"Oh . . . size five," I said, blushing a little. Brian nodded and headed over to a rack which held an assortment of hiking fleeces and began sifting through.

"And clothes a ten." He leaned down to whisper in my ear, "I noticed the label on your little red number." I gave him a little nudge back with my elbow. I was certain the redness of my face deepened a shade. I never blushed so much in my life as I did these past few days.

Brian spoke with a saleslady and after trying on a few hiking boots and clothes, followed by a pricey purchase, we were out of there. “This is serious stuff,” I said, hoping he would finally let me in on the exact plans, having stayed tight-lipped during the drive.

“It’s good to be prepared,” he said in a way that did not really reassure me. I was no stranger to walking, but not super long distances or on difficult terrain. I was up for a challenge though, kind of, just nothing too crazy.

“You will take it easy on me, won’t you?”

“That’s why I brought a tent, Lizzy.” He kissed my forehead. “I’ll keep you safe. Promise.” He winked, charming me into trusting him.

We stopped by a quaint café and were lucky with the sunny weather, allowing us to enjoy our meal on the terrace. I texted Su the address where I was going to be staying and that I most likely wouldn’t be reachable.

She rang back straight away and was over the moon I went with Brian but also a little concerned that we possibly couldn’t get in touch. But I wasn’t. I felt safe with him and tried to reassure her of that.

Brian, seated next to me devouring his lunch, overhearing the conversation, stroked my leg. “I will take good care of you, Lizzy,” he whispered.

"I know," I said, putting my hand over his. "And I can take care of myself too, you know," I added confidently.

"I don't doubt that." He sat back in his chair, smiling.

"Okay, I give," Su said, overhearing us, but not before shouting in the phone a light-hearted yet serious threat for Brian's ears.

The drive to Seatoller was breathtaking, if not somewhat of a challenging road for drivers. I couldn't believe my eyes when I saw a bus going over a narrow bridge that should really be considered pedestrian only. *You must have some good nerves to be a bus driver here.* Brian's Mini Cooper was perfect for the narrow, winding roads with sharp bends, if not somewhat daunting when a bigger vehicle passed by and your only option was going closer to the protruding rocky walls on the side of the road. If you were lucky, only your side mirror would become a target.

Several times, I thought we were there when we passed a tiny village, if you can even call them that. They were more like a few houses in a row and some sparingly scattered around the landscape. I checked my phone; not one bar was showing.

"I told you," Brian said, amused.

"You did," I smiled, unconcerned. It wasn't like I was a complete stranger to having no phone reception; drive long enough around Connemara and you will meet the same fate.

When we finally reached Seatoller, a tiny village, the imposing mountain views with the peaks covered by clouds were breathtaking. Sheep were roaming everywhere, living in harmony, grazing and maintaining the landscape. Only their spray-painted red and blue markings and shaved bodies indicated they belonged to people. One sheep had clearly made an escape from a farmer, as everywhere but his behind was shaved. "He has a nice cushion," I said, chuckling while pointing him out to Brian.

Water was gushing down through the cracks in the mountains as if it appeared from nowhere. The impressionable surrounding got me eager to get out of the car to have a closer look. As if sensing my anticipation, moments later, Brian parked the car on a gravel parking lot. We got out and leaned onto the hood of the car, taking in the towering mountain, and I could hear water flowing in the distance. "That is Bessyboot," Brian said, pointing at the mountain right in front of us. Staring at it made me dizzy. The view was *exhilarating*.

"Bessyboot." Then, it dawned on me. "We are *not* going on that, are we?!" He put his arm around me.

"Who knows?" he said, the edge of his lips tilting upward. "But first." He lifted me up on the hood with a knowing smile. I messed his hair as he leaned in to kiss my neck softly, trailing down. He knew just the right spots. When he came up and our lips met, our kisses quickly deepened. "How about your second time al fresco?" he said, his voice deep with lust.

I briefly looked around, and then followed his line of sight to the little covered area behind us.

"Bus stop?"

"Uhm. It's the bright of day?"

"You're right." He took me by the hand, planting a trail of kisses laced with promise of what's to come and got back into the car, driving ten seconds across the road.

"Uhm?"

"We are here." He winked.

Getting out with our luggage, I followed him through a beautifully kept garden into a charming old guest house. Brian quickly checked us in and we made it up the stairs to our room. He took the bags from my hands, tossing them to the side, and closed the door behind me. "Take off your clothes," he ordered, his voice hypnotic and eyes wide with desire, which told me that he wanted every inch of me. I eagerly submitted to his request and then some. Hands down, he is the best sex I *ever* had. Our bodies fit so seamlessly together, as if we are performing a dance; a very passionate and even ravenous one, that is.

After our intimate frenzy, I took in the room. It was decorated with old, dark furniture, and even the light fittings had old-world charm. The window seat looked inviting, and I strutted there, placing a soft cushion in my back, leaning against the thick walls, taking in the view.

"Nice view," Brian said.

"Beautiful."

"I agree." His voice teasing. As I looked over, he lay on his side propped up on his arm, checking me out. "There is an en suite just big enough for two," he hinted not-so subtly.

"I would not have taken you for this kind of getaway," I said, ignoring him, giving him a cheeky smile.

"Didn't you, now. How about sleeping in a tent?" he said softly, biting his lower lip while his eyes travelled to my bare breast.

"No, not that either."

"We can keep each other warm when we do."

"Oh, can we now?" I got up and he quickly did the same, took me by the hand and guided me to the en suite, ducking through a low doorway. "It is very cosy," he teased.

"I like cosy."

#

It was about 7:00 p.m. when we left the room for a meal. Dinner was what Gloria would have called 'splendid'. There were many more people in the dining room, all seated together at two very large tables, sharing news about their day. But it was all background noise to us. We only had eyes for each other.

I actually felt flutters in my stomach. *Am I falling for him?* That was a ridiculous thought. I hardly knew him.

"Excuse me." An elderly fellow diner interrupted our admiration for each other. Brian kindly helped the lady to another helping of roasted potato, lamb, and a glass of wine.

"One for your lady too?" she said with a smile.

"Well, my lady?" he asked, fully in character, looking me straight in my eyes. I returned his gaze and gracefully accepted. We were so engaged with each other that the wine in the glass almost spilled over when he poured it for me.

"I used to look at my husband like that, you know. We adored each other. He was a handsome gentleman," the elderly woman said fondly, nodding in our direction. She then began to unclasp her golden locket and opened it to reveal a black-and-white photograph of a young couple. "We were only in our twenties here," she said, beaming at us.

"You were a dazzling lady," Brian flattered her.

"I think I still got it," she said, her smile widening, revealing perfect teeth which were most likely dentures as she did a little pose, flicking her long, white hair over her shoulder.

"You do indeed," Brian replied, and took hold of one of her hands and gently kissed it. She was charmed by him.

"You have a good one here," she said, turning to look at me with her soft-blue eyes.

"Elizabeth and Brian," I said, introducing ourselves.

"Martha," she replied, holding up her glass and tipping it in our direction.

We spent the evening meal listening to the colourful life Martha had lived with her now-deceased husband. In his honour, she still visited the Lake District once a year, as he had such a love for the area and she has many glorious memories of that time, as she put it.

Brian listened with such genuine interest. I admired him for that. Meeting Martha and her enthusiasm to share her precious life stories with us was a humbling and enjoyable experience. As she retired to her room for her "shut-eye," we decided to spend some time in the common room by the open fire, finishing our drinks. Afterwards Brian guided me back up the carpeted stairs. It creaked under our feet.

Once we were in front of the door to our room, he glided his hand over my shoulder and down toward my chest to unbutton the top button of my blouse and kissed my neck softly. When we entered the room, foreplay was lengthy and dare I say, romantic, and the final act had us open-mouthed with breathlessness. It was different from other times. The intimacy and emotional connection between us was as if we had become one. We fell asleep with our bodies intertwined.

#

The sound of birds chirping and the light streaming through the slightly open curtain was our call to awaken. He stretched out his arms and sat up, looking down at me with his dreamy, brown eyes. “So, is this the longest one-night stand you have ever had?” Brian asked, smirking.

“Ha-ha, very funny,” I replied, rolling my eyes at him. “Actually, I would like to ask you something.” I sat up beside him, leaning against the headboard.

“Sure.” He sat up too.

“Why did Andrew say those things the first time we met? Why did he think you were going to hurt me?” I kept looking straight ahead, a bit anxious. “He seemed to imply you will hurt me like all the other women,” I said, my voice going into a whisper.

“Woman, not women.” His voice was serious.

“Sorry?” I asked, finally looking at him. But he was looking down at his hands, wringing them together.

“He meant one particular woman.” He sighed at length. “When we were teenagers, we both liked Gloria *a lot*, but we didn’t want to ruin our friendship. So . . . we made a pact that neither of us would ask her out on a date. Which we kept to for several years.” He paused for a while as if reluctant to go on. I was almost going to prompt him to speak again when he continued.

"But then, on my twentieth birthday, Gloria and I ended up spending the night together. We were both intoxicated. Andrew was dating another girl and he said he was over Gloria. I was at that time of my life where I was not going steady with anyone. But after we hooked up several times more, we decided to go on a real date and had an exclusive relationship for a while. Or, well, I tried.

"After several months of dating, I didn't treat her in a way she deserved. I was quite distant and I – I started to see another woman on the side. When I admitted that to her, Andrew was there to comfort her. At that time, he wasn't in a relationship anymore.

"As the months passed, their friendship developed into a romance, and, well, you know the rest." He paused again, taking a sharp breath. "Andrew was resentful toward me for how I treated Gloria, and sometimes, he still acts as if I am still that playboy. I did go through a phase where I was dating several girls at the same time . . . but that phase in my life has long been in the past."

We were silent for a while. He seemed deep in thought, and I had a few of my own. I was surprised he and Gloria had been together. I wouldn't have guessed. Processing, I didn't see him different because he dated several girls at a time, eons ago, as long as it was out in the open. That he cheated on someone, however, touched a nerve deep inside. I know the absolute devastation it brings to one's heart and the shattering emotional turmoil you go through being at the receiving end of the cheater. It is not something I ever wish to go through again.

Brian looked at me and read the concern on my face. He softly kissed my forehead.

"Hey," he said, lifting my chin with his hand and gently turning my head to look at him. "I am *not* that person anymore. I regret hurting Gloria. She is very happy with Andrew now, and I just didn't love her like that. We have been great friends for many years; it is all water under the bridge. Really," he reassured me. "Andrew is very caring and always looks out for everyone," he continued. "He just doesn't want you to get hurt, especially with everything you're already going through. And I have no intention of hurting you."

"Good," I replied, my shoulders sagging a little in relief.

"Can I ask you something?" he asked tentatively after a moment. I looked at him and gave him a small nod to let him go on. "You told your friend on the phone that night that I was your rebound. Who was he?"

I let out a deep breath and I told him all about Gordon. The engagement, the cheating, how he got the woman pregnant, and the hurt of it all. I didn't hold back until it was all out. The pain felt almost fresh again, except for the first time in ages, I didn't cry.

"I'm so sorry you went through that, Lizzy," he said, his dreamy eyes locked onto mine. He moved closer, his lips slightly parted, and kissed me gently. It was a lengthy kiss that possessed care, gentleness, and – dare I think it so soon? – love.

I had always lived by this one golden rule. I would not tell a person that I love them until the first argument had been had. Many things can be learnt by how the first argument is resolved and how you feel afterwards. If you're in love, you will know then for sure. That has always been my belief.

My first argument with Gordon was pretty silly, but real. We were going on a double date with Susan and Conor, her then-boyfriend. He was late picking me up and had no good excuse for it. I was sure he was deliberately late. He had said earlier that he would like to spend some time alone, while I wanted to go out. I had, admittedly, built up some resentment about us being late and during dinner, I gave him the cold shoulder. We had a heated argument about it on the way home.

Afterwards, we both made our apologies and understood each other's perspectives because we made an effort to relate to the other person. Not long after this, we said I love you.

Brian and I hadn't even talked about what *this* is, other than the longest one-night stand, and here I was falling for him. It wasn't just lust or a bit of excitement anymore, it started to feel deeper than that. What if we were to start a real relationship? I was leaving in eight days, how was that going to work? My mind was going into overdrive prematurely. *Back to the here and now, Liz*. It could just be a holiday fling, an amazing one at that.

"So . . . what do you have in store today?" I asked, shivering a bit when Brian pulled back the covers and jumped out of bed.

"Well, why don't we take a shower, go for some breakfast, get our gear and head out?" he said, bundling our towels together which had fallen onto the floor the night before.

"Heading out *where* exactly?" I asked, raising my eyebrows, the daunting image of Bessyboot flickered in my mind.

"You'll see." He took my hand to pull me off the bed and guide me towards the shower once more.

#

"Would you like to join an old lady?" Martha waved her hand towards the empty chairs at her table. We ordered a full English breakfast, got some orange juice from the drink stand, and sat down beside her.

"Well, what are you doing today, lady Martha?" Brian asked, taking a sip of his juice. Martha's face brightened.

"I will be taking the bus into Keswick to meet up with some old friends for an afternoon tea," she said with delight. "How about you two?"

"We are going from Seathwaite up to the Green Gable." Brian spared me a glance, lip tilting up in a teasing smirk. "And who knows, maybe even up to the Great Gable." Martha's clear, blue eyes widened.

"You are keen hikers."

I looked from Brian to Martha and back, slightly concerned about what I was in for. I had no idea what he was talking about; the names were foreign to me. Not to mention the fact that I wasn't a very keen hiker at all, even though I really did appreciate the stunning surroundings we were in.

"Well, *I* am," Brian smirked. "And I have a feeling we might have a hiker in the making," he teased in his sweet way.

"Take it easy on her, you don't want to scare her away," Martha said and winked at me, which made me smile.

The scent of the full English entered the room and moments later, it was placed in front of us. "That's one portion?" Surprised at the amount of food we were given, I just stared at it.

"Eat up, Lizzy. You're going to need it," Brian said, digging in eagerly. Everyone likes a big, delicious meal, but not so much when you're told you will need it. Nonetheless, I tucked in and managed to eat every bit of it. Lady Martha, as we had started to call her, had a much more modest breakfast.

"I will indulge this afternoon," she told us with excitement. I could just envision her and her friends having afternoon tea in a stylish manor house, getting spoiled with delicious confections. She seemed like a woman who liked to spoil herself regularly.

"I will be departing now," Martha announced when she had finished her meal and got up gracefully from her seat to pull on her mustard tweed coat. "I might see you at dinner." She held out her hand for a courteous kiss, which Brian obliged.

We chuckled once she had left. She is such a sweet, eccentric lady.

Soon after breakfast, we got ready to go. "I can't believe I'm wearing four layers of clothing," I grumbled, feeling myself burning up in the cosy heat of our room.

"It can get rather chilly on the fells, and it's going to be a windy day. You'll appreciate it later," he explained.

"Any attempts at seduction in this gear would require great diligence," I said while bending down awkwardly to retrieve my backpack from the floor.

Brian laughed, "I am up for the challenge, Lizzy." I looked at myself and then at Brian, who was similarly layered up, but looking very relaxed in it. *Not sure I am.*

#

The walk started off as a breeze, till we reached a waterfall and he announced we were going up Sourmilk Ghyll. It was beautiful to look at, and hearing the water pouring down the rocks was an incredible sound, but that's when the hike became real for me.

Halfway up, I took a moment to catch my breath and look at the valley below and once we arrived on top, I was breathing heavily and down several layers of clothes. Brian had hardly broken a sweat as we sat on some rocks for a rest. The view was something else. The sheep in the valley were little white dots in the green fields and the river just a small stream from this height. "*That*," Brian said, pointing down from where we had come from, "is Seathwaite."

More than three hours later, with the help of a very patient Brian, we reached the top of Green Gable. It was a magnificent, breathtaking view of vast mountains and lakes. It had me speechless.

Granted, some of it was from exhaustion and the relief that we were *finally* here. For a novice like me, I was rather proud. Diamond Hill in Connemara National Park was the only mountain I'd gone up before, and I recall finding that a little challenging towards the peak. This was definitely on a different level.

As I admired the view, Brian took some pictures. "Look behind you!" he said, still holding his camera. Turning around, I noticed the looming peak, high, even from our vantage point at the summit of the Green Gable. "That is the Great Gable."

I felt the colour drain from my face as I turned back to look at him. Snap! "Priceless!" he smiled broadly. "Don't you worry, we are not going up there."

That was a relief. I was spent, and we still had to go all the way back.

We sat for some time and ate our packed lunch which we had brought with us, prepared by the gourmet chefs in the place we stayed. I was ravenous. The full English breakfast was already a distant memory.

The journey back had some challenging terrain, and my feet were *hurting*. Yet, the stunning scenery made up for it. By the time we were back, we had been out for almost eight hours. I was shattered. A shower and long nap were all I could think about. But a power nap is all I could take, as dinner was being served in an hour's time.

Martha was full of praise to me for having made it up to the Green Gable and we listened to the stories other guests shared about their day and hikes they went on. After the wonderfully filling dinner, Brian suggested we go out to the nearest pub for a drink. I couldn't muster energy for it. My bed upstairs was calling for my attention and all I desired was sleep, not even a bit of fondling.

Chapter 6

"Oh, Su, I was so tired, and my feet were . . . are hurting! Thank God, Brian skipped the idea of spending a night in the tent! We took it easy on the last day. Just a nice drive through the mountains . . . and we stopped somewhere for lunch. But tell me, how's the shop?"

"It's grand. Adrianna is enjoying working full-time. I think she is out to replace you and become my new business partner," she said with a chuckle.

"Ha-ha, very funny."

"Anyhow, everything is fine, Liz."

"I am glad to hear that," I said, letting out a sigh, massaging my aching feet sitting on the bed. "So, what are you doing today?"

"I'm meeting Claire later for a spa evening."

"Ooh, I'm jealous." Feeling a little pang for home.

"You don't get to be jealous! You have a guy giving you much more than a spa treatment and having endorphins released for days."

"Uh, yeah, actually, you're right," I said smugly, imagining Su rolling her eyes at me.

"What about you?"

"Oh, I really hope to speak with Willie today."

"I hope you do, Liz."

"Me too, and later I am going back to the house. But first I'll be having some of Gloria's breakfast. It's sooo delicious," I said, grinning, just one final tease.

"Thanks for that!"

"You're welcome . . . have a good day, Su."

"You too, Liz."

My muscles ached as I got out of bed and I craved a hot shower before doing anything else. As I let the water stream over my head, my hair covering my face and the bathroom steaming up, my muscles started to relax.

Once all showered and dressed, I was a little nervous about seeing Willie and wondering where to even start talking, but the little break away had done me good for my mental state, which felt stronger. Whatever happened, presuming he would be open for a chat, I would have to deal with it. Like Andrew said, it's always better to know the truth than to speculate.

I walked down the stairs to go to the breakfast room, wondering if he was going to be there. "Welcome back!" Andrew greeted me in the hallway with a wide smile on his face and holding a paintbrush. Only Gloria was still up when I had arrived back late last night.

"Thank you."

"*How* was the Lake District?" he winked.

"Oh, it was really beautiful." I shot a cheeky smile back. Andrew's expression didn't falter.

"I'll get all the details from Brian."

"I'm sure you will."

"Jokes aside, did you have a nice time, Liz?" he said, sobering up a little. I almost forgot how quickly he could turn serious. I nodded.

"I did, thank you . . . Is he there?" I asked, stretching my neck slightly past Andrew towards the door. It took Andrew a moment to realise who I meant.

"He is here, but I am not sure if he is in the breakfast room at the moment. Would you like me to look?" I shook my head.

"No, no, that's okay. How is he?"

"He is doing well and has been in reasonably good spirits, considering. He got out of hospital late yesterday and the doctor said he will have to take it easy for the foreseeable future and make some life changes. He asked for you, you know. He was wondering where you were."

"Oh. That's nice." I felt a little weight in my chest lift. "Thanks, Andrew." He gave me an encouraging tap on my shoulder.

#

The breakfast room was, for the first time, busy with guests and filled with sounds of cutlery tinkling and soft chatter. Willie was sitting in the same spot as the first time we met, only this time, he was in his pyjamas. Our eyes quickly found each other. My stomach filled with more nerves when he gave a little smile. That was my cue to go over.

"You're looking well. How are you feeling?" I leaned over to hug him.

"Doing well. I have you to thank for that. Bless you for being there when you were." His voice was strained and when he reached up to pat my back, he let out a little moan. I quickly let go.

"I'm so, so sorry. Did I hurt you?" I asked, frantically worrying.

"It's okay, the area is just still sore." Pained, he pointed at his chest. "If only Hilda could have met you before she passed." He gestured for me to sit down. I was surprised he brought her up so quickly, and eagerly sat across from him. "It would have meant the world to her, you know." I bowed my head.

"Me too. From what I have heard, she was a wonderful woman."

"She was. She always had my heart." Before anything further was said, Gloria walked in with her trademark picture-perfect smile.

"She's here," she told Willie softly and she proceeded to help Willie up from his chair.

"I must go, but do you drive?"

I nodded slowly. "I do, but I don't have a car here."

"That's okay. I would like to show you something at Hilda's house later. How about one o'clock?" he asked without a hint of eagerness.

"Sure,"

"I will meet you here." His expression was blank as he hobbled slowly out of the room. Unease washed over me. I gazed up at Gloria, who stood ready to take my breakfast order.

"His nurse," she said, looking in Willie's direction for a second before turning back to me.

"Sorry?"

"A nurse is here to check him over, clean the wound . . ."

"Oh. That's good. He seems . . . well?"

"He's definitely improving." Gloria took my order and disappeared into the kitchen while I helped myself to some fruit and yoghurt at the open buffet, all the while wondering about what Willie wanted to show me.

#

"Are you sure you're up for this?" Andrew asked Willie, concerned, as we slowly walked out the door.

"Well, that depends on her driving skills," he said, looking at me.

"He'd like me to drive him to Hilda's house," I clarified to Andrew. His eyebrows raised and eyes widened with even more concern.

"Why don't I come along too? I sure could use a break." He tried to be tactful with the self-invite, but I knew it was to keep an eye on him, and probably one on me too. Moments later, the three of us were in the car. I so badly wanted to ask him what he wanted to show me, but I held off. Small talk about the weather and other non-personal topics got us to the gravel driveway in a short time, and Andrew helped Willie out of the car.

"We have to go to the study," Willie said, his voice crackling slightly.

I unlocked the door to the house and followed the men to the study. Andrew opened the squeaking door for Willie, who slowly made his way through. Entering after, I was met with the same distinct scent I hadn't been able to place.

"On the top shelf is a little wooden box, please help me get it down," Willie told Andrew, pointing in the direction as he made his way to the couch. Andrew and I stared at each other, acknowledging, and I reached into my handbag, where I had left it, and took it out.

"Is this it?"

"That's it," Willie croaked, surprised. He took it from my hands. "You unlocked it already?" he said, dismayed seeing the damaged lock. "I have the key, you know." He reached in his jacket pocket, feeling around, and sighed. I looked at Andrew, who stared sheepishly at Willie. He brought his hand from his pocket.

"Sit down, Elizabeth," he said in a serious tone, his face sombre, with eyebrows lowered, and his body sank into the couch. Obligingly, I sat beside him.

"Elizabeth," he began. "Your grandmother had been waiting, hoping, for the day to see you again but – but she made me promise her, if she did not get to see that day, to give this to you." He opened up the box and took out the now familiar larger than usual brass key, holding it up. "This key will unlock the small, blue door into the east tower room upstairs." He laid the key in my hand and closed it into a fist. His hand tremored and when I looked up at him, tears were filling his eyes. "Andrew, please take her up there. I am no match for the stairs right now."

"Are you going to be okay?" Andrew asked, placing a concerned hand on his shoulder.

"I am fine, I will wait right here for you." He patted the couch.

I tensely followed Andrew up the stairs, not knowing where to go myself. I hadn't been near any of the towers, or explored the upstairs, for that matter.

The first door he opened creaked with age.

"Not this one," Andrew muttered, and walked towards a narrower door beside it. When he pushed it open, we were met with a narrow spiral staircase. The steps reminded me of the time my mother and I had gone up the narrow stairs to see the bells of the

Notre Dame Cathedral on one of our holidays to Paris. Like the Notre Dame, the walls were cold, bare stone and the steps were smooth with wear and uneven in height. Only there would be a lot less steps than the three hundred and something steps we climbed then, and I didn't know what to expect to find at the end of it.

"Are you coming?" Andrew asked in a gentle voice, sensing my apprehension. I gave a weak thumbs up. It was not long before we stood in front of the blue door that Willie described. I was holding the key so tight that when I released my fist, it had imprinted into my hand. "Do you want me to open it?"

"Why don't we – sit. Sit here for a moment." The stairs were hardly wide enough to sit side by side, but the squeeze gave me the comfort I sought. I laid my head on his shoulder and breathed in. I felt so overwhelmed with anxiety. I didn't know what to expect to find on the other side of the door.

"You're shivering. Come here." He put his arm around my shoulders. "Whatever is in there, you're going to be fine, Liz. I know we haven't known each other long but we're here for you. Gloria, myself, and Brian, of course." I could feel his deep voice rumbling through his body and it somehow soothed me. I gave him a weak smile and he kissed my forehead, helped me up, and guided my hand to the lock. "Remember, it's always better to know the truth," he said, repeating his wisdom as a final word of encouragement.

It took me a few tries to push the key into the lock fully and twist it. The lock clicked and the door opened slightly. A ray of light appeared through the gap, brightening the darkness of the stairwell. One final look at Andrew and I pushed the door open.

A white cot bed stood in the centre of the round room. A wooden rocking horse was placed on a floral rug and an old-looking dollhouse was beside it. The floorboards creaked under our feet as we walked in. A small child's chair was beside the wardrobe with two pairs of pretty little shoes lined up underneath it, ballerina pumps with a pink bow on top and a red pair of shiny sandals. The wardrobe had some pink tulle fabric hanging out. The door was a little stiff to open and squeaked at the hinges. It was filled with girly-girls clothes. Everything seemed so ordinary besides the layer of dust which lined every surface. It was a little girl's bedroom.

"I don't get it?" I looked at Andrew, expecting an answer. He was silent, looking around.

"I presume this was my room while I stayed here, but what is the big mystery? Am I missing something?"

Andrew shrugged.

I inspected the room further without touching anything else, as if I was afraid it would turn to dust under my fingers. I finally made my way towards the arched window at the other end of the room. The view of the window made me realise how high up we were. *This whole, big house, with all these rooms, and this was my bedroom? Far, far away from the other rooms?* It might be a fun play den for a child, but a bedroom? It felt a bit like Rapunzel.

And why was the door locked? An eerie feeling washed over me.

Desiring some fresh air, I tried opening the window, but the hinges were not giving way. That's when I noticed that the window was screwed shut.

"Well, it was definitely your room, look!" Andrew called out. He was next to the cot and held up a small baby blanket with "Lizzy" stitched in light-pink embroidery.

"Something feels off, Andrew. Don't you think this is a strange place in the house for a child's bedroom?" He tilted his head, considering this for a moment.

"I kind of do, actually," he agreed.

"There are no pictures on the wall or – or birthday cards, or anything. I don't know what I'm supposed to see or find here, or why Willie is so shaken up about showing me this."

"Perhaps you were a horrid child that needed to be locked up." Andrew tried to make light of it.

"Ha-hah, hilarious. I really want to go back downstairs now."

The door automatically locked shut when I closed it behind us. The sound of it echoed in the empty stone stairwell, which was unnerving me to the bone. I quickly made my way down, Andrew following on my heels, to the study.

Willie had moved to Hilda's captain's chair by the desk, having her throw laid over his lap. He looked anxious. "You were not supposed to find out this way," he blurted, lip trembling and his eyes watering again. I stopped in my tracks.

"Find out what, Willie? I don't understand. I already learned that I lived here . . . which I have come to believe to be the truth. Right? So, what is it, Willie?" I asked anxiously.

"That is not your room, Elizabeth." He spoke in barely more than a whisper.

"Oh, well I presumed it was. There is even a blanket with my name embroidered on it, and –"

"Yes, Lizzy." As he looked down at the ground, I could see tears dripping from his face onto his lap. I frowned, confused.

"Was . . . was it my mum's room when she was little?"

"Lizzy," he repeated. "Not you, Elizabeth, or – " he gulped down a sob "– or your mother, Lizzy . . . Lizzy, your sister. It was her room."

His last words were barely audible as he began sobbing uncontrollably. I just stood there staring at him, bewildered, not comprehending. Andrew rushed towards Willie and tried to console him. My legs felt weak, and my head dizzy with confusion as I walked slowly over to the couch, plopping myself down.

"It's okay, Willie. It will all be okay, please calm down. You're not supposed to stress yourself right now. Please calm down." Andrew's voice was faint in my head but becoming more frantic. "Liz, please, please!" he called out. "He really shouldn't stress right now, it is dangerous for his health." His plea took a few moments to register, but eventually it brought me back from the shock and into action.

"Okay. Okay, let's go back to the car and go. Whatever it is you want to tell me or, or . . ." I didn't know how to finish that sentence. "Please, *please* calm down. Think about your health," I begged him.

Together, we were able to get him back to the car. "Let me quickly make a call," Andrew said as he closed the car door.

Willie and I were left together in the back seat. He wasn't sobbing anymore, but his face showed such profound sadness, and the occasional tear still rolled down his face. He looked weak. There was so much I wanted to ask him, and the urge to push for answers was overwhelming, but I knew I couldn't right now. It was tormenting.

Some minutes later, Andrew stepped in the car, driving us back to the B&B. "How are you feeling, Willie?" he asked, his voice laced with worry. "The nurse will come over to have a look at you."

Willie didn't respond. He leaned slowly against my body. "I am so sorry, Elizabeth," he said, his voice strained. My eyes caught Andrew's in the car's rearview mirror. He mouthed something to me, but the only thing I could make out was "okay". I reassured Willie that it was all going to be okay and that he should rest. Nothing further was said in the short journey back.

Gloria was waiting by the front door, clearly expecting us. She helped bring Willie to his room to rest in bed. Luckily, his was on the ground floor.

Moments later, the doorbell rang and I went to answer it. To my surprise, it was Brian and another man. For a moment, we just stared at each other until the other person, who I noticed was wearing scrubs, announced that he was here to see Willie. He showed me his badge hanging around his neck. "Is he in his room?" His voice had an urgent tone.

"Yes." And before I could say any more, he swiftly passed me to attend to Willie.

"Andrew rang and told me to come over immediately; that you need me. What is it, Lizzy?" Brian asked, bewildered. He closed the gap between us and hugged me. I held him so tight and just couldn't help but cry. It took me several tries to talk between the tears. "I – I am n-not Lizzy. Lizzy . . ." I inhaled sharply, unable to believe what I was about to say. "Lizzy is my sister."

He pulled back from the embrace and looked at me, perplexed. I shook my head. "I don't understand any of this, Brian, I just – don't understand. Nothing about my life seems to be real!" I sobbed as he stroked my hair and wiped the tears, but they just kept coming.

"I have no answers for you, Lizzy, or – Liz – or . . . whatever your name is. But I do know that I care about you; that's *real.*" He paused; I could hear him swallow. "Actually, I am falling for you." Before I could respond, he tilted my chin and softly kissed the tears on my lips. "I am here for you, Jane Doe."

Chapter 7

I rang Su and told her all. She could hardly believe it. For my own mother to hide the fact that I have a sister was incomprehensible to her, considering our close relationship. Su had gotten to know my mum quite well over the years, and she was right. Why did she not tell me? And where is my sister now? I had a *sister* out there, somewhere. Did she know about me?

So many questions went through my head, all of them still unanswered, and from what I learned, the less I felt I knew about my mother, and my life.

Gauging my low mood, Su looked to bring up something more light-hearted. Of course, that's when the topic of Brian entered the conversation. "I tell you to find a rebound, and you have the guy falling in love with you. Typical!" she said in her oh-so-eloquent way. Even though we had known each other for only about a week, I couldn't deny I felt the same.

#

"Are you sure you want to go?" he asked, his voice soft with concern. Aside from the bombshell that I have a sister named Lizzy, I had learnt nothing further. Willie was doing all right, but in no shape to talk to me, and anyone else who could potentially have shed some light was dead.

"I have to go," I said. No one, not even Brian, could convince me otherwise. There *must* be something there that can tell me more.

"I just want to be sure that you're going to be okay," he murmured and kissed my forehead. "Is Andrew going with you?"

"Yes, he insisted. He is such a kind person," I said, smiling a little.

"How kind?" he joked.

"Ha-ha, jealousy doesn't suit you." I gave him a nudge. "Have you seen my coat?" I asked, looking around his sitting room, once again admiring the retro décor.

"On the couch." He got it, and helped me into it like a gentleman, and gave me my handbag. Rummaging through it looking for my phone, I once again took out the small wooden box.

"Is that it?" Brian asked.

"Yes." I stroked my fingers over the engraving when a sudden revelation hit me, and I gasped.

"What's wrong?" I collapsed onto the couch. All I could do was keep staring at the engraving. "What is it?" he asked again, sounding a little more frantic, sitting beside me.

"If –" I gripped the little box tightly, trying to compose myself. "If this is my sister's and – her date of birth, then . . . then she is my *twin* sister."

For some moments, neither of us spoke. I didn't know what to say, and he couldn't have said anything that would have helped either. I just needed answers.

After some time, taking several long, deep breaths, I got up from the couch and faced Brian. "I'm off," I said with conviction, bending down to retrieve my handbag which I had dropped.

"And, Brian?"

"Yes?" he said a little gingerly.

I swallowed. "Falling for you too." His eyes twinkled and he moved towards me and cupped my face, planting the softest of kisses on my lips. "Are you going to be okay?" I gave what I hoped was a convincing smile. "Do you really want to walk? I can still drive you before my meeting starts."

"I could do with the fresh air, really," I said, going to the door to leave. "Maybe it will help clear my head."

#

It was warm outside, with the sun in full shine and not a single cloud in sight. The streets were quiet as I made my way to the house. I knew which direction to walk towards, but that was it. However, I found my way like a woman on a mission, and before long approached the gravel road to the house. Once there, I stood still for some time, taking it all in as a detective might take in the scene of a crime. I was no longer blown away by the impression or architecture. All I felt was a determination to find answers.

Having watched many detective series, it was time to put those long hours of telly to good use. "Right, first look around the grounds, take in the scene," I said aloud. I hadn't even walked around the house yet or toured the entire garden.

I briefly glanced up to the tower and swallowed, then marched off like a soldier, exploring the grounds. Taking in everything, from the immaculately kept garden to the draining pipes that came down the walls from many places, some of which were obviously in need of repair.

The house looked even larger than before. I peeked through every window along the way I could reach; silly, really, as I could just go inside. What was I looking for? What was I going to find? The first one was easy; it was answers. The second, I didn't dare to answer for myself.

Ahead of me, an iron gate opened to a walled garden at the back of the house which was much bigger than I could have imagined. It reminded me a bit of the walled garden in Coole Park back at home, only these walls were almost completely concealed by vines.

The path that circled the entire garden was neatly kept, while slightly smaller paths led the way to the fountain in the middle, now standing dry. It was a garden that one would expect at the front of a Victorian manor, to impress visitors upon entering, only artistically crafted stone statues of important figures were missing. You could just envision ladies walking around in elaborate dresses with petticoats, a tight-fitting corset to reveal their tiny waists, and of course, a parasol in their hand to shield themselves from the sun. Children would be running around the grass with perfect sugar curls and pretty ribbons in their hair, and not forgetting the gentlemen all smartly dressed in a frock coat and a top hat. All would be enjoying the pleasures of the garden and the company they kept.

It couldn't be that Andrew took care of all this on his own while working on the renovations and running the B&B. As I took a seat on one of the many cast-iron benches, I pondered on all the people that might have sat here over the decades. Would my sister have sat here? Would my mum have? If only I could travel back in time.

Mum was very much into this style of garden and house; in fact, it had many aspects she said she would have loved in a home. On the many occasions we watched *Pride and Prejudice* together, she would comment on it all; it reminded me of that. She was also a big Jane Austen fan and read her books numerous times.

I had developed the same love for Jane Austen's writing and acquired a great interest in the regency era, although I am certain my mum had romanticised that period as much as we would have the Victorian era. Now I wondered if some of the love for the time and its characteristics came from here, her home. Hilda obviously had taken great pride in taking care of her house and gardens. Growing up here as a child must have been amazing; it felt like a historical treasure.

"Right." I slapped my lap with both hands. "*Focus*." I continued my mission. This was when I noticed a little door at the right side at the back of the house, which had direct access to this garden. I made my way towards it and studied the back of the house; some of the windows had curtains partially drawn.

The door was old, with cracked varnish that had started to peel off. The keyhole was surprisingly small and didn't match any of the keys I had. "Hmm." *Maybe Andrew has the key.* Which reminded me that he should have been here by now.

I made my way back to the front of the house and soon heard a familiar voice in the distance, becoming clearer the closer I got. Andrew was pacing by the tunnel's exit, speaking on his phone. He hadn't noticed me yet.

I quietly approached the porch and sat down on the bottom step. Whoever was on the other side of the conversation, it sounded formal. There were a lot of hmms and ahas in his responses. I watched him for a while. When he finally stopped pacing and turned towards the porch, he was visibly surprised to see me. His face said it all as he awkwardly waved in my direction. Soon after, he ended the call and walked slowly to join me on the steps.

"That was Brian. He made me promise that I would look after you. He *really* cares for you." He put his arm around my shoulders and I smiled, flattered by his words. We were silent for a moment before Andrew spoke again.

"So, you think Lizzy is your twin sister, huh?" he said somewhat nonchalantly, obviously trying to keep the mood light. I nodded. "Well, we better go find some answers. It must be somewhere in the house," he replied, sounding up for the task. I liked his energy, and we seemed to be on the same proactive wavelength. He stood and helped me up.

"How is Willie?" I asked, kicking some of the gravel on the path.

"He is . . . okay, but he must avoid *all* stress," Andrew said softly, as if afraid of insinuating that *I* was the stress he must avoid. I agreed.

"Good to hear he is okay."

Eager to get a move on, I opened the front door. Andrew picked up a few dead leaves from the plants on the porch. It was like he couldn't help himself. He saw me looking. "Hilda wouldn't have been impressed with the state of these plants," he said, feeling the need to explain himself.

"Do you take care of the back garden as well?"

"Oh, you *have* seen it. Isn't it stunning!" Andrew beamed, his face lighting up.

"Yes, it is definitely a statement of a garden, very grand." Andrew's smile widened.

"I have had to hire some help. It just too much to do it all."

"I suppose this is all my responsibility now," I said quietly, the reality of it suddenly occurring.

"Well, I have a feeling you will make Hilda proud," he said encouragingly, but I had no confident reply.

"Do you have the key to the back door, going into the back garden?" I asked, changing the subject. Andrew smiled. I suppressed a groan. "*What*?"

"You get so flustered by compliments, it's cute!" he said, ruffling my hair.

Surely enough, I was blushing. I was never really good with personal attention directed towards me. If only I could control the reaction of my sympathetic nervous system, it wouldn't be so obvious. Oh yes, I researched it.

"The door is locked from the inside, as the key has been lost for a long time. Hilda insisted that one day, she would find it. 'It must be in the house,' she always said when I offered to change the lock."

"The key must be very small."

"Tell me about it." He scratched his head, looking around the hallway. "Where will we start?"

I stared at the collage of pictures on the wall again and took down the one which I believed to be me on the swing. "So, it probably wasn't you after all," Andrew said, standing right beside me.

"Yes, I suppose not," I replied, staring wistfully at the photo. "I – I wonder where she is now. And why my mum never mentioned her. Does she know about me?" I sighed deeply. "I just have so many questions."

"We'll find some answers. There must be answers here somewhere," Andrew said reassuringly. But there were so many rooms, only a few of which I'd entered and explored inside, and not even in depth.

"Do you know which room was Hilda's bedroom?" I asked, having a little lightbulb moment. "People tend to keep diaries, letters, or secrets hidden in their bedroom."

"I do . . . good to know," he teased. "I helped her set up her bedroom downstairs after she had her stroke. It's over here." He led the way past the kitchen and study to the next door and opened it wide. The room was bright, flooded with light from the big bay window, with a lovely window seat underneath and yet another beautiful view of the garden. The bed had assistive aids attached to it, and other modifications an elderly person might have needed in their room were visible.

On the bedside table, I noticed two photographs underneath the heavily fringed lampshade. Intrigued, I walked over, bending down to study them closely. A gold frame held a black-and-white photograph of a young-looking Hilda with another man. The one beside it was of my mum as a little girl, sitting outside on Hilda's lap. "Andrew," I called to him eagerly. "Is – is this in the garden here?" He took the wooden frame from me and looked at it attentively.

"I . . . believe so. You see this tree here? I think that is the hornbeam tree near where the swing is now. It wasn't much more than a sapling then." I looked at it closely, taking his word for it.

"And this is the same man, I think, from the photograph in the hallway?" I said, picking that one up too and handing it to him.

"Uh-huh. That is Charles. He was very special to her. I can't tell you much about him, but on the few occasions she did mention him, you just knew how much she loved and missed him."

"Charles. Huh. He must have been my grandfather." My mum never even mentioned his name. The more I thought about it, I realised how little she had told me about her parents, and I never enquired much about them either. That started to feel strange now, in a way it never did before.

I took the wooden frame back and turned it around and pried it open to see if there was anything else inside. "You check that one," I prompted Andrew, still holding the other frame. But both held nothing other than the picture itself. "I now know where to look if I am ever in your bedroom," Andrew grinned as he opened the top drawer from the chest of drawers. "Ahem." He frowned and wrinkled his nose from discomfort. "Maybe it's better if you go through these?"

"Why?" I asked, setting down the frame. He held up a large-sized granny bra from his fingertips with what I can only describe as a priceless expression on his face. I couldn't help but laugh. "Right, you take the wardrobe, I'll do the drawers." I let out another chuckle as Andrew sighed, relieved.

The drawers revealed much about her lingerie choices, socks, blankets, some toiletries, and even a dentures box, yet nothing was stuck to the bottom of the drawers or at the back hidden away. The wardrobe and all other furniture didn't reveal anything either. My thinking had been flawed. "So much for the movies." I sighed and sat down on Hilda's bed, wishing I had the ability to probe people's brains. Willie's, to be exact."

"The movies?" Andrew questioned, taking a seat beside me.

"Yes, in the detective movies or series, people often hide items or clues in their bedroom. Something is stuck at the bottom of a drawer, or in a shoebox, inside a picture frame, behind a mirror, under the bed . . . under the bed!" I jumped off and kneeled to look under the bed. Nothing but clusters of dust.

"Behind a mirror, you said? Wait. Here. Come!" Andrew hurried over to move the mirror, which hung on the inside of the wardrobe door. There were impressions on the wood which indicated that the mirror had been moved. Andrew slowly lifted it off its hinges while I held the door still. "Careful . . . Stop! Look!" I cried when I noticed a flash of something white taped to the door behind the mirror. Carefully, I pulled it off the door, the tape leaving behind a sticky residue on the wood.

Holding it in my hands, leaving Andrew to hang the mirror back, I meticulously removed the tape from the edges of the white envelope, not to tear the paper, before slowly pulling the flap open. Peering inside, I saw it held another key. I sighed heavily with frustration. "What is it with all the keys?"

Andrew reached for the envelope and I handed it to him. "At least we know what this opens," he said as he held the key up, showing a little white tag dangling to the side. I took it from him. "It's Hilda's handwriting," Andrew said, certain. Written in small, shaky handwriting was the word *cellar*.

"Does the house have a cellar?"

"I think so, but I have never been down there. Why would she hide the key?" He took the words right out of my mouth. I started thinking back to the plans of the house that Attorney David had sent over, but I couldn't remember if it showed a cellar.

Andrew left the room. "Follow me!" he said bossily.

"Yes, sir, Chief Inspector Barnaby!" I saluted him, which he couldn't have seen.

"Ha, a *Midsomer Murder* fan, are you? Detective Sergeant Jones!" he said once I caught up with him.

"You too! You have been holding out on me." We smiled. "Just . . . minus the murder, of course!" I added seriously while appreciating the way Andrew could make light of a situation.

Moments later, we stood in front of a low but oddly wide door, but that was no surprise from this quirky house. The lock on it, however, looked rather modern for the style of door. Andrew held out his hand for the key and once inserted, he had it unlocked with one easy twist. We were met with a dense darkness, only able to see the top of the stairs, lit from the hall we were in.

Andrew felt the walls, looking for a light switch. "We need one of those chamber sticks," I whispered; he huffed a laugh.

"Aha, here you go. Light!" he announced with pride after an audible click of the switch brought to life a flickering yellow light. I followed him down the narrow stairs where we were met by another door. I reached for Andrew's arm and held him back. It felt eerie, and I was regretting the detective series I had watched over the years.

"It'll be fine." His tone was reassuring as he placed his hand on mine, giving a gentle squeeze. He tried the handle and the door opened slightly with a screeching sound. His eyes met mine for a moment, and we both pushed it open further.

Only the silhouettes of objects were visible until Andrew managed to turn on the light. Confused and troubled were just some of the feelings I had. Why was this here? First the room upstairs in the tower, with the window screwed shut, which I had told myself was just for safety, trying to shake off the uneasy feelings it had given me. And now there's this room in a cellar of all places, with the key hidden away. Why?

It held everything a young child might like to play with maybe 25 years ago. A little metal school chair with a wooden seat stood in front of an old TV and VCR player, troll dolls and a pink, a blue, and a purple Care Bears teddy were scattered around as if they had just been played with on a big, soft rug. Taking it all in, one thing that stood out of place was a mahogany antique console table. Approaching it, my heart started to sink. It held a large, framed portrait photograph of Lizzy placed on top, a glass vase filled with artificial white flowers next to it, and a little white angel statue standing in between. "Is . . . is this – does this look like a shrine to you?" I asked Andrew, feeling sick.

"I . . . I don't know, Liz. It could just have been a special place your grandmother made where she would go after she had left," Andrew reasoned, unconvincing.

"But the angel?" My words came out as barely a whisper.

"Let's go back upstairs. There is nothing more to find here," he said, and he was right. There were no wardrobes or any places that stored anything, just lots of toys. Andrew held my hand and led me back up to the stairs. I squeezed it tightly and didn't let go until we were back in the hallway.

"I need some fresh air." I hurried straight to the front door and sat on the porch step, where he joined me.

"Do you think she is . . .?" My voice broke and I turned to look at Andrew. "Your mum said that Hilda told her that I – or *she,* I mean – left to live with another family. And it obviously wasn't with Mum. It doesn't make any sense. Why – who would . . .?" I sighed deeply.

Andrew was quiet; not a reassuring word or light-hearted comment could be said to change the mood. He just placed his hand on my lap and gave me his shoulder to rest my head on. We sat together in silence, our proactive energy completely dissipated.

Time passed by. I had no idea how long but when I lifted my head, I realised I was so consumed with my own thoughts and feelings, I hadn't noticed Andrew was upset too. His face was sorrowful, his eyes just vacantly staring ahead. "Hey, are you okay?" I asked, reaching out to stroke his arm. He didn't say anything and before I could ask again, I heard a soft crunching noise in the distance. It was Brian walking up toward us.

"Hey, guys!" he called cheerfully, not having read the mood. "I thought I'd bring some lunch." He held up a paper bag. I gave a little smile; that's all I could muster in response. "What's going on?" Brian asked when he stopped in front of us. He looked from Andrew to me, and his cheeriness fell. I was still stroking Andrew's arm that he had placed on my lap.

Brian sat beside me. Shakily, I told him about the key we found and the room in the cellar. All the while, Andrew was quiet. "I don't know why he is upset," I whispered to Brian, which was silly, really, since he could easily hear me.

"I do. Don't worry," he whispered back, reassuring me with a kiss on my forehead and telling me in many words that I was going to be okay. I wished I could believe that.

After, Brian cleared his throat softly and stood up. "Hey, Drew. Come, let's go for a walk." Andrew got up slowly and Brian put his arm around his shoulder as they walked away together, disappearing into the garden.

As I sat alone, I couldn't help but think of how many times this place had brought tears to people in the time I'd been here. Understandably, my grandmother's death was still recent and raw to everyone who knew her, but there was so much more to it all.

As many thoughts swirled around in my brain for some minutes, I tried to streamline them to gain some focus. I physically shook my head and hands and let out a big exhale.

Instead of all this searching for clues in the house, I knew what to do next: get in touch with the office of registration of births and deaths. Hapless, it being the weekend, I would have to wait . . . wait to hear what I oh so feared.

#

The wind had started to pick up and grey clouds moved in to cover the blue sky at a fast pace. The drop in temperature made me shiver and I got goosebumps all over my bare arms. Minutes later, large drops of rain began to fall sparingly and soon turned into a torrential downpour, making the earth dance with its force. Hiding underneath the porch, I searched for Brian and Andrew, and quickly spotted them running towards me at speed. As we entered the house, an earth-shaking sound of thunder startled us.

They were drenched. While they dried off with towels Andrew found, I put on the kettle in the kitchen. A little while later they entered, each wrapped in a blanket with bare legs sticking out. I couldn't help but giggle at the sight of them, and I felt my mood lift a little.

“Let’s make a fire,” Andrew said. Brian hummed in agreement. “We are not going anywhere for a while.”

As they waddled out the room, I couldn’t help the chuckle that escaped me. “Stop laughing!” they said in unison.

While I searched for some dishes and a serving tray to carry tea and the lunch that Brian brought, all I could hear was the rain. It didn’t let up. From the kitchen window, I could see water pouring down like a mini waterfall. Draining pipes were overflowing, and the thunder and lightning were rampant, and everywhere was being cooled rapidly.

Carrying the tray into the sitting room, I saw the fire was going and they both had their hands reached out near it, to warm up. It wasn’t the sophistication of the room or the abundance of textiles that took my notice this time. It was the two guys, now bare-chested, with the blankets wrapped low around their waistlines, sitting by the fire. *Oh, I wish my friends could see this right now!* It sure was a welcome intrusion from the drama and fear.

Having been with Brian had sparked my sex drive back into action, and this scene seemed like the start of a romance novel. Of course, this was a thought I would never say aloud. And I am only into Brian. But there was no harm in taking in this moment, just briefly.

"Right, tea!" I said loud enough to bring myself back to planet Earth while walking over to the coffee table to place the tray down.

Andrew didn't appear upset anymore; quite the opposite, in fact. Whatever it was, it had passed for now, and I felt it would be better not to ask. Despite this, I gave him what I hoped was a reassuring hand on his shoulder. He smiled.

It was remarkable, in a way, with all the intermittent drama since I had been here, there were still these many moments where life's joy took over, which made me feel very grateful indeed.

I sat – well, half lay down – on the chaise lounge. That's what it is for, after all, and the velvet fabric felt wonderfully soft on my skin. The warmth from the fire slowly warmed up the room and the tea warmed our bodies from the inside. The spicy wraps were the last nourishment we needed to feel okay again.

As we sat, digesting and talking about the weather, with them insisting it wasn't going to get much better for some time, Andrew left the room to call Gloria. Brian snuck onto the chaise with me, his body radiating heat. "Well, this is an unexpected turn to the day," I murmured into his ear as Brian wrapped his arms around me.

"*You* are unexpected." He kissed my forehead.

"I meant the weather." Brian rolled his eyes and smirked for a split second before he began tickling me. For a moment, I was stunned, but then quickly reciprocated with full force. "I won!" I called out triumphantly a short while later and rested my head on his chest as he lay slightly breathless in defeat. "How are you, Liz? Andrew filled me in," Brian said, sobering up a bit, stroking my hair.

"I don't know," I told him honestly as I shared my plan to get in contact with the office of registration of births and deaths.

"That is a good idea."

"I just need straight answers, however hard. All these half stories and not knowing things is driving me crazy." I tilted my head to look at him and he placed a soft kiss on my lips. We lay silent for a while and I listened to his breath calming while his strokes soothed my body.

Out of nowhere, the thought that I would be leaving in five days popped into my head. We hadn't spoken about that, about us. What *us* entails. However, this didn't feel like the right time. I just wanted to enjoy his company in the here and now. Who knows what devastation would come.

Andrew knocked on the door. "Come in," we said in unison, and smiled at each other. The door opened slowly and he walked in, raising his eyebrows at the two of us.

"Seriously?" I said, huffing out a laugh.

"Well, how should I know if you're still decent?" he replied teasingly. I got the feeling Brian had shared about the numerous passions we'd engaged in.

"So, Glor and I were talking," he continued while sitting on the armchair opposite us. "Since the weather isn't expected to improve anytime soon, and Annie is staying the night at her friends, she proposed to cook dinner, bring it over, and we can all spend the night here. It will give us plenty of time to look around, and we thought maybe a night among friends is something we all could use."

Brian and I looked at each other, pleased. I liked the sound of it. "Tell her that would be lovely!" I said and got up to hug Andrew and kissed him on the cheek. "But wait. What about Willie and the B&B?"

"I'll try to sort something now," Andrew said, nodding, and off he went with his phone. When the door closed I turned to face Brian, who had completely taken over my spot on the chaise. I laughed. "You guys are amazing."

"I am a *little* more amazing, I hope?" He gestured for me to join him, which I eagerly obliged.

"That goes without saying . . . Bri," I said, cringing a little.

"Bri?"

"Yeah, that didn't sound right. I was trying out a nickname for you." He laughed at me fondly.

“Do you have a nickname?” I wondered, reluctantly giving up on coming up with an adequate one.

“No . . . not really,” he said after a brief pause.

“Not *really*? So, you do?” I turned to look at him, eyebrow raised. He chuckled and looked away.

“I did. I had one in senior school, but it was more of an infamous one, and rather embarrassing.”

“Do tell,” I pushed, intrigued.

“Well – I was ‘Smooth’.”

“*Smooth*?” I was a bit underwhelmed. It was definitely unusual, but not something embarrassing, was it? Brian let out a long-suffering sigh.

“You see, there was this girl in my class when I was in year nine that I liked, but she was out of my league – I can’t believe I am telling you this . . .”

“Go on, keep going.” I sat up straighter, eager to hear the full story.

“Well, after a lot of convincing from Andrew and some of my other mates, I decided to ask her out. When I approached her one day during break, I was so nervous that I tripped and fell straight forward onto *her*, and . . . and my hands initially landed on her breasts before I hit the ground.”

“Pfft,” I giggled. I couldn’t help it. He smiled wryly.

“Well, that is how I got the nickname Smooth, which lasted for the entire school year.”

“What about the girl? What happened to her?”

"Let's just say she, too, was embarrassed. And that was that," he said, rubbing the back of his neck.

"Aww, I'll have to think of something sweet. It will come to me," I said lightly with a smirk. He pulled me down and lay on top of me and we kissed passionately, for a long time. Heating up like the crackling fire, he slid his hand under my dress skirt, trailing upwards, making me quiver for more. "Do you think he will knock again?" I whispered in his ear while holding his hair back with both hands.

"Probably not after our earlier reaction," he lamented.

We reluctantly stopped and laughed while we blew out our excitement as if we were doing breathing exercises. We probably only needed ten minutes. He pulled me back up and helped me fix my hair. Moments later, Andrew walked back in. We sniggered at each other, knowing we couldn't have made it.

"What did I miss?" Andrew asked, looking at the two of us suspiciously.

"Brian told me about his nickname in secondary school," I said quickly, feeling a blush rise. Thankfully, the room was dimly lit, so I doubt he noticed.

"Aah, Smooth." Andrew grinned. I gave Brian a cheeky wink.

"So, everything is sorted. Glor just wondered if you want her to bring some of your clothes. If you don't mind her going through your stuff, of course."

"I didn't even think of that! That would be great. Thank you," I said, smiling appreciatively.

"She will bring something for you too," he said, turning to look at Brian.

"Oh, great. I get to wear your fashion style. Thanks, mate!" he said sarcastically.

"Speak for yourself, mate!" Andrew rebuked.

"Well, I think you both are very fashionable," I teased. They looked my way and we all burst out laughing.

But jokes aside, Brian dressed quite dapper. Earlier, he was in a well-fitted V-neck grey sweater with a crisp ironed white shirt underneath, the collar showing, and two buttons undone, paired with a jean that fitted to perfection. And Andrew scrubbed up rather well too when he wasn't in his work attire.

"How about a game?" suggested Brian after some time. We were sitting next to each other watching Andrew tend to the fire.

"Sure," I said, sitting up a little straighter.

"I think he meant with me," Andrew replied.

"Oh?" I said, a bit thrown.

"Why don't we wait for my lady to arrive to hang out with Liz, and then we can go do our thing and –"

"Good thinking," Brian said.

"Your . . . thing? What is your thing?" I asked, intrigued, looking between the two of them, but they ignored me, as they apparently had a telepathic conversation. "Just a game we play," Brian eventually added light-heartedly.

"Hmm."

Andrew cleared his throat. "So, Liz, how do you actually feel about owning this house?" he asked, deflecting from their secretive game. I rolled my eyes but decided to play nice.

"I haven't thought about it much. It's all very surreal," I said, realising that since my arrival, I hadn't seen this place as *mine*.

"Well, I for one hope you won't sell it," Andrew said with a breeze, but I could tell there was something imploring behind his statement. His words took me a bit by surprise. It wasn't even something I had contemplated, having been so consumed with finding out the truth about my family, and well, the new interest in my life . . . Brian.

As the question sank in, the answer came easily and quickly, without any doubt. This was not a house to sell. It is an heirloom to cherish.

"No, I won't be," I said with conviction. However, I had no clue what I would do with it.

"Great. That's great!" Andrew smiled; he seemed relieved.

"You know, I don't even know where the toilet is here," I noted, feeling a bit silly.

"Well, the door is rather inconspicuous." He got up and beckoned for me to follow him. The entrance hall had many visible doors, but it wasn't any of those. On the right side of the drawing room, built into the wall panelling which held a collection of paintings, was a shape of a door. It was only noticeable up close – if you were looking for one, that is.

"Thanks," I said, pushing the door open. "This house is just full of surprises."

#

A whiff of warm food followed Gloria when she strode in with her bags. I was hungry for it. "Where would you like to eat?"

"Uh, let's bring it to the kitchen," I decided, reaching out to relieve her of some of the bags. "Thanks."

She knew her way around the cupboards and chose some fancy serving dishes. Nothing was half-measured with her.

As I helped her open the Tupperware and plate the food, I heard a commotion, a straining sound as if they tried to lift something heavy followed by a couple of bangs. I looked up at Gloria, who seemed to take no notice, or wonder about it. After a few more moments, I had to find out what was going on. I was about to walk out of the kitchen when Gloria spoke softly with a touch of amusement, "They are just doing their game."

"What game? What is this game?" Gloria chuckled neatly behind her hand and gestured for me to follow her.

"You have to see it to believe it."

The straining sound became louder as we approached the double doors. Unable to tame my curiosity any longer, I swung them open. They went quiet for a couple of seconds and stared at us before they resumed as if we weren't there. Dumbstruck, taking in the hilarious sight of the two grown men still bare-chested, but having the blankets wrapped in a way that I can only describe as giant nappies, they were sumo wrestling. It was a priceless image, and my laughter didn't stop them.

"They have been doing this since they were kids," Gloria said.

"I, for one, have never seen such ripped sumo wrestlers before," I replied, amused. "What am I saying? I have never seen one at all, except on TV."

"They have even made up their own set of rules and have been keeping score since." It was obvious Gloria had witnessed this many times, from her more composed demeaner.

A moment later, she left them to return to the kitchen. I followed her back, still entertained by the sight, the grin on my face causing a strain in my cheeks. Oh, if only my girlfriends could have seen that.

Not waiting for the men, we ate the creamy vegetable soup for the starter and had a generous slice of the rich, flavoured quiche loaded with bacon, goat's cheese, and whatnot, paired with a fresh, zingy citrus summer salad as the main course, which Gloria had plated like an art piece on the table. Once we started on the dessert, which she claimed was just for us – a delightful, airy yet rich chocolate mousse that makes women have orgasms in TV ads – the guys finally joined us. "So, who won?" I asked, licking chocolate off my spoon.

"We are not finished yet," Brian said, panting, quickly grabbing the nearest glass of water on the table and gulped it down.

"No one win-wins," Gloria interjected. "Who knows when the final game will happen?"

Brian and Andrew looked at each other and tucked into their meal. It was not until they were finished eating the soup and stopped panting completely that they joined back into the conversation.

Gloria served another decadent dessert of sticky toffee pudding, after we all had digested a bit. Merlot kept flowing into the glasses while we licked the last remnants from our bowls; it tasted divine. We got a little loose-lipped from the alcohol, and Brian was getting touchy-feely under the table. Gloria and Andrew only had eyes for each other as they were engaged in a kissing session.

"Maybe we should go explore the house? I will go with Liz, and how about the two of you go together?" Brian said not-so-subtly.

"Can you *be* any more obvious?" I whispered in his ear, and planted a tender kiss on his neck. Andrew and Gloria got up and walked off hand in hand, without a word.

"Well, where shall we go?" Brian reached for my hand, ready to escort me. I shrugged, and he confidently chose the stairway on the left side to go up. When we stood on the landing, we were met with a long hallway dotted with doors. *This house has so many doors.*

"Which one?" he asked in a voice infused with desire.

"I don't know," I whispered, almost overwhelmed with choice.

"Well, what about this one?" he said, and led me to one of the doors near the middle.

We peeked inside, in what turned out to be a bathroom, and Brian closed the door. "Not that one."

"You could use a shower," I said, giving a little wink and reopening the door. The truth was, he really could after that sumo wrestling match. I took his hand and led him inside the bathroom. "I'll take care of you," I said softly as I loosened the ridiculous nappy blanket from his waist and slid down his boxers. Brian grinned wide as I pushed him against the floor-to-ceiling cream tiles.

"I like this side of you," he said. I smiled and reached to turn on the shower. When the water began gushing down, I quickly pulled off my clothes to match his nudity and led him into the shower cubicle. "Aaah!" I shrieked. The water was freezing. Brian tried to change it, but to no avail. This was not the steamy scenario I'd envisioned.

We shivered and laughed while we bundled up in his blanket together, awkwardly making our way back to the drawing room. The fire was still radiating some heat, and the room was pleasantly warm, and before long, so were we. We had passionate and lengthy sex on the chaise lounge, after which, I rested my head on his chest, feeling the vibration of his raised heartbeat, and closed my eyes.

I mused about Brian, the amazing guy he is and how crazy my life had turned since arriving here. I made some wonderful friends, found someone that my heart not only desired, but had started to love, and I owned this grand house. Even so, there were all these dark things in my life, with uncertainty and secrecy. It was overwhelming and downright frightening. Which made me especially thankful for the highs, and with that grateful thought, I must have drifted off.

"Why do you think Hilda never told you any of this?" I heard in a whisper, waking up.

"I don't know; I considered us close. Family, even." I recognised Andrew's voice. "I suppose everyone has secrets."

"This is big, though. And we don't even know all of it," Brian whispered in response.

I didn't open my eyes and listened in on the conversation for some time. They were clearly as bewildered by it all as I was.

As I moved my arm from underneath me, I realised that I was naked under the blanket. Oh jeez. I peered from one eye and saw Brian sitting on the ground with his back towards the chaise and Andrew and Gloria sitting cosily side by side near the relit fire. I never considered myself a prude, but this was a rather uncomfortable predicament I found myself in.

I stretched my feet towards Brian's back and softly touched him. He jumped slightly and turned around, and quickly leaned over to kiss me. "I'm naked," I whispered against his lips.

"I know," he smiled with cheek. "Just wrap the blanket around you."

"Seriously! Where is my dress and my . . ."

"Bra and thong?" he finished with a smirk.

"Yes!" I said a bit above a whisper, wrapping the blanket around me tightly.

"I think you might be lying on top of them, or . . ."

"Shit, I think I left them upstairs."

"Over there," Andrew said, pointing at the occasional table. We both looked over and saw my dress, black lace bra and thong on display. Brian reached for it.

"Great. Thanks," I said to Andrew, utterly mortified. A turbulent heat rushed to my head.

Brian handed it to me with amusement written all over his facial features and turned to Gloria and Andrew, mercifully starting a conversation. They deliberately looked away, which was my chance to leave and make myself more civilised.

Returning, I found my phone lying on the ground and to my shock, it was almost 1:00 a.m. "God, how long did I sleep for?" I asked, joining them on the rug, cosying up to Brian.

"Well, we only came down an hour or so ago," Andrew said, stretching out his arm and placing it around Gloria, who had that distinct afterglow.

"What is all this?" I queried, spotting a few albums on the ground.

"I found those upstairs when we were . . . well, in one of the bedrooms," Gloria said.

"Under the bed," Andrew added. Gloria pushed her elbow in his side.

"Uh-huh." I didn't need to hear any more. I picked them up, placing them aside for now. Brian put his arm around me and we all sat there enjoying the zen of the moment.

As time went by, Gloria drifted off to sleep by the fire. I was feeling a bit peckish, as were the guys, so Andrew covered Gloria with an extra blanket and with the albums in hand, we went to the kitchen to find some leftovers to nibble on.

With forks, we picked away at the quiche and salad. I had placed the brown leather album that was almost falling apart at the seam on the table in front of me, staring at it for a short time before deciding to open it. The photographs inside were from a long, long time ago. It must have been from when my grandmother was a little girl. Each photograph was displayed beautifully on the black pages and would have come with its own stories. If someone could have narrated it, my ears would be devoted to their every word.

With each turn of the page, my eyes were met with a history of lives lived, fashions that had gone by, and interior designs that were hardly seen anymore. None of it, though, seemed to be in this house.

Across from me, Brian and Andrew had been looking at another album together, making some chatter as they do. However, they had noticeably gotten quiet. I looked up to raise an eyebrow at them when I noticed Andrew had a piece of paper in his hand.

"I . . . I'm so sorry, Liz." His voice shook as Brian appeared beside me in record speed.

"Lizzy is dead."

Chapter 8

"Ow." My head was pounding as if it met its match with a woodpecker. I couldn't distinguish whether it was alcohol, stress, or both.

I used my fingers to massage my temples slowly, hoping for some relief. It might have been better if I had taken Brian up on his offer of going home with him. He would have taken care of me. But I also needed some time alone. Time to reflect. I felt a strange sense of loss, a loss that was hard to explain.

Growing up, I didn't mind being an only child. I had all Mum's attention. Except now she's gone, having a sister would have been nice. In the 36 or so hours I knew of her, I had wondered where she might be now, what her life was like, if we had similar interests, if she knew about me, which one of us was the older sister. So many thoughts and questions had all come crashing down with the piece of paper I held in my hand. It still felt so unreal that I was looking at my sister's death certificate. She died so young.

I recalled again what Selina told me, about that one summer when Hilda said I was with another family. Of course, it wasn't me, it was Lizzy. Except, crucially, there was *no* other family. That horrible feeling I got in the cellar had materialised in front of me. It was a shrine for little Lizzy.

I wanted to know everything about her, and I was left with just the details on the death certificate, saying she died on the 22nd of July 1985. She'd only been a month shy of her fifth birthday. Her full name was Lizzy Heather Hayden. Heather, after our mum. Hilda was down as the informant, and the cause of death was recorded as accidental. Which begged the question again, why all the secrecy surrounding her life? And death? Why was she kept a secret? Why were we kept apart? It was all so much, and I needed the questions answered, and I needed pain relief now!

I slipped on some clothes, brushed my teeth, and made myself reasonably presentable. When I checked the time on my phone, to my shock, it was well into late afternoon. I had been sleeping for far longer than intended and missed several calls from Su and Brian. I sent them a quick text with a promise to ring later. I could imagine Su's reaction when I shared the news. Shock.

When I arrived downstairs, Andrew was back at work, seemingly unaffected by the alcohol intake from last night. "Good afternoon," he greeted louder than I liked and with emphasis on afternoon.

"Hi," I said unenthusiastically. "Do you have some paracetamol?"

"Aww, you're a lightweight? Are you sure you're Irish?" he teased. I pursed my lips. I wasn't in the mood for his jokes. "All right, follow me," he said moments later, still too loud for my liking, but at least he read my demeanour and kept further comments to himself.

I followed him into the kitchen. "Why don't you sit down?" he said, pulling back a chair. Within minutes, I had taken two paracetamols and had a homemade hangover remedy in front of me, which Andrew swore by and let me be. It tasted awful! How I longed for my own special hearty breakfast sandwich, grilled with a generous amount of cheese and fried egg. Always impossible to eat gracefully, but so forgiving, and perfect hangover food. I must have really poured it down. The thought made me feel even worse.

Having enough of the harsh lighting and memories of last night, I left the kitchen and snuck past the guest dining room, avoiding bumping into Andrew, whom I saw a glimpse of, and made a beeline back to my room. My curtains were still closed. I switched off the light, undressed in the darkness, and rested my body on the soft mattress, cocooning in the puffy duvet. I listened to my breath, focusing on each inhale through the nose and exhale out through the mouth, elongating them as much as I could until calmness was restored within.

By late evening I arose again, persuaded by the determination of my ringing phone. I reached toward the bedside table to grab it and answered. Su was relieved I did and upset I hadn't rung back yet. She was impatient with my slow and groggy start to our conversation as I entered the waking world and told her about Lizzy's death. She couldn't find the right words to say outside I'm so sorry, Liz. If the situation was reversed, I wouldn't know what to say either.

Brian was also happy when I *finally* rang. I kept the call short and decided to stay the night here at the B&B, as I just wasn't up for much of anything, but we agreed to meet in the morning for breakfast. He said he wanted to show me something. I couldn't muster much excitement for a surprise. Nevertheless, it was sweet.

My headache reduced significantly, and hunger had taken its place. Not inclined to socialise, I quietly got dressed, crept downstairs, and listened outside the kitchen door before peering inside. It was empty. A dim light by the counter was shining on a little note. Oh-so-thoughtful Gloria left me homemade lasagna with instructions on how to warm it up. Can this woman be any more amazing?

I woke up bright and early the next day. The birds greeted me with a welcoming concert as soon as I opened the window. There was no longer evidence from the downpour left and the fresh air was being warmed by the rising sun. It was a *new* day.

I was the first person in the breakfast room, not to eat, but for a cup of tea while I waited for Brian. The door opened and I could hear Willie's and Gloria's voices, shortly after I sat. For a brief moment, I contemplated if I should go over. Why not? I had no intention of causing him upset. I now knew my sister died and I just wanted to greet him, see him, hoping he was keeping well.

He was seated at the big dining table, having his VIP-style breakfast made by the one and only. "Morning," I said as I walked over to him. He appeared surprised initially, but gave a warm greeting, and even stood up halfway to offer me a seat, which I gratefully accepted.

"You're up early. Can I get you anything?" Gloria asked in her signature cheery way.

I held up my steaming mug. "Thank you for the lasagna. It was delicious."

"It was nothing." She waved it off and hurried on, packing up a picnic basket and filling a flask. I raised an eyebrow.

"Going somewhere?"

She looked over gleefully. "You are."

"Oh." I felt excitement bubbling up.

Willie refilled his cup with tea, pouring so slowly and carefully, the trickle of brown liquid got me watching. "Sorry you had to find out about Lizzy in the way that you did," he said, head bowed, barely speaking above a whisper. "I wanted to tell you, but I just couldn't find the words." He placed the teapot back on the trivet with a shaky hand.

"It's all right, Willie. It's all right." The last thing I wanted to happen was a repeat of the other day and impede his recovery. I placed my hand over his. He gazed up into my eyes and I gave a little nod to let him know I meant it. "Maybe one day you can tell me a little more about her, my grandmother, and what happened?" Willie hung his head again and gave my hand a slight squeeze.

"Is it ready?" Andrew asked loudly, breaking the tension as he barged into the kitchen energetically.

Gloria, who was likely accustomed to Andrew's boisterousness, didn't even look up from the food she was wrapping as she calmly replied, "Almost." Andrew looked at us and his face broke into a small smile when he noticed our hand-holding.

"Hi, I was just about to give you a wake-up call. Brian is ready," he said, sounding very chipper. It was contagious, and I couldn't help but grin in response.

"Is he here already?" Letting go of Willie, I got up from my seat.

"No, I am driving you there," he said, jingling the keys in his hand.

"Where?" I asked, hoping for a slip of the tongue.

"You'll find out soon enough. We first need to make a quick stop," he said, otherwise tightly lipped. Andrew was dressed casually but smartly with a well-ironed shirt and no paint stains to be seen on his fitted jeans. It was unusual to see him like that in the morning.

"All done!" Gloria announced triumphantly as she held a basket and bag up in the air before handing it over to Andrew.

"Have a special time, my dear," Willie said in a way that made me think he knew something about my breakfast date. I gently hugged Willie and thanked Gloria.

"See you later, hon." Andrew kissed Gloria and we left the kitchen together.

#

"No hint? At all?" I asked for the umpteenth time. Otherwise, we drove mainly in silence, with his 'upbeat' playlist still playing softly in the background.

"Nope," he said, still chipper. "What are your favourite flowers?" he asked me out of the blue.

"Um . . . it depends on the occasion, but I like the wildflower bouquet look, some Queen Anne's lace, blue cornflower, larkspur – in any colour – and some English lavender, for example," I answered, as if he knew what flowers I was talking about.

Seconds later, he pulled the car over. "If you knock on that door," he pointed it out, "Rose will open for you. Just tell her you're Elizabeth."

"Rose?" I creased my brows.

"I'll wait for you in the car." We were parked in front of a flower shop called Blooms. I stared at Andrew quizzically, who wordlessly leaned over to my side and opened the door. I did as told and stepped out and walked up to the entrance. "The sign says it's closed," I called back.

"Just knock!" Andrew shooed from the rolled-down window.

As I knocked on the glass door, a middle-aged lady soon opened. I took a deep breath. "I am – "

"Elizabeth," she said assuredly with a nod which made her loose bun, placed right on top of her head, bounce.

"Uh, yes," I said slowly, a little dazed.

"Well, it's a pleasure. Follow me." Entering the shop, I found the scent of flowers enchanting, I had missed it and loved it. It's the perfume of nature. I took a deep breath through my nose, inhaling the gloriousness of it all. The shop was beautifully decorated and filled with an array of flower arrangements, a wall display with every conceivable colour of ribbon, and a cute little card stand. I felt at home.

I trailed her through a doorway to a back room. It was larger than the one we had at Ms Bouquet and held a sizeable quantity of colourful flowers and foliage. Here is where all the wonderful creations were made. "So, Elizabeth, this is for you." She handed me a small, white envelope. "You can use anything here," she said with a smile, her dimples showing.

"Uh, okay. Thank you," I smiled, feeling dazed. Then she turned around and left the room.

I fumbled to open the envelope. The front of the card was blank, but the inside made my heart warm.

Dear Liz,

Make the most beautiful bouquet for a memorable occasion.

Love,

Brian, Andrew, and Gloria

They were unreal. So incredibly wonderful, thoughtful people. They knew how passionate I was about my job and the pleasure I get from it. This was like meditation for me. My creative juices started flowing and an arrangement came together that I was incredibly proud of. It smelled like a meadow of wildflowers you would want to lay down in on a warm summer's afternoon. "Yes," I said. "You're done."

As I entered back into the little shop area, Rose was pottering around. "Well, that looks as pretty as a picture," she said as soon as she laid eyes on it. "Before you go," she picked a bouquet from one of the buckets, "give these to Andrew." It was a beautiful arrangement with fragrant white lilies and a selection of delphinium, of which the indigo was my favourite. Such gorgeous pairing. "I'll get the door for you," she offered kindly.

"Thank you so much, Rose," I said, taking my eyes off the bouquets to look at her. Her brown eyes creased into a gentle smile and I left through the narrow doorframe of the shop.

"My pleasure, Elizabeth," she called out. I turned to give her a radiant grin.

"Are those all for me?" Andrew fluttered his eyelashes.

I beamed. I couldn't help it. "This one is." I pointed out the one.

"Perfect," he murmured as I lay them carefully on the back seat, got in the car, and Andrew drove off.

"I truly enjoyed that," I told him with passion.

"That's great, Liz. We'll be there soon."

"Where?" I chanced. Still, Andrew stayed quiet.

I looked out of the window as we drove. It was such a beautiful day. It felt like I'd experienced more sun here than I had in an entire year in Ireland. It was funny, really, as I considered England to be a rainy country also. Well, they can't compete with the west of Ireland.

A few minutes later, we turned into a small road and Andrew slowed the car down to a crawl as he pulled into a secluded clearing near an entrance where Brian was standing wearing a suit jacket. A stone sign to the right read Chapel Memorial Park Cemetery. It was not the picnic spot I had in mind. Confounded, I stared at Andrew, who just gave me an encouraging hand on my shoulder and made his way out of the car.

Hesitantly, I stepped out. Andrew got the flowers, handed me mine, and got the basket and bag before we walked to Brian. He gently placed a kiss on my lips and took my free hand. "Nice flowers."

"Did you find it?" Andrew asked in a low voice, leaning towards Brian. He nodded.

Oh. It can't be . . . can it? Did they find my sister's grave? I felt myself getting emotional as we entered the cemetery and held on firmly to Brians hand. After a short walk, past the little stone chapel, we went off the main path, stepping between crumbling gravestones, an area not often visited, until we stopped by one small grey gravestone. My eyes filled with tears as I read.

IN LOVING MEMORY OF
Lizzy Heather Hayden
08.06.1980 ~ 10.05.1985

"A life measured in memories, not in years."

Speechless, letting go of Brian, I kneeled by her grave and traced the lettering before meticulously placing the flowers so they looked as pretty as possible. "How did you find her?" I turned to whisper to Brian and Andrew.

"Willie told me, after I told him what we learned." Andrew spoke.

"Did he share anything else?" I asked, hopeful, but he shook his head. For some time, I sat grieving my sister, my sister I never had the pleasure of knowing.

"Shall we set up?" Brian spoke softly. "We thought you might like to have breakfast here, in her presence." Tears still prickled the corners of my eyes as they laid out a blanket and placed the basket on top.

I couldn't help but again feel incredibly fortunate to have met such wonderful people.

"Glor would have been here if she could," Andrew added.

"I am so grateful for you guys." I stood up and motioned for them to come forward so I could squeeze them in a firm embrace.

"Well, we're fond of you too," Brian said with a wink as we let go and all sat down for a bite. As usual, the food was amazing, but it was the company that was truly remarkable. We stayed for about an hour, eating and quietly chatting a bit. The cemetery being a sad place, it was also a place of solace, which I'd learned to appreciate greatly over the past months.

"Who are those for?" I asked Andrew, gesturing toward the extra bouquet that lay patiently in the centre of our picnic.

"I'll show you."

After we tidied, I took a moment alone by Lizzy's grave, wanting to say so much, but coming up short with words while they waited by a nearby tree. Eventually I met up with them and we walked tentatively, Andrew leading the way until we arrived by a polished black headstone – Hilda's. He lay the flowers on the ground and gently touched the headstone before whispering something inaudible.

Out of the corner of my eye, I noticed Andrew welling up, his shoulders shaking slightly. Having been so consumed with my own life and grief, I realised that I hadn't acknowledged his grieving much at all. I stepped closer to him, held his hand with a gentle squeeze, and we spent a moment in silence with 'our' grandmother. Brian had also known her well but was not as close to her as Andrew had been over the years.

Staring at her gravestone, I felt loss for not having met. All these years she'd been alive and now, she was gone. I was too late. Notably, the only reason I found out about her was because she passed away. Nevertheless, it was tragic. It helped to know she'd had some wonderful people in her life.

We left the cemetery soon after and I drove back with Brian, following Andrew's car back to his place. I insisted we go back there to thank Willie and Gloria.

#

Willie was sitting in a comfortable armchair in Andrew and Gloria's private lounge, reading a newspaper near the window. He was slouched over, his nose nearly touching the paper as he focused on it. He didn't notice me standing in the doorway. I knocked softly, so as not to startle him. If he'd been surprised to see me, he hid it well.

"Elizabeth," he said, giving an anxious smile, folding the newspaper and placing it aside.

"Willie, I just wanted to say thank you, from the bottom of my heart." I crossed the lounge, kneeled in front of him, and held his hand, which felt cold in mine. "I . . . I know you have been through so much lately . . . and things are difficult for you. I just want you to know that I am very grateful to you for telling me that I have – had – a sister, and sharing where she is buried."

He squeezed my hand. "Elizabeth." He marked every syllable of my name before sighing heavily.

I had to restrain myself from asking questions. Namely, how did my sister die? I know the death certificate said her death was accidental, but what happened? Why all the secrecy surrounding her?

What more did he know? He evidently knew more about this than any other living person. Reminding myself again of the clear instructions by his carer and doctor that he should not be put under any more stress, I kept my questions at bay for the time being, but how I wished he would share more.

I was leaving in three days, and I could never have imagined all that had unravelled. I needed to find a way to understand and comprehend it all.

"Anything interesting in the paper?" I asked, leaning forward to catch a glimpse of the headline. He picked it back up. It was the most mundane question I could think of besides the usual weather topic people engage in. I certainly didn't expect that question to make him come alive as he did.

He told me with great pride that he had been reading the *Colchester Gazette* for over forty years. "My favourite thing to do is the crossword puzzle, then I check out the TV listings and read the editorial." He beamed his eyes, scanning across the page. "I skip the horoscopes section; that's just utter nonsense!" he said with conviction. "And of course, I keep up with the national news. I'd rather read that in the paper than watch it on the telly."

"What *do* you like to watch on TV then?"

"Nothing that would interest you, dear Elizabeth." We smiled. It was good to see him like this.

"Willie." He held my gaze. "I am going back to Ireland in three days. Would you like to join me for lunch before I go?"

"Breakfast," he replied adamantly.

I raised my eyebrows. "Uh, okay, breakfast, if you prefer."

"Gloria makes the best breakfast there is and we can eat here."

"Well, there is no denying that. It's a date! How about the day after tomorrow?"

"That would be good," he replied earnestly. "Meet you at nine?"

"Perfect." Moments later, he was hunched over his newspaper again, looking content. "Thank you, Willie." He waved away my words, his eyes not trailing away from the paper.

I met everyone back in the kitchen. Gloria was for once sitting down at the table instead of wearing her apron and slaving away over the stove. I walked up behind her and gave her a full-hearted embrace. She almost spilled her coffee in surprise. "Thank you!" I said with great emphasis.

I squeezed her once more. She looked up with a smile and pressed her hand on mine. Soon after, Annie walked in and greeted me politely. I wondered if I ever had children if they would end up as well-mannered as her. She was a dote. This thought was followed by the thought of Brian, and the chat we needed to have. I was leaving soon, after all. We never spoke what 'this' is, even though we had made our growing affections known to each other. Were we going to be moving forward? Did he want to see if we had a future together? I needed to know where his head was at. It was terrifying and exciting all at the same time, which gave me butterflies.

Annie having gone to play in her room, the four of us sat together talking over some tea and coffee, when Brian quietly asked what my plans were for today.

"I was hoping we could spend the rest of the day together?"

His lips curled into a smile as he reached across the table, enlacing his fingers with mine. "Me too. Where would you like to go?" he asked, downing the last sip of coffee.

"Somewhere quiet."

"I know somewhere quiet. Although . . . you might want to bring a bikini," he said pointedly.

I raised an eyebrow. "I didn't pack one." He pursed his lips in thought.

"Spare clothes will do."

Not long after, we left Andrew and Gloria's and we were on the road, firstly stopping by his place to pick up a few things and after that, we headed off to a spot he called Mersea Island. On the drive up we were engaged in light-hearted conversation, but I kept thinking of the question I wanted to ask him that was right at the tip of my tongue. Still, I didn't know how to bring it up, and felt nervous. *You're being silly, just talk to him and say what is on your mind.*

"You okay, Liz? You seem somewhere else," Brian asked after a while, glancing at me.

"Uh, yes, yes. Yes. I'm fine," I said a little too high-pitched.

"Wow, three yesses. You must *not* be okay," he said astutely. "You said you wanted to go somewhere quiet. Is there something you want to say?" Brian asked, putting me straight on the spot without him even knowing.

This is as good a moment there is.

"Can you pull over somewhere?" My voice trembled a little over the words.

"Oh, sure. It sounds serious?" he said with a touch of uncertainty.

"It isn't. Or well actually, it is." He briefly took his eyes off the road and looked at me with narrowed eyes. I tried giving him a reassuring smile. Not long afterward, he indicated and drove into a small, quiet lane and pulled over.

"What is it, Liz?" he asked in a low voice straight after he turned off the engine.

I took a moment before unclipping my seat belt and turned toward him. "I will be leaving very soon, and I know that we haven't known each other very long, but I *really* like you." I stopped, taking a sharp breath. "A lot . . . as you know, and, and I just wanted to say that I would like, if you want to, that is, to see where *this* can go. If you want a relationship, that is. You did say you were falling for me and . . ." I rambled on until Brian slowly began smiling and kissed me.

"You're so cute when you're nervous, you know that?" he said when I caught my breath from the kiss. His face was inches from mine. "Yes, I want a relationship with you."

"I mean, just with me."

"Yes, Liz, just you." He placed a soft kiss on my forehead and glided his fingers through my hair while staring at me attentively. "I want this. Us. We will find a way to make the distance work." I beamed, excited to know that we were on the same page. "Can I start driving again or is there more?" he asked with a grin.

"Sure, why don't you turn around and drive to your apartment?" His grin got bigger and he didn't question my request, making a swift U-turn. As nice as an afternoon on a quiet spot on the beach sounded, I craved the solitary confines of his lovely apartment where it was just us.

When we arrived, the first thing I did was switch off my phone. I didn't want to be disturbed. "Just you and me," I told him. Being on the same page, he followed suit. We got comfy on his couch sitting close together, our legs stretched out on the coffee table, his hand tenderly stroking my thigh starting off a lengthy foreplay followed by sensual lovemaking. After, we chatted for hours on end. Sharing our best childhood memories, favourite movies, aspirations, and desires. We laughed as we spoke of some of our eccentric fashion choices and hairstyles growing up. He even had some hilarious pictures and made me promise to share some of mine.

In many ways, we were similar, in the values we hold in life. He was calm and open as we spoke. It was a lovely side of him to see. Although I found his goofy, playful side very endearing. I just knew he was the kind of person who could keep me grounded and uplifted, and that thought warmed my heart even further.

When we were finally talked out, it was late afternoon. My body, especially my legs, were stiff from sitting down for so long. It showed from the disconcerting sound when I got up. "You need another massage," he remarked eagerly, his face lighting up.

"Is that what we are calling it now." I pulled him up to stand and we were face-to-face. "How about a shower first and you electrify me?" I seductively whispered in his ear.

"Electrify? You sure are asking for a lot," he teased, pushing his body against mine. "I *love* this side of you," he murmured, letting out a little aroused breath.

"Love, huh? How much?"

"I'll show you." He undressed me out of the few clothes I was wearing and teased me with his hands and mouth every step to the shower.

#

I studied his face as he lay asleep, and a feeling of gratefulness swept over me. He'd been my sunshine in the storm. Going back to Ireland in a few days was going to be hard. Of course, it would be lovely to see my friends again and visit my mother's grave. I missed the ritual. I missed her. Even more with everything that came about, and we could never talk again. Leaving wasn't hard only because of Brian, but I felt I'd gained a sort of family here I wasn't ready to part from.

My only family had been my mother, and of course I valued the wonderful group of friends back home dearly, but the people I had come to know here was a different bond I experienced. There was a link we shared which had become important to me.

Andrew had become my confidant and true friend in such a short time. Willie felt a bit like a surrogate grandfather I never had, I didn't know much about, but was an important connection to my grandmother. Gloria was the glue that held everyone together, and then here was this man, lying next to me. He made me want to wake up early just to enjoy the sight of him. I took in the moment and imprinted it into my memory.

"It's creepy to watch someone sleep, you know," he mumbled in a groggy voice as he pulled me closer towards him.

"Well then maybe you shouldn't look so hot doing it," I retorted, smiling widely.

"Hot, you say." He pulled me on top of him, holding my waist, which made me giggle a little.

"I wish you could stay longer."

"Me too," I said with a pouty bottom lip. "But I have to go back to work, and it will be good to see my friends again and visit my mum's grave."

"I would like to have met her. She must have been a wonderful person." Brian said it so heartfelt, his words pierced my eyes as they suddenly welled up so easily.

"She was," I nodded, sighing. "You know, some of the wonderful memories I have, I look back at differently now; now I know there was so much more to our little existence than the happy bubble we lived in."

"She loved you, Liz, you can't fake that." He stroked my arms.

"I know." He was right. I always felt loved by my mum. "Actually, my mum had a best friend, Margret. They were very close. I think I will go talk to her when I get back, to see if she can shed some more light on things for me. If Mum had confided about any of this to anyone, it would be her."

"Just as you talk about me to your friend Su?" he said, amused.

I gave a little grin. "Yes, just like that."

"Kidding aside, I think that's a good idea, Liz." He took my hand and squeezed it. "And what about your father?"

I stared at Brian. "All I know is that he didn't stick around when my mum got pregnant," I murmured after a long moment. "I never pressed my mum about it, as it seemed to upset her, and I was happy with what we had. I never felt like I was missing something."

"You never even asked his name? Or what he was like? Where he lived?" he asked, his eyebrows furrowed.

"Well, I know his first name is Oscar," I recanted, "but I don't know his surname, and he is not mentioned on my birth certificate; that's why we are all generations of Haydens," I said proudly. "I was born here in Colchester, and since my mum got pregnant here, I presume my father might be from here too. That's all I know." I shrugged.

"Aren't you curious?" he asked in disbelief.

"To be honest, no. The way I've always seen it, he abandoned my mum and me. He never looked for us or tried to get in contact, as far as I know. My mum would have told me if he did." Brian's eyebrows lowered, unconvinced. I sighed deeply. "She would have . . . wouldn't she . . .?" I trailed off.

"Look, Liz, I am not saying your mum lied about your father. But in light of everything, it might be worth keeping an open mind to the possibility that all may not be as you have been told. Perhaps this is something to explore, if you want to, one day." Without him realising, Brian's question opened a can of worms I didn't even know I had. It was overwhelming, all the unknowns about my family.

"What are we having for breakfast?" I changed the subject. In fairness, I did feel slightly hungry. He hugged me close and kissed my forehead, accepting my not-so-subtle hint.

"Would you like to eat in or go out?" he asked in his perky way, which I appreciated greatly.

"Let's stay in for the morning. Maybe later we can go out?"

"Sure."

Barely dressed, we made breakfast together. It wasn't an activity we did in harmony at all, but we got our meal plated and had a good laugh at our inefficient teamwork. "Maybe tomorrow we should go out, or just one of us make it," he said, jesting.

"I actually have breakfast plans tomorrow," I said with my mouth half-full. "With Willie."

"Ah, okay. Well, you are just going to have to make lunch later instead," Brian said, digging into his eggs.

"Really? Do I now?" We engaged in some light banter while we ate, but I was feeling the strain of time again. It felt like a countdown. I tried hard to just enjoy the here and now, but there was no escaping it. I knew he felt it too. We said silly things like, "Absence makes the heart grow fonder," to comfort ourselves, but it only did so much.

"Have you had more thought about what you might do with the house? Outside not selling, of course," Brian wondered.

"No, not really. I need to have a proper think about everything in my life. I have so much to think about."

"As long as I am in it." He kissed me.

The day turned into one of much laughter, talking, and smooching. We managed to make the most of it, and the night had the promise of being wonderful too.

#

"I really have to *go*," I laughed as he held onto my arm while I tried squeezing through the front door, reluctantly abstaining from another kiss. "I promised Willie breakfast at nine." One more kiss and embrace and I left to walk my way to The Slumber.

Being with Brian changed me. He excited me, and brought out a newfound confidence while simultaneously a vulnerability that I only ever felt before in a *real* relationship. I had completely forgotten about Gordon since, and I could finally and truly say I was over him. I have been over him! It was liberating to be able to acknowledge this and know it to be true.

I rounded a corner onto a narrow street and was getting more and more familiar with the roads, recognising certain houses, shops, and other landmarks. It gave me a sense of comfort that I was becoming accustomed to my surroundings.

My mind began wandering with thoughts about Willie as I made my way through the leafy streets. What could we talk about? For all intents and purposes, I planned for our chat to be light-hearted, but I secretly wished he would confide in me, anything that would answer some of my lingering questions. Nothing shocking – oh no, I'd had enough of that – just enlightening.

Finally there, as I was stepping onto the garden path, Willie saw me approach from the window where he was already seated in the breakfast room. He was punctual, or just an early riser. I quickly made my way into the B&B and to my surprise, met no one before reaching Willie's table.

He got up to greet me, even when I gestured that he shouldn't. He was just that kind of gentleman. "I ate something small, was feeling a bit peckish," he confessed as he patted his belly. Remnants of scone crumbs and jam were on his plate.

"No worries. Gloria's food is hard to resist," I said, eager for some too.

"That it is."

The room was the busiest I had seen, with soft chatter and clinking filling the room.

Seated, we exchanged pleasantries, and the atmosphere settled comfortably around us. The conversation followed a natural flow. Of course, the weather came up quickly, as it does. In particular, the amount of rain we get in Ireland. I told him that sometimes the number of rainy days becomes a blur and that we complain about it more often than the rain actually occurs. This made him laugh.

Gloria had come and gone, taking our orders. She was busy, but even when rushed off her feet, she worked with grace and had our breakfast served in record time.

Willie was interested to learn more about my life in Ireland and I happily shared stories about my college studies and owning Ms Bouquet with Su. It wasn't until he asked what happened to my mother that I got a frog in my throat. I hadn't expected him to go there.

"I hope you don't mind me asking?" he said, sounding quite apologetic.

"No, no, no, not at all that's – fine." I cleared my throat and hastily downed my cooling tea.

"Did you know her well?" I'd wondered, since his distress after hearing that she died.

"No, I didn't. Hilda spoke of her often." He paused and took a bite of his toast.

I cut my sausage into bite-size pieces. "Really? What did she say about her?" I prompted as nonchalantly as I could muster. On the inside, my eagerness to know was like a firework waiting to be lit. I focused on my plate, not daring to look up, hoping he would feel comfortable enough to answer. So far, he had done most of the asking.

We both knew there was an elephant in the room, but in line with his doctor's orders, I did not pry. However, this was not really a probe, I quickly convinced myself. It wasn't a conversation that I started. Seconds, maybe even half a minute passed as he repeatedly sipped tea. I was just about to give up on getting an answer when he started talking again.

"She missed your mother dearly, and often hoped she would visit. She would talk about her a lot as a young child – in a way only a parent could." I finally looked up. He stared vacantly in my direction. "Oh, how she regretted the way things turned out, always carrying that deep sorrow with her." His voice broke and he reached for his tea again, taking another sip, avoiding my stare. He struggled. "I miss her a lot, Elizabeth. She was my best friend."

"I am so sorry for your loss, Willie." I reached for his hand and gently squeezed it. "I know how you feel." The words sinking in, he finally met my gaze. ". . . It was a car accident."

"Ah," he nodded, pained, turning his attention back to his food.

". . . I think we should nominate Gloria for some cooking award, don't you?" It took him a moment, after which a hint of a smile warmed his face with a brighter expression.

"She sure deserves one," he said, licking the last bit of his baked beans sauce off his plate. A funny sight.

"What is your favourite dish she ever made you?" I asked, leaning forward slightly.

"Well, let me tell you a thing or two about Gloria's recipes." Willie lowered his voice conspiratorially. "I know some of her cooking secrets, you know . . ." He had a cheeky smile on his face that instantly made him look younger.

We spent a good twenty minutes talking about food, and he shared his enjoyment for cooking. To my surprise, he even mentioned my grandmother's favourite dish, which he cooked for her once a week. It had no fancy name, she just called it Willie's dish. But he wouldn't give away the recipe, he only mentioned that it held a secret ingredient, which Hilda never guessed. With a twinkle in his eye, he promised to make it for me if I were to visit again.

"I can't wait," I said, touched.

We exchanged contact details with a promise to keep in touch. He looked at my address with a heavy frown. "I have never been to Ireland."

"Well, who knows, maybe one day you might. It isn't that far," I said optimistically.

He stood up and I followed suit and reached over to engulf him in a final, careful embrace. With no more words spoken, he left the room, turning around once, giving a little wave. After a shaky sigh and finishing my drink, I made my way to my room.

#

Packing my belongings, my mind was a whirlwind of thoughts and emotions. I tried pushing them aside, unable to focus on just one.

I left one outfit at the top of my suitcase for tonight's dinner with Brian, Andrew, and Gloria. They were taking me out somewhere, a surprise goodbye dinner. Part of me felt these past two weeks had flown by; on the other hand, so much happened it was surreal to think that that was all the time I'd spent here. I knew I was going to need space to process it all at some stage.

I carried my suitcases down the stairs, rolled them down the hallway, and carried them out the front door, pausing to take a moment to breathe in the fresh air.

"Déjà vu?" It was Andrew. He was crouched down in the garden at work. "That is exactly how you stood with your suitcases when I saw you the first time," he said, digging his trowel into the earth. "We will miss you, you know."

I left my suitcases and walked over, sat beside him on the grass and briefly leaned my head against the side of his upper arm. "Me too," I sighed.

He wrapped his arm around my shoulder, dropping to a sitting position.

"So, you're off to your guy, I suppose," he said, wagging his eyebrows at me. I just smiled.

"That's it! Right there, that's the smile," he said, mirroring my expression. Involuntarily, I smiled even wider. I was incapable of hiding it, even if I'd wanted to. "It's good to see you smile, Liz." He gave me a squeeze.

"Thanks," I said sheepishly, the grin still plastered on my face.

"Right, off you go, and we will see you this evening."

I embraced him tightly before grabbing my suitcases again and heading off.

"Are you sure you don't want a lift?" he shouted, mocking me when I struggled with one of my suitcases, the wheels having a mind of their own. "No. I am good." It came out less convincing than intended. In hindsight, it would have been easier if I'd left the suitcases and asked Andrew to bring them in the evening and transfer them to Brian's car, but of course, hindsight is a wonderful, useless thing.

#

We spent the afternoon chatting and laughing, with intermittent periods of silence where we just enjoyed each other's presence and shared gentle touches to show our affection. Whenever I felt the time ticking away again, I reminded myself to stay present in the here and now.

I listened to the subtle sound of his breathing and inhaled his woody, masculine fragrance. As his dreamy eyes met mine, my insides melted, and his touch and taste were moments to savour.

Brian was evasive about the evening's plans when I asked. "You'll find out soon enough," he'd said, with a grin that told me he had something up his sleeve. Whatever it was, I was looking forward to it.

#

I wore another little black number with a playful, flowy skirt and spaghetti straps trailing my shoulders, barely holding up. Brian certainly approved and if I had given him the opportunity, it would have left my body faster than I put it on.

He looked smart with his white, short-sleeved, button-up shirt and casual fitted beige trousers rolled up just above his ankle, paired with brown loafers, matching the colour of his watch. I liked his style.

Brian drove for a while. Quite a long while, actually, as we crept further away from civilization. "Close your eyes," he said suddenly while focused on the road.

"Are you serious?" I said, almost laughing until he briefly looked at me with a challenging stare.

"I can stop and blindfold you," he said with a grin, slowing down the car as we approached a junction. With an inward sigh, I closed my eyes firmly. Moments later, he made a sharp turn and drove over a bumpy road that his car was definitely not designed to drive on.

"Where are you bringing me?" I asked, starting to feel a little apprehensive.

"Keep your eyes closed, we're almost there," he insisted with an amused tone in his voice.

When the car finally came to a stop, Brian got out while I waited inside with my eyes still shut, as directed. The urge to peek was high. Once he opened my door, he helped me out and guided me over an uneven ground as I wobbled on my heels, regretting my choice of footwear. *I'll be taking these off.*

Soon after, I heard the faint crunch of approaching footsteps. Brian held my shoulders and gently twisted my body to the left. "Stop here," he said with excitement. "You can open your eyes now."

For a few seconds, I had to acclimate from the squeezing and darkness to the brighter surroundings. In front of me was an old, open barn structure, picturesquely set by a small lake with trees dotted around. Brian guided me, with his hand on the small of my back, to the porch. Andrew was standing there with Gloria, holding his arms around her lovingly. They both beamed, waving at us as we made our way up the overgrown path. Seconds later, I greeted them each with an embrace.

Three candles were lit, spaced out evenly on the chunky wooden table set for four, with enough food to feed an army. My mouth started watering from the sight alone. Brian stood behind me and wrapped his arms around my waist, holding me tight for a few moments before whispering in my ear words that I felt throughout my entire body. "I love you, Elizabeth Hayden."

I turned around to face him, cupped his face in my hands, and got all emotional as I told him I loved him too. We beamed.

"Let's eat!" Andrew said, interrupting our moment.

"And after, we have a long itinerary to fulfil before we can let you go back to Ireland, Liz," Gloria announced like a woman on a mission. I looked at Brian, still fuzzy from his declaration. He had that grin again and made a gesture that his lips were sealed. We sat down and I looked at them one at a time.

Being here, I couldn't feel more blessed right now. This happens in movies, not in real life. *Where did these people come from?* "Hey, Liz, switch your thinking brain off and enjoy the evening," Andrew said. I startled at his comment. "I know that face," he said indisputably. "You deserve to be happy."

"You really do, Liz." Brian reached for my hand and kissed it.

I welled up a little and smiled from ear to ear, deciding to embrace all the wonderful things that were coming my way this evening. "What is this place?" I asked Gloria while she poured a glass of something fancy and French.

"Oh, just an old place we break into sometimes for fun," she replied, poker-faced, while handing me the glass. "Nah, just kidding! This land is ours and we come here at least twice a month for a quiet date night. It keeps our relationship fresh." Gloria was more carefree than I had ever seen her. It might have been from the wine she drank already, but I believed it was just a genuine side of her that I had yet to see.

"It is absolutely beautiful here," I said, hiding my chuckle under a sip of wine.

"You haven't seen all of it yet," she said, dropping her voice into a mysterious tone. I leaned toward her, lowering my voice to match hers.

"So, what else is on the itinerary?"

She topped up her own glass of wine and smiled.

"Let's eat, and you will find out."

The meal was undeniably delicious, as expected. The starter alone, a fennel salad with orange wedges and mint, giving it a fresh zing, was perfect for the warm evening and went down a treat. Andrew and Gloria were very affectionate towards each other throughout dinner. "It's their date night," Brian said when I caught the two stealing yet another passionate kiss.

"Ours too," I replied, stretching out my leg to rest my bare feet on his lap, letting it slowly slide up his thigh. His facial expression morphed quickly to one of excitement.

"What is next on the itinerary?" I asked him as I softly bit my lip.

"A swim," he said, gazing longingly at my mouth.

"A swim?" I raised an eyebrow.

"Yes, let's go!" Brian said enthusiastically, and everyone got up in unison. I was astonished.

I followed them to the water. Before I could say anything about not having swimwear, they all undressed, stark naked! "Right." I just laughed. *There are no prudes here.* I watched them all splash their way into the lake with excitement. "What the hell?" I said to myself, and followed suit.

I undressed quickly and jumped off the pier into the glittering lake as they cheered me on. The water wasn't as cold as I expected it to be. I let out occasional screams when an unknown slippery something touched my feet. Brian thought it was hilarious.

"I knew you were up for this," he said teasingly.

We were in the water for a while. The experience was liberating and good fun, especially with the fondling underwater. There was a moment, as the water rippled against my skin, I had to pinch myself to prove this was real, really happening. Heeding Andrew's advice, I got out of my head again.

Andrew and Gloria swam further down the lake and came out quite a while after we did. They both walked over to the barn, holding hands, laughing and naked, until Brian handed them a towel. I didn't know if I was to look or look away, and I let out an unintentional giggle, which Brian thought was "cute." I suppose it wasn't just that they were naked, but the whole experience made me feel giddy. They disappeared again once wrapped up.

"You know, I watch this series, *Gilmore Girls*, and since, I dreamed that one day . . ." I trailed off, gathering my thoughts.

"What did you dream of?" Brian asked, leaning toward me, prompting me to go on.

"Well, there was this episode where this secret society at Yale would hold some elaborate event or stunt, just – something exciting. I always wanted to be part of something like that, just once." Brian was listening intently. "This might not be the same, but it gives me the vibes. Of course, I also really liked one of the actors that played the lead role." I giggled a little.

"Did you now? What was his name?" he asked, intrigued.

"In the series, he was called Logan."

"Well, then, for the next hour, I am your fantasy. I will be your Logan."

I laughed so hard, unable to contain how ridiculous that would be, until I realised, how often can people pretend to live their hot-guy fantasy with their equally hot guy? He kissed my neck, and I needed no more convincing.

"Right, tell me more about him," he murmured in between kisses.

"Well, he is spontaneous, fun, and a bit of a bad guy," I replied slowly, distracted by the persistence of his kisses.

"How bad?" he asked, his voice low and teasing.

"You start misbehaving and I'll tell you when to stop," I whispered in his ear. Getting up swiftly, Brian lifted me up onto the table.

"Would he have sex with you right here?" he asked, placing a wandering hand on my thigh.

"In my fantasy, he would, and –"

A sudden clinking of a glass snapped me out of it. I twisted around just in time to see Gloria and Andrew walking by, grinning.

I blushed and buried my head in his chest. It was still light out. Although I was back in my dress, it was clear what we were about to engage in.

"So, I am your Logan," Brian reiterated once they were out of sight. He tilted my head, and his lustful eyes brought me back. "And your fantasy will finally come true –"

". . . you will take charge and wow me. Take me out of my comfort zone and make me experience what it will be like," I finished.

I was so up for it now, intensely aroused by the role-play alone, and the entire experience was exciting and mind-blowing. We weren't discreet or quiet, which was more than apparent when Gloria and Andrew returned with looks and smiles that said it all.

A little while later, with the light starting to fade, the men went to gather some wood for a fire as Gloria and I sat at the table, idly drinking our wine.

"Logan, huh?" Gloria ultimately said. We both burst out in laughter. Once composed again she added, "I haven't seen Brian this happy in a long time."

"I haven't been either," I replied with all sincerity. "These two weeks have been so surreal and difficult for me. But meeting you all, it's . . . it's like I have gained a family."

"Aww, come here, you," she said, pulling me in for a hug. We chatted for a while and by the time the guys had the bonfire going, we made comfy seating by placing some pillows and blankets near the flames. Slowly, the remaining light faded away and stars appeared.

I lay down on an old quilt and looked up at the sky, taking in the night. Gloria joined me and shortly after, Brian and Andrew did too. All of us looking up at the wonders above. I could have fallen asleep, if not for the announcement of the next activity on their itinerary. "How many more are there?" I asked, slightly worried.

"No sleep for you tonight, Liz," Brian said, and Andrew and Gloria hummed in agreement as they pushed and pulled me up to sitting.

"So next," Andrew said. "Drumroll, please. It's story time!" Andrew exclaimed while the rest cheered, so I clapped along with them. "Since you're new to this, Liz, let me explain the rules. Everyone gets to tell a short story or sentence, if you will, that includes *one* true event from your life. And the others need to guess which event really happened. Simple! Oh, and we have all heard about Logan, so you can't choose that, Liz." Thank God it was dark and the colour on my face was not fully visible, because I felt redder than a boiled lobster. Brian hugged me, laughing into my shoulder.

"Do you guys do this often?" I asked Brian in an attempt to move the conversation away from the Logan fantasy.

"Not since our college years," Gloria said.

"Who wants to start?" Andrew asked excitedly.

"I think I'll watch first," I answered quickly, still fighting my embarrassment from earlier.

"All right, to my darling wife, then," Andrew announced, and gave her a quick peck.

"But wouldn't you know which part is true?" I pointed out.

"If I am certain of the answer, I will recuse myself."

"What's the price for guessing it right?"

"The truth. If guessed correctly, the person will have to confirm it. If guessed incorrectly, you don't have to tell which part is the truth," Andrew said officially. Gloria stood up and took a moment to think before she began.

"Well, I prefer to cook an amazing meal over the pleasures of my man, and sometimes, I hide my new creation and eat in the toilet."

Gloria sat down as I repeated her sentence in my head. After a few seconds of silence, I asked, "Are we allowed to discuss?"

"Yes, of course," Andrew said.

"I know the first part isn't correct," Andrew said with conviction, adamantly protecting his masculinity. I chuckled.

"So, either she hides her new creations, or sometimes eats in the toilet?"

"I would say that she eats in the toilet. She can never wait to share her new creations," Brian said confidently.

"You are right!" Gloria pointed at Brian before we even agreed to go with that answer. It was fair to say we were all tipsy at this point. "Your turn now." She dabbed at Brian.

"Okay, let me think . . . In my life, I have never cheated in an exam, eaten a passion fruit, or stolen a pillow."

"You have eaten passion fruit," Gloria quickly said.

"I'm pretty sure you cheated in one of your exams," Andrew said in an *I got ye* kind of way.

"What do you think, Liz?" Brian asked.

"Actually – I'll follow Andrew. I think you cheated during your exam."

"You are . . . wrong!" Brian said with a smug grin.

"Ah! Seriously? You stole a pillow?"

"No, no, you're right," Brian laughed. "I did cheat in an exam."

"I knew it! I knew it!" Andrew shouted in delight.

"Your turn now." Brian pulled me up to stand. I had gotten the gist of the game now. I took a breath before speaking a mile a minute.

"Okay so, one day I overslept and had to rush to work to open the shop. In my haste, I arrived at work having forgotten to wear knickers, my bra, while wearing a sheer top, or wore two different shoes."

They got in debating mode immediately. "You'll definitely feel when you have two different shoes on," Andrew said.

"Oh, and you think we don't know when we forget our bra?" Gloria retorted sarcastically.

"Won't that depend on the size and bounciness of the boobs?" Andrew tried to be smart.

"With her size? Maybe, maybe not," Brian said cheekily. To my slight horror, Andrew hummed as if to confirm. "How about knickers?" Gloria wasn't sure on that one.

"Well? Guys? What's it going to be?" I asked, tapping my foot to feign impatience. After much deliberation, they ultimately settled on forgot to wear a bra.

"Wrong," I said with a triumphant grin.

"Ah . . . uh, which one is it then?" Brian asked, clearing his throat.

"You'll never know now, will you," I replied rather smugly.

Andrew was the last speaker and he had us all wound up. "On this particular day, three people were sitting by the fire, with no idea something was approaching behind them," he whispered in a hoarse voice, adding to the intrigue. We all glanced at each other, refraining from looking behind us. "Was it a fox?" Andrew stared over us. "A spider? Or –"

We heard a rustling noise, and Gloria and I jumped up. Brian had a more collected reaction, even though he also stood up. "Just a wild rabbit," Andrew laughed full-heartedly. Gloria punched him in the arm.

"You're not getting away that easy," I told him. "Start again."

We ended up playing three rounds. It was good, silly, sophomoric fun. Although it was well past midnight at this stage, we kept the fire blazing. The heat and Brian's embrace felt cosy and wonderful. I didn't want to fall asleep anymore. I wanted to savour every hour and minute with him.

As if Andrew read my mind, he told Gloria, "Let's leave them." They said their goodbyes and walked off to the barn.

We lay on the blanket spooning as Brian played a bit with my hair. We didn't talk much, outside the occasional sweet whisper, but the togetherness had us content.

#

"Brian!" I shook him. "What time is it?" The sky above us was bright and blue. There was morning dew on the grass and a hint of warmth in the air, probably from the glowing ash that once resembled our bonfire. I felt panic sweep through me at the prospect of missing my flight.

"My phone is dead," I said aloud. I turned toward Brian, who was not in the waking world yet. I shook him again. "Do you know what time it is? Brian?" He woke up, groggy, before he sat up straight with alarm.

"We fell asleep! Okay, okay, don't worry." He searched for his phone, with no luck, and then ran to his car to check the time there. "It's twenty-four past six!" he shouted.

"That's okay! That's okay, we have time to make it there," I said with relief. "Oh no, my suitcases!"

"Don't worry, we must go that way anyway. When is your flight again?" Brian asked, gathering his things and hauling them to the car. Andrew and Gloria appeared at the edge of the barn, having woken from the commotion.

"Really sorry, guys, I have to go or I'll miss my flight. I'm going to miss you!" I said as I ran over to embrace them and thanked them for *everything.* Before hurrying off, I quickly took Andrew's hand and held it in both of mine, expressing my gratefulness. He had been such a great support and friend. Minutes later, Gloria and Andrew were waving us off as we drove away in Brian's car.

The car drive was a bit intense but with some smart driving, Brian had picked up my suitcases and arrived at the airport in just over an hour. There was enough time to get through security and make it to the gate, but no time for a long goodbye, so we had started in the car, making promises to talk daily, and planning to see each other soon.

Our final goodbye was intense and emotional, as was the sweet and gentle kiss we shared. We held hands as I slowly walked away until our fingers couldn't stretch anymore, and we parted.

Chapter 9

During the flight, I mused about Brian, feeling a bit like a teenager, giddy with butterflies in my stomach by the mere thought of him. It must have shown, as the air host gave a pleasant smile and nod while passing with his trolley.

The feeling, however, didn't last as I started to recall the entire two weeks, and all the unanswered questions were simmering, as if lying on the beach with nowhere to escape the hot sunrays, my heart beating faster than normal. The announcement that we should be landing in ten minutes brought me back and I practised deep breaths to calm my mind.

It was late morning when we landed. I gave Brian a quick call to let him know. Being back in Ireland and two Saturdays had passed since I last visited my mum's grave, it dawned on me that the dark routine I had adopted of staying in bed till noon had been broken. Much had changed.

Driving back to Galway, I listened to the radio for some distraction and company. Once I finally came off the M6, having crossed the straight, never-ending road from east to west, I didn't have long to go, and drove on autopilot to the cemetery.

The weather was drab, wet, and sombre. As I walked towards my mother's grave, a chill ran through my spine. It was eerily quiet for the afternoon, only the occasional sound coming from birds, rustling leaves, and cars in the distance. It must have been the uninviting weather.

The now wilted white rose still lay near David Mo's gravestone, blown away from where I had placed it those weeks ago. I crouched at my mum's grave, which held two withering bouquets. Only the pink carnations were still holding onto their beauty. The white rose arrangement was from Su. She had described the bouquet in detail over the phone. The other one must have been from Margret, although there was no note.

Being back here, my feelings were different than the previous visits. My sadness merged with confusion and anguish, but even so, it was good to be back.

For a while, in a daze, I forgot about the eerie quietness that surrounded me, until, that is, the heavens opened and the rain poured hard, making the earth dance. With no adequate shelter in sight, I kissed my fingers and touched them on the gravestone and made a futile run for it.

Back in the car, my hair drenched and water dripping down my face, I untangled myself out of my saturated cardigan. Everything weighed me down as I drove the short distance home.

"You're back! You're back! You're back!" Su jumped up and shouted, running towards me in the lightening rain as I got out of the car, her arms outstretched when she reached me, thinking the better of it once she saw my wet state. "You! You – " she said, punctuating each word with a push to my shoulder, and laughed. "Where do I even start? I want to know everything! Every detail! Don't even think of leaving anything out!" Su was smiling widely, and I felt myself helplessly mirroring her expression as we walked into our apartment, laughing. "This place has been so quiet without you," Su said as she shut the door behind us.

"And clean," I said as I smelled a mixture of detergents and air freshener.

"Oh, that? I only started this morning," she shrugged. "I'll get a towel. How did you get so wet? Decided you missed the rain and go stand in it?" she shouted from down the hall.

"I have missed your sarcasm!" I shouted back, unlacing my shoes and carefully setting them aside. "Went to visit Mum's grave."

"That makes more sense," Su said, coming with a few towels.

Once dried and changed, I sat on the couch with her. We were each curled up cosily in the corner with a blanket and hot drink. Cocoa—my go-to on a day like this.

"I am ready!" she exclaimed after she took an inhale from her herbal tea. "Spill it. Leave nothing out." We sat for what felt like hours, only getting up for a refill, snacks, and a bathroom break. Telling it all in one go made it sound unbelievable even to myself at times.

Su went through a range of emotions from gasping through to laughing and everything in between. "Wait, wait – let me get this straight." She gathered her thoughts. "You not only inherit a house – or, well, more like a *mansion*, which turns out to be from your grandmother who died recently – not a long time ago. You had a twin sister who died, and you don't know how, and in the middle of it all, you meet and fall for a kind hunk. Oh! And there's this man Willie who you think might hold answers to more secrets," Su finished, her face alight with disbelief. "Did I miss anything?" she asked, as if we didn't speak on the phone about any of it before.

I suppose it is called processing. I had been doing the same since.

"Seriously, this is like some movie, Liz!" she blurted out after a moment of deep silence.

"Definitely not a comedy," I muttered, unamused.

"Sorry, Liz," Su said, reaching, scooting across the couch to hug me tightly.

"Anyway," I went on as she slowly released her grip, "Brian asked about my father, and even implied that what I am told about him might not be true. I didn't have much to say to that. You know Mum never wanted to talk about him."

"Ahhh, so you think there is more there too?" Su burst out way too excitedly. I raised an eyebrow at her. "Sorry, sorry." She contained herself again, looking rather guilty. "You think, uh, that what you were told about him might not all have been truthful either?" she asked more seriously.

"I just never thought about it or questioned it before, but now," I shrugged. "I will ask Margret. She might know more, if there's more to know." There was a moment of silence where we both stared at our empty cups.

"How are you feeling? How do you feel about your mum?" Su asked sombrely, trying to not get carried away by the real-life drama.

As I sat silently contemplating how I was feeling, the only thing that came to me at that particular moment was confusion and exhaustion. "I am tired, Su." She nodded sympathetically.

"Yeah, I bet. All this mystery must be draining."

"No – well, yes. It is. But I'm actually just *tired* and I want to lie down for a while."

"I am so happy you're back," Su said, and hugged me as I stood up to go to my room.

"Me too," I replied into her shoulder. She smelled just like the shop, and suddenly I missed it, but it would have to wait.

"Don't sleep too long! We have plans this evening!" Su shouted when I entered the hall.

"We have?" I asked, poking my head around the corner. Su had that cheeky smile on her face which could only mean one thing. "Sounds good, Su. Thank you!"

#

I felt disoriented as I woke from a very deep sleep because of a noise I wasn't able to place yet. I lay still, silently trying to figure out why I was where I was, the day or time, and what I did last. It must have been several minutes before everything became clear to me, with some help from my phone.

I'd slept for hours and had two missed calls from Brian. The noise from the apartment was familiar now as I got up and stretched. Smiling, I freshened up quickly and joined the gang. They cheered rather loudly as I stood in the doorway, as if I was the guest of honour to a very important occasion.

They wasted no time getting into a party mood. Glasses of red wine were toasted, and an abundance of appetizers were on the table despite the fact that some plates had been devoured until empty.

"If you had taken any longer, I would have woken you up!" Su exclaimed.

"Let me see you!" Aoife yelled, standing up abruptly, almost spilling the wine from her glass. She stepped across the room dodging everyone's legs until she reached me, took my hand, and twirled me around, examining me. She ended the greeting with a not-so-subtle pinch to my cheek. "Yeah, as I suspected. Ravenous sex has done you good! You look healthier!"

Laughter instantly filled the room and even though I felt somewhat embarrassed, I didn't deny anything. I did give Su a pointed look for ratting me out, but she just winked and raised her glass.

As the laughter died down, Su scootched over on the couch so I could sit between her and Vi. Aoife was still standing, waving her glass about as she said, "*Well*? Tell us all about it!" She broke into a wide, cheeky smile. "At least for the ones here not having it," she said, gesturing at everyone in the room but herself. That was her way of saying that we shouldn't think for a second about putting her in that category.

"Who says *I'm* not having it?!" Violet countered loudly, making sure we didn't forget that she had been in a steady relationship for over a year now – and they were moving in together soon. Aoife scoffed with a level of drama only she could pull off.

"Well, are you having wild, passionate sex again and again in places other than your bedroom?" Aoife put to her.

"Not so much outside the bedroom. But . . ."

I shot a withering look at Su as their exchange continued. *"Sorry,"* she mouthed. Claire leaned over the coffee table and handed me a glass of red.

"You're going to need it." She said sincerely, "Great to have you back."

"Thanks," I replied, suddenly feeling a little choked up. I stood up and hugged her over the platter of cheese between us. "I'm just going to make a call and I'll join you." Claire nodded.

As I walked away, Aoife was recounting her passionate relationships over the years. "Don't tell us too much, we might think you are older than you are!" I overheard Violet say as laughter erupted in the room. That must have hit a nerve.

I smiled as I walked out of the room. *These past few weeks made me almost forget how blessed I am to have these amazing friends*. The phone only rang twice before Brian answered. "Hey, you," he said in his sweet, playful voice.

"Hey, you too . . . sorry I missed your calls."

"Forgot about me already, have you?" he teased.

I chuckled and for a little while, we got into a flow of conversation as if we were sitting together on the couch in his apartment, until, that is, I really had to go back to my friends.

To my relief, the conversation had well and truly moved on from Aoife's 'relationships' history when I returned. We stayed up until the early hours of the morning, chatting, and played a tipsy version of charades. Well, everyone except Claire. She fell asleep not long after midnight, after the biggest bombshell of the night was revealed, and it had nothing to do with my family, the trip to Colchester, or Brian. It was Claire's news.

Maybe we should have noticed earlier in the evening, but it wasn't a thought that would have crossed my – or anyone's – mind. Of course, the lack of a known partner made us less inclined to think anything when she didn't touch a drop of wine. Claire had only just found out and we were sworn to secrecy. It was exciting. She was the first in our group that was going to be a mum. As we all enjoyed our classic get-together, I sensed a change in the air.

#

The morning brought me a hangover and with it, some regret, but that didn't stop me from wanting to achieve my goal for today. After my hearty hangover-curing meal and some meds, I was ready to rock and roll. Or so I told myself, until I looked in the mirror with a frown.

The dark circles under my eyes were larger than I imagined, and the messy hair look wasn't deliberate. A bit of foundation, mascara, lip gloss, and a purposely messy updo later, I could finally give a nod of acceptance to my reflection, as if to say, *good enough.*

I gathered my things and left my room, ready for church. I really hoped Margret would be there.

As she is a devoted churchgoer, I knew this was the most likely place to find her on a Sunday morning.

Su had risen and was eating the leftover hangover meal straight out of the pan. "Where you off to?" she asked with her mouth full.

"I'm going to see Margret," I replied with a brief wrinkle of my nose in distaste. "How about you?"

"Nothing much," she said while taking another spoonful. "That's how you're going out?" Her eyes zoned in on my lower half and I looked down.

"Uh, no. Of course not!" I replied, as if it was a ridiculous question, making it seem like I was very much aware I was still in my pyjama bottoms. Su laughed, knowing.

#

People walked out from the Sunday service in a quiet chatter before dispersing into groups. Ladies were catching up on the weekly gossip while protecting their fussy hairdos from the wind. Young children that had been itching to play after what probably felt like ages of sitting down were clearing away from distracted parents, and men gathered together for a masculine chat.

It wasn't long before I spotted Margret. She always had this slightly eccentric fashion sense that wouldn't go unnoticed. A conservative outfit with funky shoes on show on one day, a simple monotone A-line dress matched with unusual, colourful jewellery and a bold headpiece on another. That was her. And today was no different as she flaunted her long, full, black skirt with an abundance of pink tulle which peeked out from under the hem with each strut, and strut she did. It was complemented by some pink tulle in a unique headpiece she wore with a sleek updo.

Margret was a vibrant woman who didn't let her age define her. She was a good ten years older than my mum was, and always seemed to embrace her changing appearance with grace. Aoife could learn a thing or two from her. Elderly gentlemen's eyes would stray from their wives as she walked past, always for a touch longer than their spouse would be comfortable with. But she was a harmless, caring person. "Just a bit of fun," she would say to my mum.

She never had children, and yet she would be any child's favourite nanny to have. Like a Mrs Doubtfire. Growing up, particularly during my teenage years, I called upon her on the few occasions when Mum and I didn't see eye-to-eye on something. Even though now I could see Margret always chose Mum's side, she would spin it like a win-win.

During-my adult life, we didn't see as much of each other. Only when she hung out with Mum while I was there, and of course, when she would visit the shop. Now that I was thinking about it, I suppose she was a bit like an aunty growing up.

"Margret!" I called out, waving my hand in the air, as she had walked over to the other side of a sea of people. Obscured by the crowd, only her headpiece gave her away. Reaching my hand a bit higher as I called her name again, I made my way to her. A few people moved aside and once in view, I saw she was standing beside a pregnant lady and to my shock and horror, Gordon stood next to her.

In that instant, I knew the pregnant lady was Monica. I awkwardly dropped my hand in dismay. It was too late to back away, I had been spotted. I *knew* I would bump into them one day. We lived in a village, after all. But never in my life would I have expected it to be here and now, at a church of all places. Gordon never went to church! "It's not my thing," he had said. But there they stood, speaking with *Margret* of all people.

The three of them were staring at me now and I had to make a fast decision – make the best of this moment and not make it even more awkward than it already felt, or skulk away.

I walked over, all the while wishing I had made a bit more of an effort with my looks. Then again, my confidence would shine through. *Yeah, right.* I tried to keep my gaze focused on Margret as I crossed the courtyard.

"Hi, Margret." I embraced her with open arms.

"So good to see you! What are you doing here?" she asked with her eyebrows raised in surprise once we let go.

"Looking for you," I replied, beaming past my discomfort. I could *feel* Gordon and Monica still standing there, close by. I prayed they would leave. Not a chance.

Reluctantly, I turned to face them. *I might as well.* "Hi, Gordon. Monica," I said quite formally. Gordon looked uneasy and mustered a, "Hi, how are you?" Monica took hold of his hand rather childishly, as if to say *he's mine now*. I resisted the urge to roll my eyes. It was an uncomfortable encounter, but at the same time, he just didn't matter anymore. "I'm grand. Here to see Margret." I pointedly turned away from them toward her.

"Are you free?" I asked.

"Absolutely." She looked pleasantly surprised.

"Great, how about we go for a bite?"

"Let's go!" She linked her arm in mine, ready to trot off.

"Good luck to you both."

Gordon managed a rather meek thank you. Monica said nothing, but her uncomfortable smile said enough.

While I walked away with Margret, I couldn't help but yell, "Hope you don't miss the pink slippers!" I didn't look back to see their expressions. I knew it was a cheap shot, but it was out of my mouth before I could think it through. Seeing them was unsettling, but there was no love lost. It's like Oprah Winfrey said, "Forgiveness is giving up the hope that the past could have been any different." I had given up that hope and looked to the future now. We didn't need to make amends for me to do so.

"To what do I owe the pleasure?" Margret inquired once we were out of earshot. I stopped in my tracks and looked her in the face, her pale-green eyes staring back at me, almost concerned.

"I wanted to ask you some questions about Mum."

"Sounds serious." I nodded in response. "Okay, let's go for that bite and we'll talk."

As we made our way, I started telling her a bit about Colchester, the inheritance, the people I met, and Brian, of course. Leaving out the part about Lizzy. She was quiet as I spoke, giving the occasional hum, so I knew she was listening.

"That's a lot of news," she said after a while. I couldn't read if she was aware of any of it. After a moment of silence, I shifted the conversation to the more mundane things in life, and we eventually decided to go to her place.

When we finally sat down with a cuppa, sandwiches, and some sweet treats, she inquired about what I wanted to ask her. Of course, I wanted to ask about my father, but I'd started to reflect on her reaction so far, or more so, the lack of it. She didn't seem surprised enough with what I told her. Her silence said something, I just didn't know what.

"Were you aware of anything I just told you?" I asked tentatively as I studied her face and body language, as a detective would. With a big sigh, she removed her glasses.

"Liz, your mother was planning to tell you this, but never got the chance." She took a deep breath. "I wasn't sure if I should . . ." She sighed again, even heavier. "If I should say anything, since she took it with her to the grave." She looked down at the tea in her mug, swirling it around.

"I want to – I *need* to know, Margret," I insisted after she made no move to start speaking again.

"You meant the world to her," she said gravely.

"I know, and she to me!"

"Well, Heather . . . your mum, divulged that when she got pregnant with you, she hid it from her mother as long as she could." She took a slow, nervous sip of her tea and placed it back onto the coaster. "One day, she became very unwell and had to go into hospital, which is when her mother, your grandmother, found out about the pregnancy."

Margret paused, tracing circles with her index finger on the rim of her mug, still not looking up. "You were eventually born by emergency C-section, and it was touch and go, Liz." She lifted her head briefly, her lips trembling. I reached out my hand to touch her arm.

"I know this is hard, but please continue," I pleaded. She gave a reluctant nod before doing so.

". . . Your mum fought hard to keep you and decided to raise you alone. She told me a story that one morning when she woke up, there was an envelope left for her with money inside and tickets to Ireland. She knew what it was for and started her new life here with you."

Margret placed her glasses back on and looked straight at me, her green eyes piercing, as if to say *that's it.* I stayed quiet, taking it all in. And she filled the silence. "You see, Liz, it was easier for her to tell you that your grandmother had died than for her to deal with the truth."

It was my turn to sigh heavily. I took a sip from my untouched cup. My face twitched, as I'd forgotten to add sugar. "That is a long time to keep a secret!" I said, struggling to understand why she hadn't shared this decades ago.

"She struggled with the lie, and wished she had a relationship with her mother." Margret shook her head. "The situation weighed heavily on her, Liz, but she planned on telling you. She even hoped to rekindle with her mother," she quickly added.

"Did she know she was having twins?" I blurted out without forethought. Her eyes widened, pushing up her eyebrows, and then furrowed.

"Twins?" Margret whispered, pale-faced. "W-What do you mean?"

"I *had* a twin sister called Lizzy, and she lived with my grandmother," I added matter-of-factly.

"You had a sister?" Margret gulped.

"Yes! She – *Lizzy* – died when she was four."

Margret was very quiet for some time. "I . . . I didn't know about that, Elizabeth. Heather never mentioned you had a sister."

She must have told someone. I felt hope draining away from my face and I couldn't let that happen. "Did she ever mention *anything*? What about my father? Did she tell you who he is? Do you *know* who he is?" I couldn't keep it in anymore.

I waited for her to look back up at me. Margret shakily unwrapped the chocolate biscuit and took a bite, chewing longer than necessary. After a lengthy pause, she tilted her head slowly to face me. The colour in her cheeks had drained even more; she looked sick.

"I certainly wasn't expecting this today." Margret popped the remainder of her biscuit into her mouth, followed by a gulp of tea. I gave a tight-lipped smile, but I wasn't going to let up. She must have noticed as she, with some reluctance, began speaking again.

"Heather sometimes spoke about your father nostalgically, before everything changed." Margret took a breath. "From what she told me, they had a whirlwind romance. He was her first real boyfriend, her first love, and she never stopped wondering about him over the decades. Where he may be now, and if he ever thought of her – thought of you both. But there was also an immense pain and anger there."

"Mum told me he left her when she got pregnant," I said with urgency, hoping it wasn't another lie.

"I think it was more complicated than that, Liz." Margaret's tone was soft in a way that would have once soothed me. "It was probably the easiest explanation at the time. Your mother told me your father was a few years older than her and your grandmother disapproved of his age, and the relationship."

"Did she ever say anything that could help me find him? I know his name is Oscar. But that is all I know!"

Margret looked somewhat uneasy. "Are you sure you want to find him, Liz?"

"I do," I said aloud, surprising myself. *Do I really? Am I ready for this?* As panic rose within, she pushed on.

"Your mum told me dribs and drabs about him over the years. He did get in contact with her, once . . ." she mumbled reluctantly.

"Really! When? How?" I perked up eagerly.

Sensing my interest wouldn't disappear anytime soon, Margret shook her head and continued. "It must be about maybe three or four years ago now, he wrote her a letter –"

"Did she say anything about what was in it? Or why he sent it?"

Margret sighed deeply. "Listen, Liz, your mother shared these things in confidence. I know she isn't here anymore to ask, but if she wanted you to know . . ." She trailed off, eyes fixed on her hands. "All I'm saying is, she had her reason why . . . and I'm not sure I should."

"I am not a child, Margret. Whatever it is, I can handle it," I insisted, knowing that if I was a child, I would have my fingers crossed behind my back. Was I ready to handle more? And without Brian and my other confidants nearby? Of course, here I had my group of friends. Yet after the past two weeks, it felt instinctively natural to think about them first for this instance.

Hesitantly, Margret got up and left the room. Moments later, she returned holding a neatly kept cream-coloured envelope.

"I don't know what is in here," she said, clutching it with both hands. "Your mother asked me to hold onto it. I never asked her why. I only know it is from your father, addressed to your mother." She swallowed audibly. "I want you to think very hard about whether you want to read this," she said, her tone serious as she handed it to me without letting go. "It could be opening Pandora's box," she added, as if worried she hadn't made her point clear enough.

When Margret finally let go, I could see that the envelope had been opened. *So, Mum read it.*

A moment of hesitation crept in, but ultimately, I just wanted to know. Whatever it was, good or bad. "It's always better to know the truth," I quoted

Andrew and thanked Margret, who seemed doubtful she had done the right thing. I placed the envelope next to me on the table, tapping my fingers on it in a nervous rhythm.

"Would you like anything else?" Margret asked, nodding towards the food.

"No thanks. I think I will be heading off soon."

About ten minutes and a heartfelt goodbye later, I was on my way back home accompanied by the envelope. Once home, I sat down on the bed, crossed-legged, hugging a pillow as I studied the handwriting. My mother's name and address were written in cursive writing with unusually large, long loops in the lettering. Aesthetically, it looked nice. However, it was not the easiest to read. It also had a return address to Colchester, something I had noticed already at Margret's. Which meant he was still there when he wrote this.

The thought that I might have seen him while I was there without knowing felt surreal. Of course, highly improbable with a population of 170,000-plus. A detail I looked up before my trip. It was crazy how I'd gone from no thought or desire to know anything about my father for decades to now, eager to know.

I took a sip from my camomile tea, purposely chosen, hoping for its calming properties, inhaled deeply, and opened the envelope to reveal the letter inside.

Dear Heather,

I have thought about writing this letter many times over, never knowing, finding the right words, and now so much time has passed. Making every word too late, but here it is anyway.

I want you to know how truly sorry I am and how awful I have felt over the years and decades for not showing up that day. I know you counted on me, and I let you down. I let you both down!

You should know it has left me with a feeling of everlasting regret, and I have often asked myself, "What if?" I did buy the ticket, Heather, and had the intention of going with you and Elizabeth to start a new life.

The embarrassing truth is, I was afraid. Afraid to give up on my carefree life, especially after talking with a mate. I am sure you can guess who. I thought that telling you what I did on our last phone call would make it easier for you to forget about me, and in some twisted sense, I believed it was the right thing to say. I am so deeply sorry for hurting you so much that day. I know I acted immaturely and selfishly, and can only imagine the hurt you've gone through.

I've spoken with Hilda on a few occasions, who, at first, didn't want to see me. I thought that after such a long time, things would be different between you two, until she told me that you had virtually no contact over all these years. I was shocked and saddened to hear this, as I had hoped you would have reconciled.

Heather, I can't make up for the past, and I can understand an apology will not mean much now. But I want you to know that I am really, truly sorry for all the hurt I have caused and my absence!

It's my hope that you and Elizabeth have a good life and you're happy and doing well.

I know that I am in no position to ask for anything, but if you could find it within yourself to reach out one day, I would love to hear from you.

Oscar Brown

P.S. Your mother gave me this photograph and was insistent I pass it on to you if I were to write. I made a copy for myself.

"Oscar Brown," I said. *Your full name*. I looked back inside the envelope for the photograph, but there was none. All I could think of was to ring Margret and before I caught up with myself, I was already dialling. She picked up after just two rings. "Are you okay, Liz?" Margret answered, her voice wobbly.

"Yes, yes, *yes*." I took a steadying breath. "I am. I was just wondering if Mum mentioned anything about a photograph with the letter."

"Uhhh . . ." She cleared her throat. "No, not that I remember."

“Oh, okay.” Trying not to sound disappointed, I thanked her again for giving me the letter, reassuring her she did the right thing.

I read over it several times, and with each read, was able to connect a few dots. It made me feel sorry for my mum, she must have been so hurt and alone at the time. Reading his words, I didn’t know how I felt about him or what to think of him, and with a shudder, copied the address under the B section in my address book, planning to reach out. His letter didn’t mention about my sister; I wondered if he even knew. *Then again, how could he not?*

#

I waited till Su was home to tell her about what I learned and showed her the letter. After which, she started searching online for him. “The next logical thing to do!” she said, looking at me like, *duh!*

“My brain is fried,” I said in an exaggerated sad voice, which went unnoticed. I was merely hushed to let her do her thing.

“Brown is a very popular surname,” Su muttered as many profiles came up. But as luck would have it, he still lived at the same address, according to the directory. Finding this out, all in one day, from reading his letter to the 13-digit landline number that glared at me through the screen – it was all very fast. My confidence was swaying as nerves took over and my hands trembled.

"I am right here with you," Su said supportively. I thought of the Pandora's box reference Margret made, which led me here. I held my phone in my now clammy hands and dialled the number as Su called it out. It rang out several times and then a sudden, "Hello?" was yelled, above the loud music playing.

I looked to Su, who gestured frantically for me to say something. *I can't do this.*

"Hello?" he said again, this time with a hint of agitation in his voice. The music turned down.

"Yes, hi. Are . . . are you Oscar Brown?" I said in the strongest voice I could muster. My heartbeat was doing overtime.

"That's me. Who is this?" he said, sounding slightly rushed.

"Elizabeth Hayden . . . your daughter," I said so nervously, unsure if my voice was loud enough for him to hear. The phone got quiet on the other end, the music now fully switched off. All I heard was shallow breathing, as if he had been exercising.

"Are you still there?" My voice was trembling.

"Yes, yes," he replied, and went silent.

I looked to Su for help, who shrugged her shoulders.

"I read the letter you wrote to my mother," I said, hoping that would start a conversation.

"I – I am so sorry for your loss." He sounded sincere in his Essex accent, which my mother had lost over the decades.

"Thank you." *So, he knew.*

"How . . . are you?" *How am I?* I wasn't sure how I was feeling right now. "Are you all right?" came his insistent voice from the other side of the line.

"Yeah, not too bad." I went with the standard response, unable to say anything else without my life's story attached to it.

"That's good to hear," he sighed. "Why did you call?" he asked after another moment of awkward silence. All the while, Su was encouraging me to speak up, waving her hands in a moving-along motion. Mouthing, *"Ask him?"*

Taking the deepest breath and drawing from all my inner strength, I found my confidence.

"I want to know what happened between you and my mum from the moment she told you she was pregnant," I blurted almost sternly, and exhaled.

"Wow," Su mouthed. I shocked myself too.

"Oh – okay. Er . . ." He cleared his throat and there was a long pause. "Since you read my letter, you know some details . . . Well –" He choked over his words once again. "Er. Your mother and I dated for about five months. In secret, that is. Your grandmother was not in favour of our relationship. And when we found out she was pregnant, she hid the pregnancy for as long as possible. I . . . I wasn't there for the delivery." He skipped to the end. "There were complications, so when she was finally allowed to leave the hospital, that was the first time I saw you."

"Where did she go after leaving the hospital?"

"She stayed with someone. And then . . . well, I suppose you know."

"We came to Ireland and you didn't," I replied in a neutral tone.

He confirmed with an agreeing, "Mm-hm."

"Who did she stay with?"

"Er, she stayed with an older guy named . . . William, I think. Yes –that was it, William. I was surprised she had found somewhere to go, because a few days before she was discharged from hospital, she cried on the phone saying she had nowhere to go. I remember that phone call well," he finished sombrely.

"William?" I snapped my head up to look at Su, mouthing, *"Willie!"* to her.

"Yes. She wasn't there for very long. I . . . visited you there."

"How did she know this, William?"

"Oh, this is all such a long time ago, Elizabeth. I – I can't believe I am talking to you." I held my breath. He sounded overwhelmed, his tone humbled. "William . . . he was a family acquaintance, I think. But your mother hadn't mentioned him before that time."

"So you visited us there?" I reiterated.

"Yes. Those were the few times I saw you and held you. I still have a photograph that your mother took of me holding you. It is very precious to me." He paused, clearing his throat. "I have just one other photograph of you when you're around four, maybe five," Oscar said desolately. I pressed on, not leaving room for emotions.

"In the letter to my mother, you said that you added a photograph?"

"Yes, that's the one. I made a copy of it. Hilda gave it to me."

"Ah. It wasn't with the letter anymore . . . can you tell me about it?"

"Uh-huh, sure. Let me get it." There was a faint 'click' as Oscar put down the phone. I covered the speaker with my palm and sighed. Su gave a close-lipped smile as she patted my hand.

"Hi, I'm back. Well, you're wearing a blue dress with white flowers on it and a white sunhat," he said some minutes later.

"Anything else? Where am I? What are my surroundings?" I looked wide-eyed at Su, who furrowed her brows, puzzled.

"Well, umm," he started off awkwardly. "You're sitting on a swing in your grandmother's garden. I know it because I pushed your mother on that swing before. You see, late at night she would sneak out and meet me there. It was the perfect spot, as it couldn't be seen from the windows in the house." Oscar gave a little chuckle as he reminisced.

"Why do you think she gave you that photograph?" I asked, unmoved. Su's mouth formed a silent "oh" as a lightbulb switched on in her mind.

"I don't know, Elizabeth. Why are you asking?" His tone was confused.

"Just wondering," I said shortly, giving nothing away.

"I did find it somewhat surprising, because Hilda told me that she and your mother still weren't on good terms. But maybe, for a period, that must have been different," he finished thoughtfully.

As he spoke, I knew for certain he didn't know about my twin sister. He believed it was me in the photograph. It made me wonder how and when Mum found out. Had she known all along? Then again, how could she not . . .

"Are you still there?" Oscar asked nervously.

"Yes, yes. I am."

"Look, Elizabeth, I know you have lots of questions," he said after a moment. "I-I'm feeling rather overwhelmed right now and, er, I have people coming over any minute. Would it be all right if I ring you . . . maybe tomorrow? I'm *really* happy you reached out to me," he added quickly.

"Sure."

I gave him my number and we agreed on a time he would call. When I hung up, Su was already vibrating with curiosity.

"Well?" she asked.

"Well, what?"

"How do you feel? You just spoke with your father for the first time!" Her hands jolted, reaching across the table.

"He doesn't know about Lizzy," I said, flat-line.

"Elizabeth! You just spoke with your father who you haven't known your entire life. How. Do. You. *Feel*?"

I glanced at Su, who was very serious. She was right. I'd just spoken with my father. It hadn't sunk in yet. "How was I?" I asked her, not knowing.

Su didn't hold back, throwing her hands up in exasperation. "You interrogated the guy!"

"I did?" I replied vacantly, staring at the phone in my hand, recalling some of the conversation. "Oh, God, I did," I said, feeling distressed, and it was at that moment I felt myself getting emotional. "I spoke with *my father*!" Tears pricked my eyes, and soon they were rolling down my cheeks. Su stood up and held her arms out to come in for a hug. I lay my head on her shoulder as she held me in an embrace.

"Maybe he thinks *you* don't know," Su said in a low voice.

"What?"

Chapter 10

It was well into the early hours of the morning before exhaustion forced some calm within. The day had been such an emotional one. Contemplating my family, figuring out the puzzle that had become my life, held me in the arms of an emotional adrenalin spike with a whirlwind of thoughts.

I was certain Hilda and Willie were in cahoots. Su, who had fallen asleep several hours before, laughed at me for using the word *cahoots* – but agreed it appeared that way. And if they were, it was likely that one of them would have left the money and tickets to Ireland for my mum. But *why*? Why did Hilda and Willie want her to leave? Did it have something to do with Lizzy?

Why was she left behind? And how come my mum hadn't even told Margret? Isn't that something you would tell a best friend? Or was it such a big secret it would never have left her lips, best friend or not?

I wondered where she would have kept the photograph. I'd packed up everything from Mum's house before the sale and found nothing that would have alluded to the fact that I had a sister. Then again, a photograph could be hidden in plain sight, I would just have presumed it was me.

Thoughts of the tower room and the shrine in the basement surfaced again too. It made me feel uneasy. That was where *she* lived. Every time I came closer to having an answer in all this – whatever all this was – other questions came up.

I was wrecked when my alarm roused me from my sleep, the photo albums I'd taken out scattered around. Su, who also slept in the living room, didn't look much better than I felt. "I rang Adrianna, she will open the shop. See you at noon," she mumbled, making her way to her room wrapped in a fleece blanket.

"Thanks!" I shouted after she shut her door. I picked up the albums and contemplated looking through them again, but couldn't muster the energy, and retreated to my bed.

#

With my first step in the door, I breathed deeply. Oh, how I missed it! The floral scent was enticing, and the sight sparked my inspiration for endless creation.

"Elizabeth!" Adrianna skipped over with welcoming arms, going for a big hug.

"Hi," I smiled, looking around once she let go. "The shop looks great!" My eyes were drawn to the hand-painted ceramic vases Su commissioned from a local artist. They were beautifully displayed in the middle of the shop.

"What do you think?" Adrianna beamed, pleased with herself.

"Gorgeous. Just gorgeous."

Her smile grew even wider. "Well, I'll be off," she said some minutes later, and with the same skip in her step, she left the shop.

I spent many happy hours that afternoon with the flowers, making orders, and one of my favourites – helping customers with their special requests. Su was mainly at the desk doing the paperwork. It was a wonderful distraction from everything. Being back at Ms Bouquet reminded me of how fortunate I was to be able to do the job I love.

For me, a bouquet is never just a bunch of flowers put together. They are an arrangement of harmony that brings to life a sentiment, a story, a gift for a person, and days of pleasure.

"Are you ready to go?" I asked once finished.

"Almost!" Su shouted from the office. "What time is your dad – er, father calling again?"

"*Dad*," I said to myself. It sounded so strange. A word that hadn't come from my mouth my entire life had suddenly become part of my conversation and vocabulary.

"Eight o'clock!" I tried not to think about the call too much, and I was undecided if I wanted to bring up Lizzy.

"Okay. I'll lock the back."

Minutes later, we were on our way home. It was lashing rain and miserable. The lovely warmth I experienced in Colchester had become a distant memory already, and I couldn't wait to get inside our apartment and take a hot, steamy shower.

As I rubbed jojoba body oil on my skin afterwards, my longing was for Brian, for his hands to give me a relaxing shoulder massage. I didn't get fully dressed straight away. Instead, I lay in my bed, set an alarm for 15 minutes, and closed my eyes for a bit. Not sleeping – just daydreaming and calming my mind.

From our call earlier, I knew Brian had some friends over; otherwise, I would have rung him. I imagined the warmth of his hands and embrace, and channelled the safety I felt with him and words he might have spoken to comfort me.

How things have changed. Not long ago, I would have closed my eyes and envisioned my mum, her comforting embrace, encouraging words when difficulty struck. Now, when I tried to call on her for guidance, all that came to me were questions.

My alarm rang, which had become a harmonious tune since I changed it that night we set

Gordon on fire, so to speak. It felt like only a few minutes had passed. It wasn't long before *the call.*

Quickly dressed in comfy sweats, I was off to the kitchen to make a soothing camomile tea again. To my surprise, Su wasn't in the kitchen or in the living room watching TV. But when I peeked in her room, I found her fast asleep. She'd said she would be there for the call, but I couldn't in good conscience wake her up. She had done so much already.

I waited with my phone on the dining table and warmed my hands on the mug of tea, inhaling the scent to calm my nerves. As 20:00 showed up on my phone, my heart skipped a beat and I stared at it, waiting for the ringtone. By 20:06 I was still waiting, and anything but calm. You would think this isn't the kind of call to be late for.

By 20:12, my tea half finished, I was well and truly getting worked up. By 20:17, I was about to give up on him when my phone rang displaying his number. I let it ring several times before answering and couldn't mask the annoyance in my hello.

"Hi, Elizabeth. It's Oscar, your, your . . . *father*," he added in a slow and unsure voice. "How are you?" There it was again, that difficult question to answer.

"I don't know, to be honest. How are you?" I returned as calmly as I could.

"I'm good. Happy. I'm happy you got in touch," he said with some glee in a pitch higher. Silence fell on the line for some moments.

"Yeah, me too," I finally replied, straining to sound sincere, but feeling unsure.

"I . . ." Oscar took a deep, shaky breath. "I was so shocked to hear about your mother. I am so very sorry."

I let out a heavy sigh and wondered, "How *did* you actually hear about it?"

"What do you mean?" he replied, equally confused.

"How did you find out my mother died?"

"Er – I got a call from a woman one evening. She told me the news," he said vaguely.

"From whom?" I blurted.

"She didn't say her name, I think. She just said she was a good friend of your mother's."

"No name? And she knew how to get in touch with you?"

"No, not that I remember. I don't . . . why are you asking?"

I took a slow, calming breath to allow myself a moment to think. "Just wondering. That's all," I finally said in the most nonchalant tone I could muster.

"Are you sure that's all?" His voice was kind, and I cleared my throat.

"It's just that I learned a few things recently, which has made me question some things, and I just wondered who contacted you," I said, also keeping it vague.

"What have you been told about me?" he asked with apprehension in his voice.

"Nothing much, really, just that you left when Mum got pregnant. End of story."

"Oh well, okay. All right." He took a deep breath. "The story is longer than that. Would you like me to tell you?"

"Sure. I would like that." I took a sip from the cold tea and listened as he started telling me what happened those many years ago, and the guilt he carried around. It was much of what I read in the letter, with his sincere remorse and regret conveyed more profoundly than his written words on the paper could ever explain.

"I don't know what you're looking for in terms of a relationship, but I would really like if we could have one and get to know each other better," he finished hopefully, after talking at length about him and Mum. I was taken aback. I hadn't contemplated what I wanted out of this other than some answers.

"Sure, okay," I replied after a short pause, unsure of what else to say.

"That's great! Really, really great. I am so happy to hear that." His enthusiasm radiated through the phone.

"Mm-hm, me too," I said with a soft smile, warming to him.

"You look so much like her, you know."

"As a baby?"

"Yes, well." He went quiet for a while. "No. I . . . I saw you some weeks ago."

"What?" I tightened my grip on the phone.

"Ahem . . . you – you see, I went to visit your mother's grave to pay my respects, and, and well, you were there. I recognised you immediately. Elizabeth, you look so much like your mother . . . you were there with another person," he added as I tried to rejig my memory.

"Wait – were . . . were you the person that left the white rose with the card?"

"Mm-hm," he quietly confirmed.

"I completely forgot about that day. You were crying at my mother's grave. Why . . . why did you walk away?" I asked, shocked it was him.

"I didn't want to make your life any harder, Elizabeth. I always believed if you wanted to find me, you would."

I thought about it for a moment. *Would I have if not for all this?*

"How did you know where she is buried?"

"I asked the woman on the phone."

"What did she sound like?" I hankered to know.

"Uh. Um . . . I really can't remember. Sorry. The phone call was such a shock."

"How did you know she liked white roses?!" As soon as the question left my lips, I remembered what Su had said about me interrogating him. "I'm sorry, I just have a lot of questions," I quickly added.

"No, no, that's all right. I understand that. Let me tell you how we met."

"Okay." I leaned back in my chair.

"Well, it was a rainy day. Not just any rain, it was pouring down. Your mother ran into the shop where I had a weekend job at the time and bumped straight into me." He let out a little chuckle, reminiscing. "I was holding a bucket with bunches of flowers, which fell all over the ground. She was so apologetic and helped me pick them up. We had this moment, this movie moment, where we stood and *saw* each other – *oh,* I can still see her face." His voice sounded thick, and he paused for a few seconds.

"Her fringe was dripping all over her face, but when our eyes met . . . they were mesmerising. She was so pretty. Your mother was so pretty. Uh," he sighed.

"Anyway, she was so flustered, and I was taken by her. I gave her a flower from one of the bunches, a white rose. And that is how it all started, from that day." He cleared his throat. "That's why I got her a white rose."

"You know, they have been her favourite flower for as long as I can remember."

"*Really*?"

"Yeah." My eyes welled up a bit as I answered him, and it went quiet. "Oscar? . . . Dad?" I called out, unsure and quietly to him for the first time. I had not thought of calling him that before, but at that moment, I felt a connection to him. A few tears rolled down my face.

"Yes, Elizabeth?"

"Do you know anything about . . ." *Lizzy* was on the tip of my tongue. I wanted to ask him, yet something held me back.

"About what? Elizabeth?"

"Uh, nothing. Sorry, I should go. I . . . still have a few things to do for work," I lied.

"Right, yeah, of course, sure, sure. Where do you work?" He sounded a little deflated.

"I own a floral boutique, Ms Bouquet, with my best friend."

"Ms Bouquet . . . Ms Bouquet, you said?" he muttered as if in deep thought. "Wait, is that in the village near where your mother is buried?"

"Yes, it is. You know it?!"

"I think that's the shop where I bought the rose for your mother. A friendly young lady helped me," he said slowly as he recalled her. "She had long, curly, reddish hair, I believe. Is she your friend?"

"That's Adrianna, our employee. I can't believe you were in my shop! If it was another time, I might actually have met you," I gasped.

"I can't believe it either. A love for flowers must run in the family," he said almost breathless with delight.

"What do you mean?"

"Well, I don't know a lot about your grandmother, but she loves plants and flowers, and her garden is something else . . . Have you seen her since the funeral?"

"Er, sorry?" I straightened up in my chair like a meerkat on lookout.

"She *was* at your mother's funeral?"

He doesn't know. I sighed with a heavy heart. "Uhm, well, actually . . ." I trailed off, unsure how to break the news.

"Are you all right? I'm sorry if I said something wrong," he said, noticing my discomfort.

"Uh, no, not at all, you didn't. It's just that, well – you see, my mum told me that my grandmother died when she was sixteen years old."

"Died?!"

"Mm-hm . . . and I only recently found out that that was not the case, but she did pass away about a month and a half ago. I actually never met her. She . . . had a heart attack. And I don't think she knew Mum passed away." My vision went blurry from a few fresh tears. I gently wiped them away.

"I don't know what to say – I'm so sorry to hear that," he mustered after a long pause, sounding stunned.

"Yeah. Me too. Uh, anyway, I really must go." It all felt a bit too overwhelming at this point.

"Yes, yes, of course. Can I call back another time?"

"Sure. I would like that." *I really would.*

"Are you sure you're all right?"

"Yes, thank you." I tried to sound reassuring. "I, I just have to go. Bye-bye."

"Bye, Elizabeth."

After hanging up, I rubbed my eyes, then worked my way to my temples with a simultaneous circling motion to relieve the tension. Some minutes later after some slow, purposeful breathing, I picked the phone back up and rang Brian. *I could do with a good distraction.*

"Hey, you!" he answered happily after only two rings.

"Hi, how are you?" I asked, flatter than intended.

"Better than you, I think. Judging from the sound of your voice."

"Oh, I'm okay. Just feeling rather overwhelmed. I just spoke with Oscar . . . my – dad. It was going to take some time to get used to calling him that.

"Yes, of course. How did that go? Easier than yesterday?"

"Uh, yes. Well . . . it's just all a bit much." I shared the highlights of the conversation. "But I don't want to talk about it anymore right now. Let's talk about you."

"Okay. But might it be best just to ask him about Lizzy?" he said with caution. "It's better to know, Liz – and for him, too, if he doesn't. And he would probably be confused if he doesn't."

"How so?"

"You just told him you never met your grandmother, but the picture he has, the one he believes is you, is in her garden. Right?"

"Oh God. I didn't even think of that. It's all so messed up," I sighed.

"You can make it less so. For the both of you."

After a long pause, I hummed in agreement.

"Now, how about you?" I repeated. "How are you?"

"Good. I had a busy day, but a good one. You remember that potential new client I was hoping to take on? The one with the advertisement style and ethos that's so right up my street?" he said with enthusiasm.

"Hm, the one you couldn't tell me the name of?"

"Yes, well, I closed the deal today," he chuckled, delighted with himself.

"That's fantastic! Congrats!" I cheered. "So . . . who is it?"

"That is still confidential," Brian said unwaveringly.

"Seriously?"

"Yes," he laughed.

"Right, I won't ask again."

"I miss you, Liz."

"Miss you too."

"You have any plans this evening?"

"No, Susan is asleep already, and I think I'm going to put on my comfy PJs and do the same soon."

"How about you put on something nice instead?" Brian said, putting on his flirty voice.

"Seriously?" I giggled.

"I am very serious."

"Okay, sure, I can do that." I let out a little chuckle.

"Good. I'll call you back in five minutes," he promised, his voice eager, and he hung up.

#

I woke up smiling to myself as I stretched out my arms and went for a hot shower. Just as he had told me to do before we ended our call last night. I couldn't keep the grin off my face as I washed my body, recalling the intimacy, despite the physical distance between us.

Invigorated, I decided to dress a bit more put-together than I usually would for work, wearing some dangle earrings, a lipstick colour other than nude, a V-neck top that flattered every asset in a classy way over a tightly fitted jean and low-heeled black boots. Comfortable, yet stylish. I took a selfie and sent it to Brian alongside the caption: *Ready for work X*

My phone buzzed soon after with: *Me too. You look good!* I felt flattered. Seconds later, another buzz. It was a picture of him still in bed, smiling.

Jealous ;) I replied, which was quickly followed up with: *Have a good day Liz X.*

You too, Smooth :) I chuckled softly to myself. He rang a moment later.

"Smooth?" he repeated with a laugh as I answered the phone.

"I believe after last night, your infamous nickname can be nothing but that anymore."

"Ah, you liked it that much, huh?" he replied, cocky.

"I did." Heat rose to my cheeks, but thankfully, no one could see.

"How much?" he asked, eager for me to elaborate. I chuckled. "I bet you're blushing right now."

"Wouldn't you love to know," I said less confidently than I would have liked.

"I love it when you get all flustered."

I smiled, feeling even more so. "I've really got to get going," I said after some more banter.

"I know. Bye, Liz."

"Bye, Smooth."

#

It was another gloomy day for the month of July, only drier. The shop was relatively quiet in the morning and when the excitement from the night before had worn off, my focus went to Oscar.

I went through scenarios in my mind, knowing very well that it was futile unless I actually asked about Lizzy. Remembering Brian's words helped me to decide and gain the courage. This evening after work, I was going to ring and put the question to him, I affirmed with myself as I placed a flower display by the window with a decisive nod.

As I looked out, to my surprise, Margret was pacing in front of the store. I reached over the azaleas and tapped my knuckles on the window. It startled her. She slowly walked in the door.

Margret would have usually come once a week to get flowers, mostly at the weekend, leaving the standard greeting for Adrianna to relay to me. However, since Mum passed, she would come more regularly on days I was working.

"Hiya." Margret held me in an embrace and squeezed me tighter for longer than usual. Her peacock feather headpiece slid down her hair as we untangled.

"Hi. Are you okay?" I asked her, placing it back in position.

"Yes, yes – I was just a bit worried, that's all." She took a step back and composed herself. "Since I gave you that letter, I just . . . felt I needed to check on you."

"I am fine, I promise. It is all a lot to take in, but it's good." Margret looked doubtful. "I promise! Really, it is, and guess what?" I put on a smile.

"What, Liz?" she said, her face not relaxing.

"I spoke with him, you know." Margret stood stiff. "To Oscar. My father."

"You did! You have?" Her eyes were larger than I'd ever seen them. If she was a cartoon character, they would have popped out dangling on a spring. "How?"

"Su was able to find his number in no time, with the return address from the letter."

"I thought you wanted to know a bit more about him. Not actually get in touch this soon?" Margret said, looking unsettled, picking imaginary fluff off her royal-blue coat and stroking it down.

"I really appreciate your concern." I placed my hand on her shoulder. "And you looking out for me." She gave a subtle nod. "These weeks haven't been easy, but I am so glad, Margret, that you gave me the letter." I reached for her hands and held them, beaming with appreciation. "In fact, I am calling him again this evening. I built up the courage to ask about Lizzy. I don't believe he knows. But he should, right? He deserves to know."

Margret released her hands from mine and walked over to the wooden stepladder near the window and sat down. "Are you sure that is a good idea, Liz?" she asked, her voice trembling, once I stood beside her. "All this is in the past. Sometimes, things should stay there."

She sighed heavily. "Your mother and grandmother are not around anymore, nor is your sister. What good will it do?" Her tone was almost pleading.

I looked at her for some moments, her shoulders slumped, as if a tremendous weight was coming down on her.

Why does this matter so much to her? "Is there something you are not telling me?"

"No, dear." Margret looked up at me with glazed eyes. "Your mother meant the world to me, and I don't believe in opening old wounds and digging up the past when, very obviously, your mother had chosen to keep them hidden."

"The photograph that was with the letter you gave me, was of Lizzy. My father made a copy," I said, feeling the need to argue my case.

"It was?" She gasped and a few tears rolled out from her eyes as she closed them tightly for some moments. "Well." She opened them and wiped them away. "Then there must be a reason she never told me, or you. I am not in support of this," she said in an almost motherly tone, tinged with bitterness.

I took a step away from her, taken aback by her demeanour; it was so out of character.

"Sorry, Elizabeth, but I value your mother's choices and wishes without knowing why, and so should you." Margret looked at me sternly, which soon followed with more tears. It then registered with me. She was hurt, hurt by my mother, her best friend, whom she had known for decades, yet never confided or entrusted her with her deepest secrets.

I bent down and gave her a big hug. "I know it hurts. Trust me."

"Just promise me you will let it be?" Margret mumbled, her face pressed on my shoulder. I promised. A little white lie, for her sake.

"Right, I am going to cheer you up, wait here," I ordered after a quiet minute or so and got to work on a colourful arrangement of gerbera daisies in orange, purple, hot pink, and light pink, and to add some fragrance to the cheerful display, some yellow roses to finish it off. The bouquet was bold and bright, just like her – well, the usual her. "Here you go," I said with a wide smile. Margret's face brightened as she held them near her nose for a delightful inhale.

"You look different. Something is different about you," she said after studying a few of the flowers.

"Oh, I just made a little extra effort today," I said, brushing it off.

"No, that's not it. Something else," she said, looking at me, trying to pinpoint what it was.

"She is in love!" Su shouted from the back.

"Are you now?" Margret said, pleased. "Well, good for you, it suits you. You must introduce us someday." She squeezed my hand as she stood up, thanking me for the flowers, and with that, she was on her way.

No sooner had she left, Su walked up to me, stopping opposite the counter, eyeing me cautiously. "I heard all of that. Are you okay? Are you really not going to ask about Lizzy?"

"Yes, I am fine." I gave a little smile. "And I am still going to ask him. I just said that to appease her." Su nodded approvingly.

"Good. Good! And you better be okay! Since we both know why you look different," she said sarcastically with a smile, "*All* that excitement you're getting!" She winked, not too subtly. I couldn't hold back a grin. *He very much excites me.*

#

The afternoon passed by quickly, with heightened anticipation and some nerves washing over me for the pending phone call. Like déjà vu, Su sat across from me. I felt grateful to have her support and I was determined to follow through this time, like a river bursting its banks. It was going to happen.

I dialled Oscar's number and put the phone on speaker before I laid it on the table. It rang numerous times before a young girl answered. "Brown family," she spoke cheerfully. Su returned a raised eyebrow at me.

"Hello, anyone there?" the high-pitched voice inquired. Su quickly nodded at me, gesturing to say something.

"Uh – yes. I would like to speak with Oscar, please?"

"Who can I say is calling?" she asked, good-manneredly. For a moment, I hesitated on what to say.

"Elizabeth. It's Elizabeth," I said in a low voice as if I was unsure of my own name.

"Elizabeth!" she repeated oh-so cheerfully, "I'll get my dad, one moment."

"Dad!" I mouthed to Su. She shrugged her shoulders, her eyes wide. We could hear her call out to him several times. "Phone for you, it's Elizabeth," she whispered not quietly enough when he had arrived.

"Hi, Elizabeth," he answered after clearing his throat.

"Hi . . ." I was thrown off on what to say. Calling him *Dad* didn't come naturally just now.

"Hi. How are you?" Oscar asked. His voice broke and he cleared his throat again.

"I have a half-sister?" I asked outright, with hardly concealed surprise.

"Uhm, it's more complicated . . ." There was a rustling, and then I heard him whisper, "Scar, can you give us a moment?" A few seconds later, I could make out the sound of what I thought might be a door closing.

"I was hoping to tell you." He cleared his throat several times again.

"Do you need to get some water?"

"No, no, I am fine." And with one final "ahem" he continued. "You see . . . you didn't ask about my life or if I have a family." I looked up at Su, who tsked at me. "I was just waiting for the right time to tell you more about me. If you want to know, that is?" he added hesitantly.

At that moment, I realised how consumed I had been with myself; I hadn't even considered he might have a family of his own and I could have half-siblings. I felt rather selfish and stupid.

"Yes, I'm sorry. I do . . . I would like to know. Uh – are you married?"

"No, not married."

"Divorced?" I guessed.

"No."

"Oh, I'm so sorry. You're widowed?" I said sombrely.

"No, no, no, not that either." He sounded a little amused.

"Oh?" I said, looking up at Su, who mouthed, *"Let him talk!"* and motioned for me to shush.

"Scarlet – that's her name – is my late brother and his wife's daughter. They died in an accident when she was only three years old . . . and since then, I have raised her as my own."

"Oh, I'm so sorry for your loss . . . for both your losses."

"Thanks . . . It has not been easy, but as the years pass and daily life continues, we keep moving forward, I suppose . . ." he trailed off.

"How old is Scarlet now?"

"She will be eight in a few months. What about you, Elizabeth? Do you have any children? Or anyone special in your life? You never mentioned . . ."

"No children, but I am seeing someone."

"That's nice," he said, as I didn't elaborate further. There was a lengthy pause.

"Actually, I wanted to ask you something," I finally said, gathering every inch of nerve. Although our conversation had started off rather unexpectedly, I would not allow myself to have it end without asking about Lizzy. It was how to phrase the question that got my tongue momentarily twisted.

"Okay. What do you want to ask?"

Well, to hell with it. "Um, well . . . I wanted to ask, or – do you know that my mother had twins?" I held my breath in anticipation.

"No, I didn't know she had more children. Wow, twins!" he breathed. "So, you have more siblings." Even in his surprise, he sounded pleased for me.

"No, I mean, *I* was a twin . . ." My voice trailed off softly.

The line got so quiet you could hear a pin drop. When Oscar spoke again, I could hear doubt wash over his words. "I don't understand what you are getting at, Elizabeth. Are you trying to tell me *you* are a twin?"

"Mm-hm."

"You're telling me you have a twin brother or sister? Impossible!"

"Yes, Mum gave birth to two girls. Me and my sister, Lizzy." I spoke slowly and the line went very quiet again.

"You . . . you're saying your mother had twins when, when she had you?" he asked, confirming he understood.

"Yes. I know it's a shock."

Another lengthy silence followed. Susan gestured for me to continue talking.

"I, I . . . only found out about her a week or so ago. She . . . Lizzy, passed away a little shy of her fifth birthday." The words caught in my throat as I shared another piece of the puzzle with him. Little sobs interrupted the silence on the other end of the phone. The sound made me well up. Even Su looked watery-eyed listening to it.

"I am so sorry. I didn't mean to upset you. I know it's a big shock." I sniffed through my words. "I wondered if –"

"Why did she never tell me? Why? Why? I don't understand. She only brought *you* home from the hospital," he asked in a broken voice.

"I'm not sure if she knew then. I have an inkling she might have known later on, but I think Lizzy was kept from her. The . . . the photograph you copied, the one you sent with the letter that is missing, that's not me, it's Lizzy. I was never there." I let out a shuddery breath. "And, *and* I know what I am about to say might sound even crazier, but I believe the William you spoke of, and my grandmother Hilda played a part in it all. I just don't understand *why*." Tremulous, I continued to tell him what I uncovered on my visit. Meeting Willie, the house, all of it.

Oscar had been oblivious to it all. He was riddled with sadness and disbelief, needing time for it all to sink in.

The call ended with me feeling drained. My eyes were raw and my head was spinning. I cupped my face in my hands and repeatedly sighed. Part of me was disappointed, as I secretly hoped he had something to share with me. That he'd known even something that might have meant nothing all these years, yet now would have made sense or meant anything at all. But all I had done was give him despair. It was impossible not to feel dejected.

Before I could process another complete thought, I picked up the phone again and rang Andrew. Up until now, we texted occasionally, and he'd dropped a few words or a line or two about Willie. Su gave me a tight, comforting hug and left the room.

"Hey, friend!" Andrew answered, upbeat.

"Hi, Liz!" Gloria shouted in the background.

"Hey, is this a good time to call?" I tried to match their cheery mood.

"Sure, we're just finished rounding up the day and getting ready for a glass of something red."

"Right." With that said, I wasted no time pouring myself one.

"How are things there? Are you totally lovesick?" Andrew asked smugly.

"Ha, ha, very funny!"

"Well, *are* you?" he asked, digging for news.

"Brian is!" Gloria shouted into the speaker.

"Yes, I miss him!" I said with a smile.

"I bet you do! Liz i-is love-sick!" Andrew sang in a childish voice.

"Are you sure you haven't been drinking already?" I laughed, somewhat embarrassed.

"You better come back soon!" Andrew replied, pointedly avoiding my question. "When *are* you coming back?" he asked, suddenly more serious.

I sighed. "I don't know, to be honest, but I need to speak with Willie," I said, all humour gone.

"He's gone to bed already," Gloria chimed in.

"No, not tonight. I have his number. But I just wanted to ask you first if he would be up for a conversation. A serious one. I really need to ask him some questions, and I believe now more than ever, he is the last person alive that could give me some real answers." It all sounded very dramatic, but it was the truth. "Maybe one of you could stay with Willie while I speak to him?" I proposed.

"Let me talk to him tomorrow and I will call you," Andrew said.

"Thank you! Thank you! I really appreciate that."

"Are you okay?" Andrew asked with concern.

"I am managing. Let me not disturb your evening more."

"Nonsense, tell me. I have a few minutes for a friend," he said, thoughtful as ever.

I told him all about the conversations with my father and the letter. He listened attentively, occasionally providing comforting words and lightened the mood with his inherent charm on the right occasions.

"I'll get it!" I heard Gloria shout in the background when the doorbell rang.

"You're having visitors?" Before Andrew could answer I heard a faint, familiar voice and beamed.

"I have a lovesick woman on the phone here!" Andrew called out with glee.

"Hey, you!" he said moments after some inaudible whispers.

"I'll call you tomorrow!" Andrew shouted from the background.

"Thanks!" I yelled.

"She said thanks!" Brian said back to him, and then, in an intimate voice, "So you miss me, huh?"

"I do." I wasn't going to beat around the bush.

We chatted for a few minutes before he joined Andrew and Gloria while I got settled for a lazy evening in front of the TV with Su.

Chapter 11

"Coffee or tea?"

"Coffee please."

"How have you been?"

"You know you just saw me yesterday, right?" I told Margret.

"I know, I just wanted to make sure you're okay." She placed the saucer with the small, rattling cup of coffee on it in front of me. Moments later Pooky, her friendly tabby cat, jumped on my lap, purring for attention. "Where were you hiding the other day?" I stroked her little head, which made her purring even louder.

"Probably snoozing somewhere," Margret said as she poured herself some tea.

"Thank you for inviting me over, and for your concern, but I am fine. Really." The truth was, it felt more like a summons than an invite. The morning text read: *Why don't you come over during your lunch break? See you then, Margret.* "You needn't worry, Margret, I mean it."

"That's good to hear. I am glad you have decided to leave things in the past, where they should stay. We owe it to your mother!" she said with conviction. I hoped my face didn't look flustered, as my cheeks sure felt warm. I looked down at Pooky, stroking her and making little chatter at the cat while praying for a poker face.

Margret's stance was strong and I, for one, had no intention of appraising her of anything until I knew everything. The complete story. And maybe even then, I wouldn't. I took a careful sip from the hot coffee and finally gazed up at her as she placed little dishes with a selection of bite-size food onto the table.

"Is the coffee all right?"

"Oh yes. Perfect." I brushed my fingers across my lips. "Just burned my tongue a bit," I said, hoping that would explain away if there was any redness left showing on my cheeks.

"You're not in a rush, are ya?" Margret raised a brow as she sat opposite me on the round wooden table.

"No, I have time. You went all out, it looks delicious. Thank you!"

"I had some help from the shop," she admitted.

"You look extra nice today, did you go somewhere else other than the shop?" She was dolled up more than usual, with heavier makeup and a pearl jewellery set that complemented the kind of French look she had going on, very stylish.

"Someone special maybe?" I asked cheekily, putting the focus on her.

"No, no, not many suitors these days. All the good ones seem to be taken. But you never know where you might bump into someone," she said, hopeful, while pricking an olive that had a mind of its own.

"I am sure you will find someone." I took a mini pastry and added a dollop of clotted cream beside it. I was more in the mood for sweet than savoury.

"Let's talk about you! Tell me about this man that is making *you* smile these days."

"Okay." I couldn't help but grin. If she hadn't noticed me flush earlier, she did now.

"His name is Brian."

"Good, strong name. Continue," Margret said with approval.

Time passed quickly as I told her about him and to my relief, we had a light-hearted conversation until I needed to head back to the shop. I declined her offer to bring some of the leftover food with me twice, but ultimately gave in on the last hurdle while I stood just outside the open front door.

"Just give me a minute and I'll pack some up." Margret hurried down the hall. "Susan might like some too!" she shouted moments later from the kitchen as a phone rang. I habitually reached for my pocket when I realised it wasn't mine, it was the one on the console table near me.

"Your phone is ringing!" I shouted from the doorstep after hearing the fifth ring.

"They will call back if it is important!" she said without a care.

And that was when it happened. Where all my thoughts turned into a daze of disbelief. Leave a message after the beep, a recording said. BEEP rang through the hall followed by an urgent voice. "Margret, we need to talk. Call me!"

Margret stood on the other side of the hallway now with a Tupperware of food clutched in her hands. Having heard the same, she tried to hide her shock and read me, to see if I knew.

He said only seven words, but it was enough for me to recognise his voice.

"Was that . . .?"

Margret marched towards me and shoved the Tupperware into my hands. "You shouldn't be late, thanks for coming!" and she shut the door with considerable force.

It went so fast, yet it felt as if I was in a playback slow-motion scene. Her march towards me, each large strut noticeably becoming louder as her heels touched the floorboards. The plastic box landing in my hands almost by magic, the slam of the door, and finally the sound of the lock hitting the latch, amplified.

There I stood, shocked. It took me a few moments to spring into action. I banged on the door. "Hey, Margret! Open up!" I shouted as the Tupperware dropped to the ground with a crack. She ignored me as I continued banging and ringing the doorbell for what felt like minutes. I called out through the letterbox, pleading for her to come talk to me, and as I lowered my face and peered through the opening, I thought I could see her shadow at the far end of the hallway. "Margret, open up, *please*!" I stood up and cupped my hands, leaning in to look through the opaque window. I could see her move and then disappear completely. "Margret!" I yelled several more times in vain, when I noticed I had attracted some stares from the people in the street.

As a last attempt, I got out my phone and rang her landline. I could hear it ring and go to the answering machine. "Margret, talk to me!" I begged for some time to the machine, until ultimately, I gave up.

On my way back to the shop, my brain was like a washing machine on spin cycle. "What the fuck!" I said out loud. I generally wasn't one for cursing. "But, what the fuck, fuck, fuck!" I just couldn't comprehend what just happened. I even momentarily entertained doubting what I heard, but I was right, obviously, given Margret's reaction.

As I pushed the door open to the shop with much less grace than I usually would, Su walked over at a quick pace. “You are late. We are very busy!” she said in a harsh whisper.

“Willie called, and –”

“That’s great, but can we talk about it later! Two people are waiting for service.”

“Willie called Margret,” I said, monotone.

“Okay. I don’t understand, but I need you to focus and help serve these customers. I have somebody waiting on the line!” She pointed to the back.

I stared at Susan. “I don’t understand either.”

“Right.” Su grabbed my arm and pulled me aside. “I have no idea what is going on, but get a grip, will ya! We have a store to run and whatever it is, we can talk about *it* later!” she said with a face like thunder. I knew whenever she had three prominent lines show up on her forehead, it was serious. She was mad, and it snapped me out of my daze.

“Sorry, Su.” I gave her a half smile to let her know I was back and for the rest of the day I tried my hardest to put on a happy customer service demeanour. Su hardly spoke a word to me throughout, other than about shop matters.

After I brought the last flower display and sign inside, Su switched off the light, turned on the alarm, and locked the door. She still had lines on her forehead when she looked at me. “Are you coming?”

"No, I must do something first. I'll see you at home later," I said in a gentle voice, feeling bad for the stress I caused her. "Su, I'm s–"

"Fine." And with that, Su was off.

#

I couldn't go home to sit and ponder. Margret likely wasn't going to answer my phone calls, so I had to go over there and stay outside the door until she would talk to me.

When I arrived, the curtains were drawn while it was still bright outside. Only her large aloe vera plant and two pink orchids were in sight. Even Pooky wasn't in her favourite place, her little bed on the windowsill. I couldn't see anything from the front door, and the upstairs curtains were all drawn too. I rang the bell and knocked several times on the door and peered and listened through the letterbox. Utter silence, nothing.

Luckily, the evening was dry and not cold as I sat waiting on her doorstep. I sent her a few messages and rang several times too, just on the off chance she might reply or answer.

I even rang Willie. I didn't care at that moment if he was up for it. But it was all in vain. His phone was switched off. I thought of ringing Andrew to get to Willie when I heard a strange scratching sound on a window. From the corner of my eye I saw Pooky, not in her house, but the neighbour's.

Without a second thought, I rang their doorbell. Pooky got all excited and scratched some more. I rang a second time as nobody opened, waiting for what felt too long. I stepped carefully into the garden, allowing me to peer through the living room window. There was nothing to be seen other than a seventies-style interior that wasn't my cup of tea.

"Can I help you?" A voice startled me. In my attempt to get quickly back to the garden path, I tripped and stood on a rosebush.

"I'm so sorry! I saw Pooky in your window, and I am looking for Margret, and . . ." I tried desperately to perk up the rosebush, being careful not to get pricked by the thorns.

"You're the one making that racket earlier," she said, looking wide-eyed, her eyes amplified by the thick lenses in her glasses. She stared from me to the bush and back. Her grey hair was neatly pinned in a ballerina bun, and she wore clothes that I could only describe as *conservative*.

"Yes, sorry." I stood up straight, towering over her petite frame. "I just really need to see Margret."

"I don't know where she is, but she left in a haste about an hour ago." The bespectacled woman looked at her pocket watch and nodded to herself. "As you can see, I am looking after the tabby." She gave a brief wave at Pooky, who was still at the window.

"Where did she go? For how long?" I asked breathlessly.

"I don't know." She picked up a light-pink rose from the ground that had broken off. "Not today anyway. She left with two large suitcases and gave me a large bag of cat food. Margret never talks much about herself, and I don't pry. It did seem urgent," she said with conviction, now tending to her flattened rosebush.

"I'll say," I mumbled.

"Pardon?

"Nothing. I am very sorry about your roses." She nodded as if to say I was forgiven. "Could I leave my number with you in case she gets in touch?"

"Sure." And with that, I was on my way home.

I didn't hold out much hope it would yield anything; after all, Margret was ignoring me. What the neighbour said got me thinking. She indeed never spoke much about herself. I had known her for as long as I could remember and could describe her as a chatty, bubbly, outgoing person, a real presence in a social gathering, someone that liked quirky fashion, but how much did I actually *know* about her? Very, very little.

Her faith was an important part of her life. She was involved in some charity work through the church, and she adored children. That was about it. I knew nothing about her family, if she had any siblings, where she was born, nothing. It hadn't dawned on me until now. But the one thing I did know was that she knows Willie. But *how*?

#

Su was lying stretched out on the couch with a glass of wine on the table and the bottle right beside it. From her obvious silence, I knew she was still mad at me and the last thing she would care to do was listen to any more of my life's drama. I let her down today.

"Hey," I said in a friendly "please forgive me" voice when I stepped closer. She didn't acknowledge me.

I walked around the couch to see her, but she didn't turn away from the TV. "I'm sorry about today, Su."

"So you should be!" Su's voice quivered as she met my eyes. Hers were blotchy, as if she had been crying for a while.

"I really am sorry." I kneeled in front of her. "What's wrong?" I asked, wiping away some fresh tears.

"Nothing really. But you're not the only one with things happening in your life," she said softly. I prompted for her to lift her head up, and I sat down as she lay back on my lap. I stroked her head, her brown, curly locks bouncing back after each brush.

"I'm sorry, Su," I said again from the heart. "What is happening in your life?" I prompted her after she stopped her soft sniffing. She pulled up her legs and sat up, sharing the fleece blanket with me.

“I want to tell you something,” Su said shakily. “Actually, I have been wanting to tell you, earlier, but . . .”

“What is it, Su?” I spoke gently, trying to encourage her.

“It’s nothing bad. It’s . . .” She got a tissue to blow her nose, straightened herself, and looked at me, staring deeply into my eyes.

“Liz.”

“Yes, Su?” She reached to hold my shoulders and gave me a weak smile, inhaling.

“I have been seeing someone, and I’d like you to meet her.” Su’s voice was serious.

“That’s great, Su! I am so happy for you.” I took her hands off my shoulders and held her in a firm embrace.

“You heard me, right?” she mumbled into my hair.

“Yes, Su, I did.” I pulled back and gave her a smile.

“You *knew*?”

“I have had my suspicions you might like both.”

“Why didn’t you say anything?” Su smiled widely with a wash of relief on her face.

“Why didn’t you? You know me!” I fist-bumped her arm.

“Ouch.” She laughed.

“So, tell me all about her!”

"Well, her name is Avril, she is a year older than me, and she is an artist." Su eyes sparkled as she spoke and she swiftly brought out her phone, showing me pictures of them together to add to the many stories that followed. There was no doubt she was smitten. I felt so happy for her and a little shocked when she told me they had been dating for *five* months, and I hadn't known! And also, a little disappointed she didn't tell me sooner, but with my mum passing, the drama with Gordon, the other big bombshells in my life and nerves on her side, Su said she found it difficult to share her *happy* news.

By the time the wine bottle was close to empty, Su was all talked out about Avril, and ended with one short announcement I hadn't seen coming.

"We are planning to move in together, Liz." I could tell by the look on her face that she was anxious for my reaction.

"Oh . . . that's great . . . I'm so happy for you!" I said, processing. I *was* happy for her. But I couldn't help feeling sad for me too.

"I know how you feel," Su said.

"What do you mean?"

"I felt the same way when you moved in with Gordon." She gave a weak smile and we hugged, holding on tight to each other. I recalled the day I moved out. Su fought back tears, and even though we saw each other at work, we spoke on the phone in the evenings almost daily for at least the first month. *I am going to miss her so much.* I felt teary, squeezing her even more.

"So," Su said after a while. "What is this about Margret and Willie?"

I took a deep breath and lifted my head off her shoulder. "Margret is AWOL . . . and I think I should go back to Colchester. I want to know, for once and for all, everything! The entire story. I *need* to know! But of course, not before meeting Avril." I gave her a quick nudge. Su grinned.

"AWOL, you said?" She shared the last drops of wine between our glasses and listened while I recalled the lunch with Margret and what transpired after.

"You should go!" she affirmed after I finished. "You can meet Avril anytime, she isn't going anywhere," Su said with a smirk. And with that, she got the laptop out and searched for a ticket.

"What about work?" I asked her twice as she typed away.

"Adrianna will probably be delighted to have more hours again, and I can call in a favour if needed," she winked, briefly taking her eyes from the screen. I didn't need more convincing. "Do you . . . think Margret has gone to –?"

"I have been thinking the same thing."

"Make sure you get your answers." Su looked up from the screen and squeezed my hand softly, and about ten minutes later, my flight was booked. After which, Su went to ring Avril to tell her that she finally told me. She was radiant as she left the room.

I rang Brian to tell him the news. I was hoping to stay at his place, not only for obvious reasons, I also wasn't ready to stay on my own in that massive house. "Of course," he replied before I could even finish asking, and I felt an instant swoony sensation in my stomach. I swear he could see me smile through the phone line as it went quiet. "Can't wait to see you," he said, breaking the seconds of silence.

"Me too. Me too." I grinned sheepishly. "I should ring Andrew to give him the heads-up and get packing."

"Hmm," Brian agreed, and with that, we said our sweet goodbyes.

"You read my mind," Andrew said upon answering the phone. "I was just about to call you!"

"Were you now?" I smiled at the timing.

"Yes. Just to tell you that Willie was a bit evasive, to be honest, about when he might be able to talk with you."

"No worries, Andrew. That's why I am calling. I'm flying over tomorrow."

"Tomorrow!?"

"Yes, I want to talk to him in person, but I was hoping – do you by any chance have time tomorrow to sit in? I will fill you in more later."

"Yeah, sure. Will you be staying here? Because we have –"

"No, no, I'll be staying at Brian's."

"So, tomorrow!" he said again.

"Yes, please don't tell Willie. I prefer he doesn't know."

I ended up telling Andrew everything over the phone after all, as he insisted he had time to listen. He was gobsmacked. Before we ended the call, we agreed to meet in the evening.

"I can't find anything! Nothing is clean!" I complained later that evening as I marched around the apartment, stressed. Su was rather entertained. "You only care because you're staying with your *boyfriend*," she sang childishly, a sure side effect of the wine. The second bottle was nearing empty.

"Why did I go for the early morning flight? I have no time to wash and dry these." I held up my favourite jeans. I loved the way they hugged me around my butt, just showed it off well. "I'm sure he prefers you out of those!" Su said, loose-lipped.

I laughed. "Go ring your girlfriend again, will you? You're no help!" She smirked, hinting that she might just do that.

"And she might stay here for a bit while you're away." She beamed with delight. I couldn't believe I hadn't noticed how in *love* she was. *Or did she only now feel comfortable enough to show it?*

Packing was a chaotic affair. Nerves about speaking to, well, *confronting* Willie, and the excitement of seeing Brian again so soon, made my stomach feel funny.

I hardly slept a wink. So much for a beauty sleep to look my best! The flight was quick, as I closed my eyes soon after take-off and opened them after what felt like minutes later as we landed. Still groggy, I got off the plane and quickly went to the bathroom to brush my teeth and fix my hair and makeup before coming out through those doors. The ones that have a half-moon shape of people waiting on the other side. All looking for their person or persons with the same expressions, anticipation. Hoping the next time the doors slide open it's who they are waiting for. I walked through *that* door and stood in the middle of the half-moon of people scanning the crowd for my person.

It wasn't long before our eyes met and smiles filled our faces as we walked toward each other, a bit like a movie scene. And oh, it felt amazing. Brian's embrace, lips, and scent instantly familiar and wonderful. He took my suitcase and held my hand in his as we walked to his car.

Between chatting, gazing, and occasional lap touching, the drive to his apartment passed swiftly. He carried my luggage inside and I followed him through the door.

"You can use that drawer and basket for your clothes if you like," Brian said as he placed my suitcase beside the bed, as if it wasn't a big deal – only it was. He had made some space for my stuff. I was impressed, and he knew it. Just as he knew the reason I came back so soon was for a different reason than him, we agreed it was a wonderful side effect.

We had the entire afternoon for ourselves before I was going to meet Willie and Andrew, yet it was difficult not to think about it. Nothing made sense, and with Margret still MIA and ignoring all my calls and texts, the anticipation of a pending confrontation – which was definitely going to happen – was consuming. No amount of intimacy could have soothed me, which is why we kept our affection PG – until later, we agreed. "If you can keep your hands off me?" Brian had joked. A crappy movie, an early dinner tappas-style and a solo shower later, I was ready to go.

Brian opened the car door for me like a chauffeur, even holding onto my hand as I stepped inside. Granted, the car didn't look the part, nor did he stay professional when my dress hem went higher up than anticipated sitting in the low, small seat. Still, he was considerate and charming, engaging in some random talk on the short drive. But none of it eased my state. I was tense as hell.

Familiar with the roads, I knew we were getting close. Then it came, one more turn and we entered the street. I was sweaty, and not just from the warm weather and lack of modern technology of this vehicle. As he parked right in front of the gate, I just stared out of the window. "You ready?" Brian asked, touching my shoulder encouragingly.

"Uh, yeah. I suppose." This wasn't like one of those reality TV series where people find long-lost relatives and you could see their nerves and excitement accumulate for the big meet-up. I just felt nervous and anxious, with no clue what was waiting for me, or if he would even tell me. I didn't allow myself to contemplate the latter for long. I'd had enough of this crumb-feeding. I needed the entire meal, all of it!

Brian took my hand and kissed it softly. I got out of the car and watched him drive away. He had some work to catch up on, since he had spent the afternoon with me. I opened the gate and slowly entered the garden where I had sat not so long ago. No sign of ongoing- renovation work was visible anymore. "You're here?" said a familiar voice. It was Andrew calling from the breakfast room window before disappearing and reappearing with Gloria by the front door. And soon we were all holding each other in an embrace.

"No Brian?" asked Gloria.

"No, he has some work to do."

"No Brian," Gloria stated wide-eyed to Andrew when they let go of the bear hug they held me in, as if he hadn't heard. He nodded. They linked their arms with mine and with a tight squeeze through the doorway, guided me into the kitchen and physically sat me down on a chair. "Coffee?" Gloria asked high-pitched and a bit loud, standing near me.

"No, thank you, I'd like a tea, though. I don't think caffeine would be a good idea at the moment," I laughed nervously.

"How was Brian's? I am sure good," Andrew rambled before I could answer while he and Gloria frantically moved around in the kitchen, moving pots and dishes, both acting a bit strange while waiting for the kettle to boil. Gloria served a teapot, cup, and saucer with uncharacteristically little care and vigorously wiped the countertops several times over. There was hardly a conversation happening for some minutes. I poured myself a strong cuppa and felt uneasy as I blew it to cool down. *Not the welcome I'd anticipated.* "Did I come at a bad time?" I finally gathered the courage to ask.

"No, no, no – not at all," Andrew said hurriedly.

"Oh. No," Gloria added. Clearly, I had.

"Hey, Andrew? Gloria? What's going on?" I asked, troubled. They paused for a moment from their frantic kitchen chores display and looked at each other, then promptly continued again without a word. I watched on in disbelief.

"Guys! What is going on? You are both acting strange!" I said with a stern voice, not taking this weirdness any longer. Andrew stopped stacking plates and a moment after, Gloria stopped too, and they shared another silent glance that I couldn't decipher.

"*Please* tell me."

Andrew nodded at Gloria, and she reciprocated after a long pause and sat down, side by side opposite of me, and exchanged another look. "Did something happen?" I prompted them. *It was obvious it had.* I waited for one of them to start talking. I mean, it must have been something to do with me, otherwise, anyone would have said it was something private or personal. *Right?*

As they sat quietly, their eyes briefly met again, as if they were waiting for the other person to say something.

"Whatever it is, please tell me. It can't be that bad. Where is Willie? Is he in his room?" My desperation was reaching a high point.

Andrew audibly inhaled and exhaled. "You should call Brian and ask him to come," he said with a firm undertone, and eyes that said *do it*. Gloria lifted her head enough for me to see surprise written all over her face before looking back down, fidgeting with her apron.

I didn't know what to think. Andrew wasn't one to shy away from difficult things, with his mantra it is always better to know the truth. I reminded him of that, but to no avail. They were in some form of shock or something.

I took my phone out and rang Brian. Funnily enough, he answered. "Hey, are you okay?"

"Far from it." I stood up and walked over to the counter, to put some distance between myself and the anxious couple who were slumped in their chairs. “Better than Andrew and Gloria, though,” I whispered.

“What do you mean?”

“Brian, I don’t know what is going on here, but I need you to come, please? Please?”

“On my way,” he said without another thought, and hung up.

“He is on his way,” I told them.

“Good,” Andrew mumbled as he and Gloria shared yet another brief glance.

“You can tell me anything. It’s better to know the truth, right?” I appealed to Andrew once more. He fidgeted in his chair, but both stayed silent. “Okay,” I said, defeated. “I am going to greet Willie while we wait.” Before I could get to the door to leave, they zoomed around the table and blocked my exit.

“He – he is not here. And . . . and someone else is staying in his room now,” Gloria said, her voice wavering.

“Oh, where is he?” I asked, disconcerted by their sudden action.

“Doctor’s appointment,” Andrew said as they remained standing in front of the door.

“This late? Is he okay?!” I worried. “Who is driving him?”

I was met by silence. “Come on, guys. Tell me what is going on!” I snapped at them. Gloria was frozen in her position while Andrew uncomfortably shifted his feet.

"We will. Let's wait for Brian."

"We will?" Gloria squinted at him.

"Yes, we will!" he said, slightly agitated. "Not that," he added, muttering under his breath, but I could still hear him.

They made no sense whatsoever. It was like I entered an interactive play during the second act, clueless of what happened beforehand. Both seemed anxious, upset, angry, the lot. Mirroring my own feelings. They sat again, after I did so, resigned to wait for Brian. What else could I do?

Not soon enough, the bell rang. Andrew rose swiftly and opened the kitchen door just enough to squeeze himself out. Gloria peered at me as if to say, *stay here*. I didn't move. Brian got ushered into the kitchen moments later. He leaned in and gave me a brief kiss before sitting beside me. "What's going on?" he asked no one in particular. All I could do was shrug my shoulders. Andrew sat back on his chair beside Gloria. I took a sip of my now cold tea. "What is going on, my friend?" Brian asked Andrew.

Andrew straightened his shirt and met our bewildered gazes. Then a soft sniff shifted my focus to Gloria. Tears pricked her eyes and trailed down her cheeks. Andrew welled up too and placed a comforting arm around her.

"Come on, guys, talk to us?" Brian pleaded, reaching his hand out to his mate.

"You said you would," I reminded Andrew in a friendly tone.

"Liz, would you mind stepping out? I'll have a chat with them," Brian whispered after their silence dragged on.

"No!" Andrew and Gloria called out, half jumping from their chairs in a panic.

I froze. "Why don't you want *me* to go out?!"

"Where's Annie?" Brian asked seriously before I got an answer. I felt embarrassed I hadn't thought to ask.

"She is staying with a friend," Gloria mumbled when her tears let up. I let out a small sigh of relief.

"Okay. Do you have many guests staying?"

"No," they both said.

"Someone new is in Willie's room. He's gone to the doctor," I told Brian quietly.

"This late? Is he okay?"

"That's what I asked," I said, almost indignant.

"Well, is he?! Andrew? Gloria?" Brian asked.

"We – we have to tell you something," Andrew said, nervously tapping his fingers on the table.

"Isn't it two somethings?" Gloria mumbled under her breath, and he shushed her.

"Just tell us," Brian and I said almost in sync. Andrew got up to get a drink for himself and we waited impatiently for him to start.

"What do you have to tell us?" Brian encouraged them, his calmness wavering.

Andrew paced up and down the kitchen, stopping as if he would start to say something, but didn't.

"Why don't you take Gloria for a chat and I will stay with –" Brian jerked his head towards Andrew.

"Sure." I walked over to her and held her arm to go. "Come, why don't we leave the guys to talk?" Gloria didn't budge from her seat.

Brian signalled to me for us to step out of the room instead. "Don't go!" Gloria cried, not leaping from her chair this time, but sitting defeated with her head resting in her hands.

"Bring them," Andrew said as he put his glass down with a clank and walked past us and opened the door. Defeated, Gloria got up, her face pale, as we followed them to the door of their private lounge. Andrew opened it so slowly, peering around the widening opening, I was almost expecting something to escape. *But what?*

Free to enter, Brian and I curiously and anxiously looked around as we walked inside, sunlight flooding the room. Aside from the comfy armchair I'd seen Willie sit in while reading his newspaper, now upgraded to a fancy recliner with a cupholder, I didn't see what the big mystery was.

"Andrew, what is—"

"Wait here," he ordered, sort of apologetically. Then placed his arm around Gloria's shoulder and they left the room together.

“What on earth is going on?” I exclaimed, frustrated.

“I am as confused as you are.” Brian put his arms around me. “I have never seen them behave like this before.” We stood in the middle of the room until we heard some commotion and footsteps approaching. Gloria opened the door. “You might want to sit for this,” she said, avoiding eye contact.

We sat down on the small two-seater leather couch like two obedient children. “There is someone I want you to meet.” Her voice was shaking. “This . . . this is my mother.” Gloria stepped aside from the door as the words barely left her lips and we turned to face an empty doorway. For several seconds, no one came through, but I could hear a presence of someone standing close by, a shuffling of feet, maybe.

“Just come in, please,” Gloria hissed.

Slowly, a shadow appeared in the corner of the doorframe, approaching closer until she stepped in the middle of the doorway. I gasped so loud I forgot how to breathe for a moment.

She stood hunched over, a far cry from the confident posture I knew her to have. Gloria welled up again. “I . . . I . . . found out today that *she* is my birth mother,” she sniffed between the tears, her hands covering her face.

“Oh! That’s wonderful.” Brian rushed over and hugged her. “I didn’t know you were looking for your birth mother.”

"I wasn't," Gloria mumbled, barely audible.

"Oh . . ." Brian said, letting go, but still delighted for her.

I tried to stand up, but my legs felt too heavy. Opening and closing my mouth several times, trying to speak, nothing would come out as I looked at them. Andrew, having joined us, caught my stinging eyes and tapped Brian on his shoulder.

With a sudden burst of adrenaline running through my veins, my faculties awakening, I managed to rise to my feet and practically leaped towards her. "Margret. *This* Margret! Margret, who has no children, is *your* mother!? *You* are *her* mother!?" I shouted in her face while pointing my finger at Gloria, enraged. Margret tried to evade eye contact.

"This is the Margret that you . . .?" Brian caught on.

"Yes! She was my mother's BEST friend! Right?! *And* the person Willie rang!" I announced in case that wasn't clear. Andrew tried to take my arm as he held Gloria, trying to console her too, but I pushed it away.

"Wait!" I laughed out loud like a lunatic at the ridiculousness of it all. "So let me get this straight. When Willie rang saying you needed to talk, it was about this?" I threw my hands in the air. "Then why have you been avoiding my calls and texts, huh? I don't get it, Margret. And how is it that you know Willie? *How*? Tell me!"

My blood was boiling. If I was a lobster, I would have turned red before hitting the boiling water. I could shake her. I was so done with secrets, so done. The last and only time I ever came close to this level of fury was when things unravelled with Gordon.

Brian held me from behind and pleaded for me to calm down. "Give her a chance to talk," he said quietly.

"She better talk!" I retorted. "You better talk!" I directed my anger at *her*. Hearing my own voice, it didn't sound like my own, more like a lioness. Brian turned me around with a level of force that took me by surprise.

"Look at me." His voice low and firm. Breathing heavily, I slowly met his hazel eyes. Mine were probably shooting red lasers like a supervillain in a movie. He gave a little awkward smile. "It's all going to be okay," he said, his eyes trying to hold mine before I looked back at her again and Brian led me a step back.

"I think we should all take a seat," Andrew said as he guided Gloria to sit on the recliner and he rested on the armrest beside her. Brian put a comforting arm around me as we sat back on the small couch and Margret made her way to a single chair across from us.

The room filled with silence, only the occasional sniffle from Gloria's crying. I tried to focus on my breathing, looking down, and stopped to think not only about myself for a moment. I didn't know Gloria was adopted. I didn't know anything, for that matter.

"I am sorry, Gloria," I said, breaking the silence, gazing up at her. She gave a little nod, her eyes red, swollen, and glazed over.

"Why have you . . . what . . . how – how do you know Willie?" I asked Margret again some minutes later, as calmly as I could muster, when no one spoke. "And can somebody please tell me if he is okay?" I looked at Andrew and Gloria, pleading.

"He'll be fine, Liz," Andrew said softly.

"So, he isn't fine now?"

"He – is my brother," Margret whispered.

"Sorry, you said what?" I asked, certain I didn't hear that right.

"William – Willie – is my brother," she repeated in the same hesitant tone but a little louder.

"Willie is your *brother*!?" I gaped. "I . . . that . . . that doesn't make sense . . ."

"Yes, he's my older brother." Margret looked up, her eyes briefly meeting mine, and I felt anger rising again.

"How old are you *really*?" I demanded to know. After a pause, she started explaining that her mother had her later in life. While I listened to her feeding snippets about her family and growing up in Colchester, I tried to stay calm, but I felt very uneasy. Something wasn't right. Not right at all.

"How did you end up in Ireland?" I interrupted. "You sound Irish!"

"Oh, Elizabeth, this all happened so long ago and there was never a right time . . ." She trailed off. "And then with your mother passing . . . Forgive me," Margret pleaded, her hands in prayer position.

"Forgive you for what?" I snapped, agitated. "I am done with half-truths. Done with driving myself crazy with confusing thoughts. Tell me!" I shouted while reaching my arms at her with a shaking motion. Brian placed his hand on my arm as she recoiled in her chair for what felt like minutes before she finally started to talk again.

"I . . . I gave Gloria up for adoption in my late twenties. Which is one of the biggest mistakes of my life." She sobbed into her hands. Not one of those little sniffs, a full-blown sob.

Gloria broke again too, and it was impossible not to be affected by the sound of their sorrowful cries.

Andrew, the good Samaritan, after taking care of his wife, got Margret a glass of water and handed out tissues around the room.

Once she managed to calm herself down, she looked at me with swollen, red eyes, a few tears still appearing, then looked at Gloria and continued. "I told you why I placed you up for adoption, but I haven't told you everything that happened after that." Margret gazed from Gloria to me with a pained expression. Her lips trembled and her knees bounced seemingly involuntarily. "After . . . after I placed you up for adoption, I was in a bad, really bad place, and was very depressed." Her throat closed up, and she took a gulp of water. "I also found out I wouldn't be able to have a child again." A single loud sob escaped her as she tried to compose herself.

Brian gently squeezed my thigh, encouraging me to be patient, noticing my restlessness. "When I met *your* mother in the shop staring at baby things," she continued, "in our brief conversation, she revealed she was pregnant, and I realised she was Hilda's daughter. Who . . . who I knew through William," Margret added in case we hadn't already joined that piece of the puzzle. "You have to understand, I wasn't in a good place and – and William found out what I was planning, you see," she rambled, skipping ahead.

"You met my mother and then what? What did you plan?!" I asked, which was followed by another thigh squeeze from Brian, just that bit harder this time.

She placed her hands over her face again, letting out another sob. "I . . . I planned to take you."

"You – WHAT?"

"I wanted to raise you as my own. I wanted a baby." Margret's words were barely audible through her cries.

"You had a baby," Gloria said, laced with so much hurt. "You gave me away!"

Margret couldn't meet either of our eyes as Gloria sniffed away relentless tears again. While she was understandably heartbroken, I was fuming.

"Margret!" I snapped so fiercely while standing up. "You tried *what*? You wanted to take me as yours? What, did you follow us to Ireland and stalk us? Pretend to be a friend all these years? When were you going to take me, huh? Tell me! What was your grand plan!" I stepped forward, wanting to shake the words out of her. Brian held onto the back of my dress, restricting me, before he clapped his hands on my shoulders, coercing me to sit back down.

"No, NO! It was not like that, Elizabeth!" She was shaking her head profusely.

"Then what was it like?!" I was blinded with rage and sitting on the edge of my seat. Brian softly hushed me to calm, like a parent would try to soothe their crying child. But that wasn't going to work anymore.

"What was it like, then?" I asked, feeling completely disgusted by her.

"William, and your grandmother, were good friends, even back then. He'd always loved her but could never confess this. Not after what happened."

"What happened?! What was it like?!" I shouted, ignoring the unrequited love story. *If you don't start spelling it out soon, we will need a safety barrier to stop me from shaking it out of you!*

"I . . . I planned to take you once you were born, but William found out about it, reading my diary." Margret finally continued as if she heard my inner thoughts. "It was William who gave your mother the money and tickets to go to Ireland, hoping you would both be safe there, away from – "

"You!" I growled.

She gave the slightest nod. "And to protect me as well. I wasn't in a good place, Elizabeth, you must understand," she repeated, looking at me with wide, blotchy eyes.

"Understand what! That you planned to kidnap me from my mother?"

"But I didn't! I couldn't. I begged my brother to tell me where you were and promised I would make it all right." She paused, taking another gulp. "And then when I met your mother in Ireland, she didn't seem to remember me from our encounter – " Margret sighed heavily. "I did change my look," she muttered under her breath.

"And your accent!" I sniped at her with utter contempt.

"She . . . she was so nice, and a natural at being a mother, not at all what I expected. You were so precious and, and . . . she was desperate to have a friend, being all alone in a new place."

"Because of YOU! She was alone because of you." My voice caught in my throat and my mind was swimming with thoughts of what could have been.

"I just couldn't tell her. There were times I tried, but I couldn't bring myself."

"You couldn't, or you wouldn't?!" My teeth were clenched as I spoke.

"I never had a friend like your mother before. I felt happy again, and so did your mother," Margret went on.

"*You* felt happy again. I could have grown up with my family around me and because of you, I never had any of that!" I cried angrily, hot tears pricking my eyes. "You took that away from me!" I felt Brian's hold on my dress again.

"That's not true. Your mother had no intention of staying at home!" she cried defiantly.

I chuckled with a bomb load of sarcasm. *Was she seriously trying to defend herself as if she had a leg to stand on*? "You don't know that! They could have worked things out. I could have grown up with a father around, and a grandmother! I could have been with Lizzy! You took that away from me! How could you! You are evil! EVIL! Do you hear me!"

Brian gripped my shoulders, knowing I was ready to launch on her again. Reluctantly I sat back a little, shaking. "I am grateful my mother will never know the horrible, evil person you are!" I added in despair.

Margret cried uncontrollably for what felt like a long time. I looked at Gloria, who was pale as a ghost only with red, swollen eyes as Andrew held her in his arms. Brian was softly stroking my back, having released his grip.

"What about Lizzy, huh? What about my sister?"

"I . . . I didn't know about her for a long time. William hid it from me." She spoke through her cries and blowing her nose.

"I wonder why!" I mumbled, leaning fully back into Brian's arms. Suddenly overcome, my hurt and anger spilled over like a burst dam and I cried too, until the built-up emotions had subsided.

"You should talk to Willie. He will be able to tell you more," Margret offered, her voice shaking. "We haven't been in touch much over the years . . . I am a disappointment to him."

I swiped the last remaining tears from my stinging eyes and met hers. She went on.

"He called after your visit and his health scare. He was worried you would find out about me – he'd also discovered some years ago that Gloria was the baby I put up for adoption. Rose – I called you Rose." Margret turned toward Gloria when she dropped that information. "William wanted me to know in case he wouldn't get a chance to tell me."

Gloria stayed silent, looking exhausted and numb, while the room turned quiet. *This is happening. This is real.* I would have described my life over the decades as rather happy not so long ago. The small, simple, content life that I was living was now anything but that. It had been entirely shaped by the actions of others and I would never fully know what could have been.

"Where is Willie?" I asked once again.

"I can take you to him," Andrew offered. "If that's okay with you?" He looked at Gloria, who was tucked under his arm. She looked so small.

"I'll take you." Brian kissed my hand, which he had been holding for the last while.

"You should let Andrew take her. He still has to sort out his medication," Gloria said, adding an unconvincing, "I'm fine."

"Will you stay with her?" Andrew stared pleadingly at Brian while nodding to his wife.

"Of course!"

I didn't care who brought me. I just wanted to see him.

We got up and Brian hugged Andrew with a strong pat on the back. "Take good care of her."

"You too."

Minutes later, we stepped in the car, leaving Margret alone in the lounge as Brian and Gloria had made their way to the kitchen for a stronger drink. Andrew held the steering wheel with such a strong grip, his knuckles turned white. He took a purposeful breath. For a brief moment, I wondered if he should drive, but I wasn't in a state myself to reliably follow road rules. *A taxi maybe*?

"I can go myself if you prefer to stay with Gloria. Just tell me where to go and what medicine he needs."

He looked at me, relaxing his jaw. "No, it's fine," he said before turning the key and putting the car in gear. I felt some relief, not really wanting to go alone.

"Where is he?"

"At his house. The doctor visited him there. He is okay, but I don't like him being alone for too long."

"Why didn't you just say that earlier?"

"Say what?" His eyes were fixed on the road ahead.

"That he has gone to his house! When did he go there?"

"After the whole showdown with Margret showing up earlier today. It all got too much for him."

"Right, of course." I nodded. I still wondered if this was all happening myself or if I was going to wake up any moment now. *Please let me wake up.*

"It is a big shock for Gloria too, more news than she was looking for. Not something we needed today of all days . . . I suppose there is never a right day, is there?" Andrew let out a deep sigh before a purposeful inhale and exaggerated exhale, and with it, I noticed his hands relaxing on the steering wheel.

"I suppose not," I said as he did. "What do you mean today of all days? What else happened?" I asked a little warily.

He briefly glanced at me with a forced smile on his face. "Nothing. How are you holding up?"

How am I holding up? "I have no idea . . . I feel like screaming." I rubbed my eyes, which stung. I could feel how swollen they were.

"All right, that sounds like a solid plan. I'll count down from five," he said straight. I stared at him, trying to gauge if he was joking, but then he began counting down, with a hint of a smile as he did. *Oh, what the hell.* I quickly inhaled. *I am going to do this!* I screamed as soon as Andrew hit one. Banging the dashboard with a clenched fist, I screamed out in pure anger and frustration, shouting more curse words than have probably left my lips my entire adult life while stamping my feet like a child throwing a tantrum. I had read about primal therapy in a magazine once, not thinking much of it. Now, here I was, actually believing I might need it desperately.

It wasn't until I let it all go – my throat instantly sore as if I had sung along with Sepultura – that I squinted at Andrew through my long, wavy locks which covered my face. He looked calm and focused on the road. "Feel any better?" I could see a curl in his lips.

"Fine," I said after a few breaths in a hoarse voice. Not sure if I felt upset that he didn't join in, embarrassed that I did, or actually grateful. Because, my God, did it feel good to let it out!

I pulled down the sun visor and in the tiny mirror saw my red, blotchy face, eyes, and swollen eyelids. It was even worse than I had imagined. Not a pretty picture; more so deranged-looking. I pulled my locks back over my face and in this disguise, rested back into the seat with a sigh, closing my eyes.

When the car stopped moments later, I peeked through my hair. It was only a traffic light. Andrew gave a little tap on my lap. "We *are* almost there." He placed some of my hair behind my ear. "Remind me to never make you angry," Andrew said while driving off with a grin, which I reluctantly mimicked.

"Thank you for driving me," I said as he quickly pulled over to the side of the road. I looked around the street and then at him.

"We're not there yet." He sighed. "Liz, please, please take it easy on Willie. His health is a priority."

"But he sent me and my mother away!" I burst, dropping my gaze.

"I know, Liz, but that can't be changed anymore." Andrew took off his seat belt, turned to me, and reached over gently to tilt my chin up until our eyes met. His eyes were wide open as he spoke slowly and seriously. "Let him tell you if he is willing, and please, *listen*, Liz. You can't truly listen when consumed with anger." He spoke like a therapist. Which, at this point, I concluded I needed one.

"And remember, you can scream again on the way back." I found myself just nodding in agreement, without protest, as if I was hypnotised by his blue eyes. When the spell broke and his gaze left mine, I suddenly started to breathe faster and faster, uncontrollably, feeling sheer panic.

"*Breathe,* Liz." He held my shoulders. "Breathe, breathe with me . . . slowly in . . . and . . . out . . . in . . . and . . . out," he repeated until my hyperventilation turned into something like an out-of-breath jogger panting, which eventually became slower, calmer, and longer breaths with Andrew's guidance. "That's more like it," he said softly. "Keep that going, you're going to be fine." His words came out weary. He started the engine again and a little later, drove off. I was still counting my breaths until I could speak again.

"Thank you."

"You're welcome." Andrew looked tense, his jaw clenched again.

"I'll do my best to stay calm."

"That's good to hear."

"How are you?" I asked to distract myself.

"Not great right now, Liz."

"I'm sorry. You must be so worried about Gloria and here you are, driving me."

"That's all right. I had to go to him anyway, and I could use the breather."

"Ha, very funny," I said, which made him relax just a little.

"Glor and I are going through some things at the moment and now this . . . it's all a bit much." He opened up, sounding upset.

"Oh. I'm so sorry to hear, Andrew. I did wonder a little if something else was going on too . . ." I said softly. "If you feel like talking, contrary to what you might believe of me, I can be a good listener."

"I am sure you can, Liz, but this isn't the time." He let out a sigh. "We are here."

A knot formed in my stomach. Andrew parked in front of a narrow end-of-terrace house. There was no front garden, just a sidewalk. "Are you ready?" he asked once he switched off the engine.

I looked out of the car window to the house, the knot in my stomach tightening even more.

"Hey."

I turned to him, and he cupped my face in his hands, our eyes locked once again. "You've got this," he said in earnest. "You're strong and beautiful – I mean –" I raised an eyebrow. "You got this, Liz!"

"I've got this."

He got out and walked over to my side and opened the door, holding out his hand. A chivalrous move that was welcomed. I wanted to speak with

Willie so badly but I needed a few more seconds to just breathe. Andrew kneeled before me, his hand still stretched out. Without saying anything, he gave an encouraging nod and I placed my hand in his. "I've got this."

Moments later, we stood in front of a white PVC door with an opaque window in the upper half and Andrew unlocked it. "Willie, it's me!" he shouted as he opened the door with a shove, it getting caught on the doormat. With wobbly legs I followed him in, closing the door behind me.

"In the kitchen!" Willie called out.

"I have Elizabeth with me."

I followed Andrew through the long, narrow hallway, and moments later we were all in the kitchen together in awkward silence. Willie sat on a chair at the small, round table, and there was only one other chair. The kitchen was petite, dark, and outdated, with imposing laminate wood effect cabinets covering three walls, a countertop made out of small brown tiles that looked like a first DIY job, and a small window letting in some much-needed light.

"How are you? What did the doctor say?" Andrew spoke in a rush as if to make up for lost time.

"I am fine. Take a seat." Willie gestured toward me. I was almost hiding behind Andrew in the cramped space. I squeezed through and sat down while Andrew swiftly moved to fill a kettle.

Willie tapped his fingers nervously on the table, avoiding eye contact, and I could feel my rage building within.

"How was your flight?" he managed to ask.

"Fine."

"I'll get your medicine now," Andrew said.

"Thanks. How is Gloria?" he asked with apprehension, turning to look at him.

"She is going to need some time to process, Willie."

"Of course." He bowed his head.

"How are you, Elizabeth?" he asked after an uneasy pause. There was *that* question again, and I ignored it.

"Willie," I said with an authoritative tone as I sat straight up in my chair, shoulders back and chin up, trying to project confidence. "I *need* to know about Lizzy!" Andrew dropped the medicine bottle and froze. We heard it clatter to the ground and roll under the table, stopping by my feet, but I kept my posture.

Willie cleared his throat several times and I thought he would start to speak. He didn't. Andrew thawed and reached for the bottle underneath the table, giving my ankle what I believed was a cautioning squeeze, but it was too late. "I know all about Margret. Who she is, what she planned to do – the money and ticket you gave to my mother, all of it. What I don't know or understand is why my sister was kept away. I am very angry and hurt,

Willie! I *need* to know everything so I can fully process. I need to process!" I slapped my hand on the table, harder than intended, to get his full attention.

"Elizabeth!" Andrew called out.

I couldn't take my eyes off Willie, who looked between us, eyes wide with distress.

"I know! I *know*, Andrew, but I need to know, once and for all, I need to know the truth! All of it. You owe me that." I briefly reached for Willie's hand pleadingly, clasping my warm hands in his icy fingers. "You *owe* me that." My eyes welled up and some tears flowed freely.

"Willie," Andrew said calmly, placing his hand on Willie's slumped shoulder. "You will feel better too, once it is all off your chest," he murmured in a soothing voice that even calmed me down a bit. Willie looked up at Andrew and cleared his throat again before facing me.

"Lizzy." Her name came out groggily from his mouth. "Lizzy," he started over. "She was a *surprise*. No one knew your mother was having twins, including your mother, as she hadn't gone to her appointments." He sighed heavily and I feared he wouldn't say any more. "Hilda, your grandmother," he thankfully persisted, "was convinced your mother wouldn't be able to handle two babies, and since your mother didn't know she'd had twins, with the emergency C-section and all, she convinced hospital staff – or, well, one person working there in particular – to let her bring Lizzy home."

"They just let her take her? How?"

Willie nodded. "Your grandmother had it all worked out. She did promise she would tell your mother someday." He sighed again and cleared his throat. "You see, Lizzy had to stay in hospital a bit longer than you. She was in the neonatal care unit in an incubator, as she was unable to keep her body temperature up, and also needed to gain some weight. Hilda collected her when she was finally discharged from hospital. By that time, your mother had already left with you to Ireland, being none the wiser."

"Who was this person that helped her?" I leaned forward to hear him, not wanting to miss a word.

"An old friend who worked in the maternity ward," he replied vaguely. "That's all I know."

"So my mother never knew about Lizzy?"

He cleared his throat again and Andrew gave him a glass of water and put his medicine on the table. Taking a few slow sips first, he swallowed the pills one by one with more water until it was all gone. My gaze met Andrew's, and I gave him a little nod to say yes, I know, I'll take it easy. He looked relieved.

"She . . . she held her once in the hospital. She of course thought it was you." I turned my focus back to Willie. "Hilda arranged it."

"Why? For some twisted sense of justification?"

"Your mother was a minor, and your grandmother was . . . resourceful and influential," he said, looking at his empty glass.

"I'll say! And manipulative. And a liar!" The words left my lips reasonably calmly but without forethought, and the back of my neck prickled with barely contained anger.

"She thought what she did was in the best interest of your sister and your mother at the time." Willie sounded like he needed to defend her, adding to my fury.

"Wait – so how was she going to keep her a secret? Is that why Lizzy's room was all the way up in the tower?" Andrew placed a mug of tea for me on the table and got a small, black foldable chair from beside the fridge. He sat down beside me and placed a hand on my leg and gave it a gentle squeeze, as if to say you are doing fine, stay calm.

"Initially, but . . ." he sighed. "I convinced Hilda that I could make sure you were okay and go with your mother and father and start a new life, be the little family your mother wanted, as she was dead-set on not going home. Your . . . your father not going with you to Ireland was a real shock, and not something we had any control over."

"So she was part of it? It *was* the two of you after all?" I said, keeping my voice as steady as I could.

"Let him finish talking," Andrew whispered, playing the role of mediator.

"I deeply regret my part in this, and your grandmother was heartbroken, especially since the death of your sister. At times, she couldn't bear it." A tear slowly made its way down his cheek, which he wiped with a trembling hand. "She tried to tell your mother many times, and finally did some years ago when she came over for a visit."

"My mother visited?! When?"

"I think it's about five years ago now." Willie's voice wavered.

"So, she knew about Lizzy?"

"Yes."

"Yes?"

"Yes," he said with more assurance.

"And Margret?"

Willie shook his head. "No, Margret never knew about Lizzy until you told her."

"How did she die, Willie? How did my sister die?" I leaned in again, closer to his face, watching him. Andrew got up to get Willie more water and he took a shaking sip, avoiding eye contact.

"It was an accident. A tragic, tragic accident, Elizabeth," Willie whispered, trembling. "Lizzy loved going to the tower to play . . . she was such a little princess. One day, she was up there by herself playing while your grandmother took a shower. We think she . . . she must have climbed on the rocking horse, standing on it to look out the window. The latch gave way and . . ."

I gasped, covering my face with my hands, dreading what he was going to say next.

"She . . . she fell out." He choked on the words. "Your grandmother never forgave herself, Elizabeth. She never entered that room again." There was stunned silence that seemed to last forever. Andrew placed his arm around my shoulder.

"Is that why the window is screwed shut?" I lowered my hands. Willie nodded. I cried for my sister, the sister I never had the opportunity to know. Andrew pulled me in close to his chest where I lay my head, his shirt absorbing my tears.

"Your grandmother wanted you to know about her," he said once I had calmed somewhat. "If you like, I can show you some pictures and tell you a bit more about her sometime? I'm so, so sorry, Elizabeth." He sniffed through his own tears.

Andrew reached out to Willie's hand. The thought of my mum, so heartbroken when she found out about Lizzy, the daughter she never even knew she'd given birth to but was gone, filled me with overwhelming grief. I missed her so much it ached; I also ached for my twin sister.

I so wished she'd told me. This brought to mind again the trip my mother planned for my thirtieth. *Maybe that's when she would have.*

"Do you know which one of us was born first?" It suddenly felt important to know.

"You were."

My little sister. I sipped some of my tea and did my best to soothe myself. Andrew's arm stayed firmly around my shoulders, like a comforting blanket. "I would like that." Willie dared to meet my eyes. "I would like you to tell me more about Lizzy one day and to see some photographs." He reached his free hand out over the table. I wasn't ready for that and froze with hesitation. I wasn't sure if I would ever be ready. But I did want to keep the dialogue going, and for that reason, I held out a hand and briefly touched his. Willie sighed with relief and more tears flowed.

Not long after, I left Willie's house and waited in the car while Andrew made sure he was settled and had everything he needed until the following morning.

"Are you okay, Liz?" Andrew asked once joining me in the car and driving off.

"Yeah," I replied, disengaged, staring out the window, replaying the visit over in my head. After some time, he pulled into a sandy road and parked the car.

"Liz." He placed his hand on my lap. "I know you're not okay. No one would be in your situation. I just want you to know I am here for you if you want to talk." I gave him a weak, grateful smile.

"I know you are. Thanks." I briefly placed my hand on his. He reached for the glove compartment and opened it. "Thought you could use one." I nodded appreciatively as I noticed the pack of cigarettes. "Why don't you drive somewhere we can sit down. If you have the time that is?"

"I have. I know where to go." While Andrew took on the road again, I called Brian with a short update. I was still trying to process it all myself.

"Margret has gone to her room, and Brian and Gloria are watching a game show on TV together," I filled Andrew in from the phone call.

"I know, I briefly spoke with Gloria before coming out." As the drive continued, we were quietly engrossed with our own thoughts, until he parked.

I chuckled a little despite everything when I realised where we were. "The famous – or infamous – bench?" he asked.

"Let's go with famous."

It was the same bench where Andrew found me smoking the first time. The evening had turned a little chilly as the sun started to set. We smoked a cigarette each in silence. "Penny for your thoughts?" he asked as he offered me another.

I took it. "Too many thoughts. It's a lot to take in." I sighed with a heavy heart.

"This is as good a time as any," he said, putting his cigarette down and standing, taking my hand to pull me up with him.

"For what?" I asked, not up for *any* surprises.

"Aaaah!" Andrew screamed at the top of his lungs. I smiled. He squeezed my hand, hinting for me to join in. He didn't have to ask me twice, nor did I care that people could hear us. I took a deep breath and screamed with him until my lungs were emptied and I involuntarily started to cough. *Smoking was definitely not the wisest thing to do*. I took another small drag, ignoring my conscience, and blew it out with some difficulty. Andrew slid his hand through his dark-blond hair, which looked darker in the dimming light, and gazed at me intensely for some long seconds. We went for another go, grinning a little when a passing couple stopped and stared.

When we sat again and I let go of his hand that I'd held onto in a strong grip with our fingers intertwined, a sudden wave of overwhelming sadness hit me and I bawled like a child that had fallen off their bike. Tears, snot, everything – uncontrollable bawling. Andrew tried to calm me as he held me in his arms. I heard him tell the occasional passerby I was all right. His shirt was stained with my tears when I eventually pulled away.

"I'm sorry," I sniffed, having finally stopped to look at him. He moved some strands of my hair that had stuck to my face.

"Don't be. It's all going to be okay." Andrew turned his gaze away from me, but not before I could see the sadness in his eyes. "Let's go," he said, and we got back into the car and silently made the short distance to the B&B.

#

Inside, Brian was still on the couch, with the TV at a low volume, while Gloria was asleep with her head resting on his lap. It had been quite an evening. I felt and looked like crap. Brian carefully slid a cushion under Gloria's head and stood up. She moved briefly but didn't wake up. I hugged Brian tightly. He stroked my head and wiped away the occasional tears that fell.

"You guys can stay here, if you like?" Andrew offered as he kneeled beside Gloria.

"My stuff is at Brian's, and I really, really don't want to see Margret . . ." My lips quivered.

"Let's go," Brian said, gathering his coat and keys while I thanked Andrew for all he had done for me this evening, and promised to call tomorrow.

In the car, I briefly filled Brian in with more detail about the visit to Willie, but I didn't want to talk about it any further, so we didn't. Throughout the drive, when he could, he placed his hand on my arm, giving it the occasional stroke. His touch was comforting. I was exhausted, completely exhausted.

Back at his place, I took a long, hot shower. If I had brought comfy sweats I would have worn them, but stupidly enough, I'd only packed getting-it-on nightwear, which was definitely not my current desire. I got one of Brian's shirts to wear instead, which still gave a sexy vibe, but it was the comfort that I really wanted out of it.

In bed, I lay with my head on Brian's chest, listening to the beating rhythm of his heart. His radiating, warm body was the last thing I remembered before falling asleep.

#

The morning brought with it a raw awareness as I replayed the events of the evening over in my head. All the puzzle pieces had been gathered and finally put in place. Two stories were my life now. The one I knew and lived, the other, my unlived history, which left me with nagging questions of what-ifs. Wondering what would, or could, my life have been like.

On top of the what-ifs was the feeling of hurt and anger of how Margret, Willie, and Hilda used their power and deception to influence my mother's and my life's course. I had a wonderful childhood and life till not so long ago, and this unveiling made me question it all.

"What would you like this morning?" Brian asked once he noticed I was awake, his shape visible through the voile curtain. I pushed hard to take away all those feelings and thoughts, mentally shaking them off, not wanting to deal with them any further for now.

"You!" I said candidly, desiring the distraction.

"I meant for breakfast?" He peered through the opening of the curtain with a curl on his lip and questioning eyes. “Are you sure that is what you want right now?” he asked after some *moments* between us.

“Yes,” I said with certainty, and got out of bed to quickly freshen up. My eyes were still swollen and red, but besides that, I did a quick nod to the mirror, I looked good.

When I returned, he was in bed, ready for me, and we enjoyed each other in a way we had done many times before. Dopamine was released in abundance, and really, what better medicine is there?

Our *real* breakfast was not as mind-blowing, but the soda bread with avocado, fried egg, and bacon was delicious.

“We should go visit them after,” Brian said, making us one more cup of coffee. I knew he meant Andrew and Gloria, and I agreed. I wasn’t the only one going through major stuff. Gloria’s life was shaken as well. But the possibility of running into Margret gave me palpitations. I swallowed hard. They had been so supportive, the least I could do was be there for them too.

#

The walk over to the B&B we had settled on over coffee quickly turned into a drive as the weather changed into a wet and windy Irish-like day. When we arrived, I noticed that Andrew’s car wasn’t parked outside.

Gloria opened the door wearing her apron, holding a spatula, and quickly turned around before a greeting could leave our lips. Exchanging a quick look, we followed her to the kitchen. I made a mental note of the closed doors on the way with some relief. If Margret was there, at least I didn't see her.

Once in the kitchen, I let out a gasp that made Gloria look up at me with a quick feral stare. Her hair was a mess, as was the kitchen. The top and bottom parts of the oven were on, all five burners had something boiling or frying away, and the counters were covered with dishes galore. Chopping boards and more spices than I would know what to do with were scattered all over the place. The room was stuffy, and the different aromas in the air were a confusion to the senses.

"Expecting a lot of visitors today?" I asked in a light-hearted tone as I glanced at Brian, whose eyebrows had shot up taking in the room.

"No. Are you hungry?" Gloria said in a monotone voice, frantically mixing the concoctions on the stove.

"Stress cooking," Brian whispered in my ear as an explanation.

"That's a *thing*?"

"I have seen her do it before, but not to this extent." He tapped my shoulder, hinting that I should sit down. "The kitchen is where she feels comfortable." He continued to whisper a little louder with the blender going on full speed.

"Where is Andrew?" I asked Gloria once it had stopped.

"Picking up Willie . . . my uncle. He is my uncle," she said with absurdity, looking up at the wall as if it had something more than nothing on it.

"And Margret?" I asked hesitantly, silently praying she wasn't around.

"My mother? Ha, oh, my mother." Gloria's voice was loud, filled with contempt as she waved tongs in the air. "She went for a walk." A long one, I hoped.

"Hey, you want to sit down for a bit? Take a little break?" I prompted, hoping she would.

"Not yet." She began to name all the dishes she was making, pointing at each one with her tongs.

"Let me," Brian said to me in a low voice. He walked up to Gloria, standing closely behind her and held her arms until she laid down the utensil. "Look at me, Glor," he said calmly, calling her like Andrew would. "We will switch everything off. Nothing will burn, but you can use a little break." She stayed motionless for a bit, contemplating, until she finally leaned her head back to his shoulder and surrendered. As Brian helped her to a seat, I quickly switched off all the appliances.

"You're good," I whispered, impressed when we all sat down.

Moments later, the door opened, and Andrew and Willie walked in. Gloria sprang up in a haste and returned to her cooking.

"I tried," Brian sighed.

"Hey, at least you got her to sit down." Andrew patted Brian's shoulder in thanks. Little did he know how brief it was.

Willie sat on the chair beside me. He looked frailer. I dimmed my negative feelings towards him and said hello with a tight nod. He weakly smiled and focused his gaze at Andrew and Brian, who took a seat across from us.

"Willie, would you like something to eat?" Andrew asked in a strained, positive voice.

"I'll get it!" Gloria shouted, ignoring Willie as he thanked her. He stared at her, which went unnoticed and made him well up. He brought out his handkerchief and dabbed his eyes.

"It's all right," Andrew tried to reassure him. "It is all going to be all right." His last words didn't come out as convincing as he probably would have hoped.

Andrew signalled with his eyes for me to say or do something. While the truth was, if Willie was a young man, I probably would have caused him some sort of physical harm yesterday, but he wasn't. He was frail, guilt-ridden, and grieving my grandmother. That, and the four pleading puppy eyes, with Brian having joined in, got me to stretch out my hand and place it on his shivering one.

"Andrew is right, it's all going to be okay," I managed to muster.

"Yes." Gloria marched over. "It is," she repeated with an angry undertone.

"I am so sorry, Gloria," Willie said as she placed a sizzling oven dish on the table, avoiding eye contact.

"I know you are," she said after placing the final dish down. "Now we're going to eat!" Gloria instructed, leaving no room for argument.

It wasn't long since Brian and I ate breakfast, and I had little space for the three-course meal that was on the table. Not to mention more pots were still on the fire. Eyes wide, I looked from Brian to Andrew and back at the many pots and dishes in front of us as Gloria took a seat at the head of the table.

Andrew started plating food and we all followed suit except for Gloria, who just sat staring blankly out at the table. When he offered to plate her some, she turned her plate upside down without saying a word. We ate in an uncomfortable silence, as attempts at small talk were even more awkward than the silence itself. When we emptied our plates, I said a silent prayer for no more food.

"Brian. Elizabeth." Gloria called out our names and looked at us in turn with an unreadable expression. "We need to talk with you." She gestured at Andrew.

"Not now, *Gloria*! Let's do this later, in *private*," he almost snarled at her, not so subtly hinting at Willie's presence.

"I can go to the other room . . ." Willie offered, catching on.

"No, it's fine. Or do whatever you want," Gloria said with disregard.

"I really think we should do this later," Andrew insisted. I looked at Brian questioningly, but he shrugged his shoulders.

"We have to tell you something and we're going to discuss it. Nobody gets to leave until everyone has had a chance to say what they have to say about it *and* the food is all finished." I got goggle-eyed at the food comment. Gloria got up quickly to inspect the pots on the fire.

"I thought you said it was *stress* cooking, not hijack cooking!" I whispered across the table. Brian shrugged his shoulders again. Willie pushed his plate to Andrew. "Add some more." He spoke quietly with a concerned expression, afraid to upset the lady of the house any more than he already had. "And I'll leave the room." As he pushed his chair back and got up with some difficulty, I took his plate from Andrew and followed him to the lounge where he sat in the fancy armchair. "I am a bit tired," he said, trying to get it to recline. I helped him pull the lever and as I did, he placed his hand around my wrist, holding it in a soft grip. Gazing at him, his remorseful expression said it all. No sooner had I given him a little nod than he closed his eyes.

I left his food on the little coffee table and draped a woollen blanket over him. Walking back through the hallway, I wondered warily if Margret had returned. Thankfully, I didn't see her. Opening the door to the stuffy kitchen, dread filled me at the thought of more food. Brian moved to where Willie had sat, and Andrew was pouring whiskey. "A bit early, no?" I said, sitting down.

"Well," Andrew said after giving us all a shot, ignoring my remark. He and Gloria chucked it down instantly and gestured that we do so too. "We are *walking* back today," I said to Brian before we did the same. It burned down my throat.

"I wasn't expecting to have this conversation now," Andrew started. "And like this." He paused, unscrewing the bottle again, pouring himself a second shot and draining it down. "Glor and I had an unexpected long, frank, and difficult talk yesterday, before all the other things that happened, that is, and we decided that we should tell you, share our feelings . . ." He looked at her, and she gave a subtle nod.

"One that could change our friendship and lives. *All* our lives." He moved his gaze from Gloria to us. Instinctively, I reached my hand out toward Brian, who laced his fingers in mine. We stared at each other with a level of unease. I hadn't a clue what this was about and from Brian's expression, he was at a loss too.

"Okay?" I said warily.

"You see," Gloria interjected, tapping her fingers on her glass. "It involves you both because of what you mean to us . . ." She waited to attract Brian's gaze and I stared between them, until I noticed eyes on me.

Epilogue

10 years later

"Are you excited?"

"Of course I am!"

"That's what I love about you, Liz. You don't worry about getting a year older."

"Well, I'm like wine and cheese, the older and more mature, the better I get."

"You sure do, hon."

"Are you ready?"

"Almost, I'll see you there." He kissed my hand and my ring, the one that had bound us together for nearly five years now. As I looked at my reflection in the mirror, fixed my hair and touched up my makeup, I felt amazing. Having embraced the little crow's feet appearing and the odd strands of grey hair over the last few years, I was excited for celebrating the big four-o.

As I made my way down the grand staircase, my long, flowy, navy-blue dress swayed with each step. I smiled wide as my hand glided down the railing and all eyes were on me. This was my Oscar moment in my own house, the house that I had called home for the past eight years.

"Happy birthday to you! Happy birthday to you!" They burst into song on Su's command and ended with cheers all around. There was so much love around me. Everyone had a glass of bubbly in hand and made their way outside. Gloria pushed Willie in his wheelchair, making sure he had a front-row seat for the event. The four carved columns were stunningly decorated with white roses and ivy, as was the table which stood underneath the entrance with a three-tier chocolate cake, decorated with shades of purple violas all around. Anything but ordinary.

"I'd like to say a few words." Everyone went quiet. "I am so happy to see so many people here to celebrate Liz's birthday. Anyone that knows her, knows she *loves* her birthday." The crowd erupted in laughter. "I just want to say," he held up his glass of champagne, "I am very proud of you. Here's to many more happy years. Happy birthday, sweetheart!"

"Thanks, Dad," I said in his ear as I hugged him.

"Speech! Speech! Speech!" Brian called out, and others soon joined in.

"All right, all right!" I smiled as I raised my hands in the air. I picked a glass of the bubbly off the table and took a moment to look at all the wonderful faces around me.

"Firstly, I'd like to thank you all for being here to celebrate my fortieth birthday on this gorgeous day. It has been ten years since I first set foot in this place, and it has been an unforgettable journey since."

"You can say that again!" Brian shouted playfully, which found him on the receiving end of a shove from Gloria. I smiled at them widely.

"Some of you know me since that day, others I have met over the past few years and a special few of you –" I looked at my girls from back home, standing together "– much longer." They cheered loudly and raised their glasses in the air.

"I want you to know I am very grateful to each and every one of you for being part of my life." There were more loud cheers. "And finally, to the man that holds my heart, the one that is always by my side. My confidant in life that puts up with me every single day." I turned to him and held his hand. "I love you. You make every day special. Thank you!" and gave him a passionate kiss. "To Andrew, everyone! Cheers!"

The End

Acknowledgements

My first shout-out must go to none other than my daughter Paris! She sat for countless hours editing with me and has been there every step along the way, eager to read the next chapter. I have enjoyed every second of our time spent together and will forever cherish the memories. You're my grammar queen, and I have learnt so much from you in the process. Without your help, I wouldn't have acquired a hilarious English blooper list and would still be writing "Brain" instead of "Brian", and "smile grin to grin". Thank you, kiddo! Thank you for your time, enthusiasm, praise, and guidance. You're amazing!

Thank you, son. To hear you say you're proud of me makes me the proudest mummy!

To my three youngest girls, eagerly wanting to be old enough to read this book. Thank you for always asking how the book is going and how many pages I have left to do. For being extra quiet so I can concentrate and not disturbing me when I am working, unless it's something really important like, can I have another ice-cream.

Thank you, Schatje, for your care and kindness throughout my writing journey. I know if you read my book in the same length of time it has taken me to write it, I should and will feel honoured.

To my family and friends who have asked and wondered over the years if this book is ever coming to fruition. Well, it finally has! Thank you for your interest and patience. I hope you enjoy reading it as much as I have enjoyed writing it.

Finally, a big thank you to FirstEditing, especially Lee Ann, for her hard work in giving this book its final polish.

Printed in Poland
by Amazon Fulfillment
Poland Sp. z o.o., Wrocław

44084469R00210